Horror on Hoy

B K Bryce

This first edition published in 2019
by FM-Neverton Publishing

ISBN 978-0-9956681-4-0

Every effort has been made to conform to
historical opinion about the time however Horror
on Hoy is completely a work of fiction.

FM-Neverton publishing
Old Post Office, Quoyloo, Orkney. KW16 3LX

With special thanks to Jo Dolby for her assistance.

The Marna Mystery series is set in the Heart of Neolithic Orkney, a World Heritage site which contains some of Britain's most important Neolithic remains. Within an area of a few miles lies the preserved village of Skara Brae, the stone circles of Brodgar and Stenness, the remains of the village of Barnhouse and the magnificent chambered tomb of Maeshowe. The site of the Ness of Brodgar lies between the two circles. Ongoing excavations there are changing our perceptions of the Neolithic era. It is a monumental complex, in use for over 1,000 years, containing ornate buildings of a type hitherto unknown for that time. It was a significant place, with people coming together from across Orkney and further afield to feast, trade and celebrate the political and religious events that defined their complex society. Excavations continue and new information continues to be thrown up. The Marna Mystery Series aims to give a flavour of the time.

HORROR ON HOY

Orkney

Northern
Isles

Eynhallow

Skara Brae

Ness

Orphir

Settlement   Dwarfie
at Rackwick Stane

Hoy

South Ronaldsay

HORROR ON HOY

Chapter 1

Crash.

Marna's bones thudded against her flesh as the noise thundered through the air. Her friend Sylva laughed.

'If you lived here, you would get used to the sound.'

'It isn't the sound,' Marna answered. 'It's the shaking. It feels like the earth is trembling.'

'I know what you mean. It is a shame to cut down trees that have grown here before our grandparents were born, especially since we have been on Hoy less than a year. The hawthorns are pretty when they are in blossom and smell sweetly.' Sylva looked towards the near distance where the stream she was washing pots in flowed out from the valley of hawthorns, hazel and birch trees among a blanket of bluebells.

'There are plenty of trees here on Hoy,' Marna said. 'That is one of the reasons Quint and the elders at the Ness chose this area for the settlement. It is also beside the sheltered bay.'

Sylva laughed again, but this time there was an edge to her amusement. 'Their decision had nothing to do with our needs.' She gestured with a move of her head towards the hills. 'These hills are laden with fire stones. They are one of the few sites we can gather them. Those are what the Ness want.'

Marna followed Sylva's gaze to the grey outlines of the hills with the valley cutting between them, which she could see every day from her home at the Ness. Their bald heads rose up to the blue sky in a show of defiance and she had never imagined people working there. The rumbling as another tree fell brought her thoughts back to the ground. 'Chopping trees keeps the men busy,' she said.

'You sound more like your mother every time we meet,' Sylva said.

Marna showed her opinion of the comment by splashing her friend with water from the stream.

'My mother has taken leave of her senses,' Marna complained. 'She is gallivanting with her new husband in Stonehenge, further south than anyone from the Ness has journeyed before. Patro is inspecting stone circles and dolmens. Apparently he is regarded as an expert on positioning monuments in alignment to the stars.'

'I can tell you don't approve.'

'Patro can choose to visit where he wants, but I would have expected my mother to stay at home and keep day to day life running smoothly,' Marna grumbled. 'She is a grandmother now.'

'Thork told me he had a daughter,' Sylva cut in, urging Marna to tell her more about her brother's baby. Marna hadn't finished moaning about her mother.

'At least she promised to bring me back brassica seeds for my studies. I told you I was trying to find a food we can grow early in the season, despite the poor weather and lack of light in spring.'

'Yes.' Sylva's tone lacked the enthusiasm Marna hoped for. 'Having a step-father who is head priest must help. It gives you a high standing at the Ness.'

'Mmm.' Marna glanced out to sea to avoid answering. Her eyes caught the shadow of a boat on the water. 'Are you expecting visitors?' she asked.

'No.'

Marna screwed her eyes to focus on the outline. 'Maybe I'm wrong, but that looks like a boat trying to enter the bay.'

'The tide is going out,' Sylva said. 'The sea is rough. A small craft will struggle to land.'

'There's another one.' Marna said. 'I can see three.'

'Three?' Sylva looked where Marna pointed. 'It is odd for travellers to approach the village this way. The waters in the Pentland Firth are treacherous. There are rocks close to the coast that are hidden by the waves and the currents meet from the east and west to settle their differences. They do not care who gets in their way. If you are coming from the Ness or Skara Brae it is easier to row across to Moaness, as you and Thork did, then travel here on foot. A sled could carry a heavy load and an ox to pull it would fit in one of the larger boats.'

'I doubt that,' Marna said. 'Patro left his beloved pony at the Ness to avoid the mess it makes on a sea journey.'

'That would have been your mother's idea,' Sylva replied.

Marna kept her eyes on the boats. The oarsmen had worked out a system, rowing with the waves as they heaved towards the shore. They were making good headway towards the shallow water in the bay. 'Perhaps they are not coming from the Orkney mainland,' she mused. 'They could be from Caithness.'

'Why would travellers from Scotland come here?' Sylva asked. 'There is nothing to trade. The stones we gather are sent to the Ness.'

When the boats reached the rock marking the low tide line, Marna dropped the pot she was holding and grabbed Sylva's arm. 'Hurry, we must warn the others.'

'What? Why?'

Sylva's objections tumbled from her mouth as Marna pulled her from the edge of the stream. She tripped on strand of water reed and Marna let go of Sylva's arm to avoid being dragged with her into the water.

'Come on,' Marna urged, helping Sylva to her feet. Her friend wiped her tunic. Marna didn't wait.

She sprinted towards the huddle of rough, timber-built houses set in a semi-circle a quarter of a mile inland of the bay. They were clad with mud and animal dung then wound tight with sewn sealskins to protect against the wind and rain, but that would not hold against the current danger.

When the settlers had arrived the previous autumn, the Ness masons had quarried stones from the cliff and built a substantial workshop. Then winter came and the masons returned home. Little more had been achieved. The initial supplies of grain and cured meat had run low. There was insufficient light to reach the higher ground where the deer could be hunted. Survival had been the goal, not expanding.

Marna took care over the stony ground, but she was a quick runner. When she was close enough to be heard she started to shout warnings. A woman with a child in her arms appeared at the door of the first house.

'Pirates,' Marna panted. 'There are pirates in the bay.'

The woman put the child down. She looked beyond Marna and cursed. The child ran indoors wailing. Moments later three women appeared armed with stones and knives.

'Someone will have to tell the men. We need them here, now,' the eldest of the women said.

'I'll go,' Marna said. 'I can run fast.' There wasn't time to waste on discussion. Leaving the women to organise their defences, she sprinted from the settlement and uphill towards the woods. The track hadn't been cut back since the settlers arrived. The gorse branches scratched her legs, but she kept going until she reached the edge of the wood. The sound of her brother's voice, twice as loud as anyone else, guided her to where the men were working. They had stopped cutting the trunks to eat and tell stories. Marna burst into their circle as Thork was demonstrating how he brought down an auroch – in his dreams. There wasn't time to contradict him.

'Pi...pi...ra...' Marna was out of breath. She flapped a hand towards the settlement.

'What is it, sister? A year at the Ness and you've started hearing voices?' The others laughed at Thork's joke.

Marna grabbed the sleeve of his tunic and tugged it to help her recover her breath. 'Pirates.' She forced the word out. 'In the bay. Three boats.'

'Three? How many men?' a man asked.

Marna shook her head. 'I don't know. I counted six in the nearest boat.'

'What makes you think they are pirates?' Thork said.

'We don't have time to talk,' the first man

argued. 'Let's go.'

The men threw down their food and skins of water. They were on their feet, gathering up knives and axes.

'Stay here,' Thork warned Marna. 'Hide among the trees. Don't come out until you hear my voice.'

Marna nodded her consent. She waited until the men were halfway down the slope, running to defend their homes and families then sped after them. She stopped at the bank of the stream to pick up a stone. A few paces later she discarded it in favour of a heftier one. The surface was smooth and fitted in her palm, ready for throwing or hurtling down on an attacker's bent head. She bounced it in her palm before continuing.

The raiders had reached the houses. The women were surrounded. The roars of the attackers terrified them into dropping their weapons. Marna heard screams and children crying. A lad of about eight, who was too young to help the men with the tree felling, had raced to rescue the two village cows. One had a young calf and the boy struggled to control it. His mother shouted at him to flee.

The circle of pirates broke as the village men

charged down from the valley, wielding their weapons and threatening with their battle cries. Marna was used to village scuffles when the young folk had drunk too much ale, but she hadn't witnessed close fighting between real enemies before. The air was ripe with the smell of sweat and blood. Her heart beat ferociously and her stomach felt like she had swallowed the stone she was carrying. A tremor rushed from her ears to her toes. She couldn't look away.

Alekander, Sylva's partner, towered over the other men and his longer legs carried him into the fray first, followed by Thork. Her brother was more adept at throwing hunting spears than swinging a battle axe, but he had strong arm muscles and the tree felling had given him practise in wielding the weapon. The man he was attacking staggered back holding his face. From where she stood, Marna could see blood ooze between his fingers and congeal on his knuckles.

One of the fallen man's comrades turned on Thork. Marna wanted to rush to her brother's aid, but her feet were stuck as if held by mud. Alekander spotted the danger. He thrust a stone between the pirate's shoulder blades, slicing a gash from his back. Marna's warning had given the women time to gather weapons from the village store shed. Whenever an axe or mace was lost in the body of an enemy, they were able to hand the men new ones.

The pirates seemed unprepared for resistance. The crew in one boat hadn't come ashore, giving Marna the strange feeling that they knew the men would be out of the village, but that was impossible. When they saw their comrades were losing they turned their boat and rowed off. The fight did not last long. Three of the raiders were on the ground, while five others retreated towards the remaining boats as fast as their wounds permitted. One rower had been left in each of the boats to stop them being dragged out to sea. The five men scrambled into the nearest boat and the rower pulled away. The women from the settlement had followed them to the shore and threw stones into the water.

'Look over there,' Marna shouted as she spotted the last two raiders head along the bay towards the third boat. They were dragging someone with them. Tears of rage clouded Marna's eyes and she couldn't make out who it was. From the shape, she could tell it was a woman. Her words didn't reach over the cacophony. She had little energy left, but the emotions gushing through her forced her legs into action. She jogged towards the shore. Her brother was near, waving his axe and jeering at the enemy as they fled.

'Thork, do something,' she called. 'They've taken one of the villagers.'

The settlers were cheering their victory and allowed the injured pirates to leave until Alekander spotted Marna jumping and waving. He glanced across. The two men had reached their boat and were hauled aboard. It took both attackers to control their struggling prisoner, but with a lighter boat and an outgoing tide, the oarsman was able to manoeuvre the boat without their help.

'I'll stop them.' Thork drew back his arm and prepared to hurl a mace. A hand stopped him.

'You could hit the woman by mistake,' the man explained.

'It's Sylva,' Alekander cried. He lurched towards the sea and waded in. Even with his long legs, the boat was too far out to reach. He stood, thigh deep with the waves lapping at his tunic, gaping in horror as the outline of the boat faded.

Chapter 2

'Hurry, we can launch our own boats,' someone shouted.

'That would be no good, Ralfe,' another man answered. 'We have lost them. We don't know where they are heading.'

It was true. Marna could no longer make out the boats against the rolling of the waves. 'We have to do something,' she said, joining the group of settlers.

'We need to patch up our wounded,' an older woman answered. Having only been in the settlement for three days, Marna didn't remember everyone's name, but she knew Peria. She was the woman who had scolded her for using firestones to start a fire. Firestones were intended for the Ness and permission was needed to use them. Thork had also fallen foul of her tongue. Peria had told him off for talking loudly when the children were asleep. She was the one who made the decisions in the village, whether the others knew it or not. 'First we need to deal with them,' Peria finished speaking.

All eyes turned to glare at the defeated pirates. Alekander made his way towards them and the others followed. One of the men was lying face down on the ground with blood congealed round a deep crack on his shaven head. He didn't stir when Ralfe kicked his side.

'I reckon we don't need to worry about him,' Thork said. 'He's dead.'

The other two men were sitting on the ground. One rocked to and fro while the second nursed his wounds. Suddenly, the man who was rocking lunged forwards to reach for an axe dropped among the grass and heather. Alekander slammed a foot down on his hands. He bent to grab a handful of the man's hair.

'Where have your midden-faced friends taken my wife?'

The man didn't answer and Alekander pulled his head back until the bones in his neck creaked and he groaned.

'We're not telling you anything,' his companion answered.

Alekander let go of the first man's hair and pushed him to the ground before rounding on the speaker. He punched him in the chest and the pirate flinched. Marna could see he was little more than a boy. His voice was high pitched and trembling. His right shoulder was set at an odd angle and Marna winced when Alekander gave it a shove.

'Talk or I will gouge your eyes out with this knife,' Alekander threatened.

The villagers circled round. Ralfe and Thork joined Alekander in the centre and they stood over the prisoners. The boy didn't speak and Marna feared Alekander intended to carry out his threat. He raised his knife.

'You had better talk fast,' Alekander said. The boy glanced towards his companion.

'Kill us and be done with it.' The first pirate spat. There was blood in his spittle.

Ralfe took a step towards him, mace in hand. Thork put a hand on his shoulder to prevent him from swinging it. 'This is the first raid I have witnessed, but at the Ness I have heard reports of more. Quint and the elders dismissed them as false rumours. Now I believe they were true. These men are our proof. The priests will demand to know what happened here and they will not be pleased if they find we have killed men who could give them vital information.'

Thork's argument was convincing. Ralfe lowered his mace, but Alekander stood glowering at the pirates.

'Killing them won't help us find Sylva,' Thork said.

'Neither will sparing them,' Alekander replied. 'They have no regard for decency. If they tell the priests anything, it will be lies.'

'You spoke the name of Quint,' the older prisoner said. 'I will speak with him.'

'What do you know of the Ness and Quint?' Thork demanded.

'What don't I know?' The man tried to chuckle, but coughed up blood.

'The reputation of your priests has travelled far,' the younger pirate said. 'We trust we will get fair treatment from them.'

Marna found the idea of pirates expecting fair treatment odd. They were the enemy - she hadn't thought of them as being human.

'Nobody asked you, whelp,' Alekander rounded on the lad, slapping him on the side of the face. When the boy looked up Marna saw his eyes were red and watering. He gritted his teeth. As well as his shoulder being out of place, there was a gaping wound on his leg that needed attention.

'What of Sylva?' Peria said from behind

Marna. 'Will she get fair treatment from those beasts?'

'We are not animals. The woman won't be harmed as long as she does what she is told,' the older pirate assured her.

'Why should we believe you?' one man called.

'Kill them now.'

'No, let the Ness do the dirty work.'

Tempers were still hot from the attack. While Thork tried to calm the settlers, Marna returned to Sylva's hut to fetch the herbs and medicines she had brought from the Ness. Before leaving for Stonehenge, her mother had prepared balms of horsetail and squeezed the sap from kelp. They would both be needed for healing. Sylva's woollen shawl, which she had dyed, was hanging on a beam to dry. It was the first thing Marna noticed when she entered the hut. The smell of the pine bark used as a mordant to fix the yarrow dye caught in her throat. Sylva had wanted a bright yellow shawl.

Poor Sylva, she thought.

The pirate may have been telling the truth when he said she wouldn't be hurt, but Marna knew it was impossible for Sylva to do what she was told for long. When they both lived in Skara Brae, Sylva

16

would argue for days with the village leaders.

We'll find a way to rescue you, Marna promised.

When she returned outside, the discussion hadn't progressed. Most of the villagers had wandered off to tend to minor injuries and comfort children. A small group were left to guard the prisoners and decide what action to take. Thork assumed the role of leader. He raised an arm to gain attention and quieten Ralfe and Alekander.

'Taking the prisoners to the Ness makes sense. This settlement is here because of the Ness. The priests have a right to decide on serious issues.'

Marna groaned. She knew that the villagers did not feel they owed allegiance to the Ness.

Ralfe was the first to answer. 'We came here because the priests offered us land, animals and tools to build houses, farms and boats,' he said. 'They promised to send stone workers and craftsmen to help us. The hills behind us may as well be mountains and the stretch of water between us a mighty sea. We have received no aid since the winter solstice. What houses and boats we have, we struggled to build ourselves. We have no skins, whale oil, pots or needles. We have no grain seeds fit to grow on this harsh land and the two cows and calf they could spare us don't make a herd. The older beast is dry. We haven't had a drop of milk from her and the calf is a weakling. Where are the fattened pigs they promised? Our purpose here is to gather wood and haematite that is all.'

Marna could tell her brother was about to launch into a long-winded defence of the Ness. To stop him, she stepped into the centre of the ring.

'Arguing will not get Sylva back,' she said. 'We need men and boats, more than we have here. We have to get word of the attack to the Ness.'

Marna's words made sense. Ralfe replaced his mace in his belt.

'How long will it take to get them there?' Alekander asked, looking at the wounded prisoners. 'We need to rescue Sylva before she is harmed.'

'If we leave now, we can reach the Ness by evening,' Thork calculated. 'I am willing to make the journey and speak up for the settlement. I'll need three or four others to come with me to make sure these scum don't escape.' He aimed a kick at the older pirate. The man dodged to the side, but was caught on the ear.

'Are we all agreed?' Ralfe looked round the

gathering. His eyes fell on Peria. She gave a small nod. The others said 'aye'.

'I'll go with you,' Alekander said. 'I'm not going to let these animals out of my sight.'

'I will too,' Ralfe said.

'What about you, Phalt?' Peria asked.

The man beside Ralfe ran a hand through his fair-hair, which was darkened by blood. 'I am willing,' he agreed. 'I am a strong rower.'

'I shall come as well,' Peria said. 'You will need a woman to make sure you fill your bellies during the trek.' She prodded Phalt, 'And stop you from dawdling along the way.''

'Is that everyone?' Thork asked.

'I'm coming too,' Marna spoke up.

'Don't be silly,' Thork rebuked her. 'We have one woman. What need do we have of another?'

'If you want to get to the Ness by this evening, you will be glad of my help. The lad will not travel fast with his shoulder dangling and his leg half off.'

The young pirate smarted at being called a lad and he tried to back away when Marna bent to examine his leg. Alekander brandished his knife.

'We only need one prisoner. If his injuries hold us back, I won't hesitate to use this.'

The boy slumped and allowed Marna to proceed. The wound on his leg ran down the side of his calf below his knee, but missed the joint. The torn skin exposed his leg muscle, which was bleeding. Marna had yarrow among her mother's healing potions. She had seen her mother apply it directly onto wounds to stop the blood loss. The boy bit his lip as she pressed the dried leaves onto the edges of the wound.

'It is madness to waste precious healing herbs on the likes of him. Our folk need treatment too, or have you forgotten about that?' Peria complained.

Marna looked round. The village women were attending to their men folk. The men had taken the pirates by surprise, giving them the upper hand. One man's arm was bruised, but no-one had a serious injury.

'I think they will be fine,' Marna said. Peria huffed before marching to her hut to prepare for the journey.

Once the blood flow was reduced, Marna dabbed away the dirt that had gathered in the boy's wound. The cut wasn't as deep as she had feared and after rubbing in healing oil, she covered it with a felted wool dressing and bound it in place with strands of reeds. The boy struggled to get to his feet. Marna offered him her hand. He hesitated, but his leg was weak and he accepted.

'You too,' Ralfe said to the older man. 'Get up.'

'I'll fetch ropes to tie them,' Phalt said.

'I need to attend to the lad's shoulder before you use these,' Marna said, blocking Phalt's way when he returned with the rope. The boy was reluctant to let her touch his arm, jerking away when she came near. She feared his shoulder was out of joint and removed her shawl to tie it round his neck and arm in support.

'When we get to the Ness, Jolty will be able to help you,' she told him. 'He is skilled at setting bones and returning them to their rightful places. He does it with ropes and weights, I've seen him.'

The boy winced.

'I guess it hurts, but Jolty is a good man. He's my grandfather, well, sort of. He is Patro's father.' She hadn't got used to her widowed mother's marriage to the head priest. 'I'm Marna. What's your name?'

The boy looked towards the sea, as if hoping for rescue.

'We are going to be together for a while. We have to walk to the bay at Moaness, row across the water to where the sea edges close to the Stenness Loch then head north to the Ness.' The boy wasn't listening. 'I suppose I'll have to call you "Little boy",' she said. 'Or "Silly boy".'

The lad grunted. 'I'm not telling you my name.'

'That's an awfully big mouthful,' Marna said. 'What about "Nottelling" or "Notell"? My father had a dog called Nuttal. That sounds better. He was a bad dog, not like the one I have now. Pip is…'

Her story was interrupted by Ralfe. 'We don't have all afternoon to chat,' he said, snatching the rope from Phalt. 'Out of my way.'

The older prisoner had already been bound. Ralfe tied Nuttal's hands and feet. Thork had gathered his belongings while Marna dealt with the lad's injuries. He returned as Ralfe finished securing the prisoner.

'Not so tight on the feet,' Thork said. 'We need him to be able to walk.'

'I don't mind dragging him by the hair,' Alekander said.

'I know you have the strength, but we don't

22

have time,' Thork answered, believing Alekander meant what he said.

Peria strode from her hut and dropped two sacks on the ground. 'I have packed food and water skins,' she said. 'There is a third sack in the hut.

Ralfe and Thork picked up a sack each. Alekander fetched the third sack, which was heavier than the other two.

'We should go now,' Thork said. He looked to the sky. 'There are dark clouds gathering.'

'Wait, I have my belongings to collect,' Marna said. She had intended staying three more days, but with Sylva gone, there was no point returning.

Her brother gave an exaggerated sigh, but he knew by the look she gave him not to make a scene.

Marna hurried to Sylva's hut and gathered her dyes and pouches of powders. Her large pot was ideal for steeping skins. She had spent ages lining the inside the way she wanted, but she would have to leave it until later. Thork had carried it over, but he wouldn't be willing to carry it back, claiming there were a host of potters at the Ness who could make her a new one.

As she collected her instruments for scoring patterns on the wool, she spotted the whalebone comb her mother had given Sylva as a wedding gift. It was displayed on a wooden table Alekander had made. Sylva had spent the past four days moaning that she didn't have a proper stone dresser like the one she was used to in Skara Brae. Sitting next to the comb was an ornate knife carved from a deer antler that Patro had given Sylva, feeling that would be more useful on Hoy than a fancy hair comb.

Marna thought about taking both items for safe-keeping. With Sylva kidnapped and Alekander away, the house would be empty. Shelter and storage space were in short supply and the others would find a use for it. The knife and comb could get lost. She slipped the knife in her bag and was about to take the comb when Alekander pushed through the door.

'There is no time to admire jewellery. We need to leave.'

Marna set the comb down.

Outside, the two prisoners were tied together, with the older man in front. The party formed a line and Thork led the way, with Ralfe beside him, holding onto the rope that was attached to the first pirate's wrists. Alekander gathered the end of the rope that was tied to Nuttal's ankles and gave it a tug. Phalt moved to stand behind him.

'I suppose we had better get into line too,' Peria said to Marna. She took hold of Marna's sealskin sack and walked up to the men. When she reached Phalt she handed him the sack. 'Here, you are always showing off your muscles, carry this.'

'Watch my arm, woman. I scraped it in the fight.' Phalt complained. He took the sack and shook it. 'What have you got in here?'

'Pots,' Marna answered. 'Please be careful, they are easily broken.'

Thork set a brisk pace towards Berriedale woods and Marna imagined he was hearing his drum beating in his head. She never failed to be amazed at how easily her brother was able to take charge of a group. He had moved from Skara Brae to Orphir the previous year to marry Caran and already he was their drummer, elder and priest.

Phalt was ahead of her, puffing like a boar at the end of a chase. By the time they arrived at the small waterfall where the stream picked up pace, everyone was ready for a drink.

'We can't linger here,' Ralfe said. 'Can't you see the mist coming down over the hills?'

Marna could see it and knew the others could, but she didn't understand why he was worried. Mist was a common feature and the path to Moaness, although rough, was a straight one.

'There was a rock fall two days ago,' Ralfe explained. 'We will need to go the longer way round the side of Ward Hill.'

The older pirate took an intake of breath that sounded like the wind whistling.

'What is wrong?' Thork asked.

'Perhaps you are too young to have heard of the Dwarfie Stane?' The older man said.

'The Dwarfie Stane, what's that?' Marna asked.

'Nothing to worry about,' Ralfe assured her. 'It's an ancient tomb carved in a solid block of red sandstone that lies a stone's throw from the path. It is no longer in use.'

'There are tales of giants living inside,' the pirate insisted. 'Everyone in Wick knows of them.'

'So, you are from Wick,' Alekander jumped on the man's words.

'I didn't say that,' the man mumbled. He glanced at Nuttal.

'I'm not afraid of giants,' Thork said.

'I have passed it many times while gathering stones. The tomb is sealed,' Ralfe said. 'If there are giants, they can't see out. They won't know we are anywhere near them.'

'They will hear the racket you make,' the older pirate said. 'His voice can be heard halfway out to sea.' He glared at Thork then rounded on Marna and Peria. 'I don't trust these gabbling women to be quiet for more than it takes them to seize a breath.'

'I don't intend keeping quiet because of giants. If they come near me, they will regret it,' Peria answered.

They had travelled a mile when the mist descended with the speed of a bird of prey swooping on a vole. The party kept to the rough track made by the settlers when they searched for grazing ground for the cows. Marna could barely see two paces ahead of her and walked smartly to make sure she didn't lag behind. She kept Peria's faded grey cloak in her sights. Nuttal struggled to keep his footing and Phalt prodded him with a hazel branch.

'Watch his shoulder,' Marna protested.

'If anything happens to Sylva, it won't just be his shoulder he has to watch.' Marna recognised

Alekander's brusque voice, but he was too far ahead to see. She held her tongue until the boy tripped on a loose rock and fell. The older pirate was dragged down on top of him. There was a crunching sound and the lad let out a shriek of pain. The older man rose, but Nuttal remained down, despite Alekander pulling on the rope to raise him.

'We can't go any further,' the older pirate said.

'We can't stop here,' Thork said. 'It is too exposed. There is a wind blowing up and it looks like we are in for a hail storm.'

The wind was reaching gale force and Marna found it hard to anchor her feet, but as the clouds parted, Peria pointed to a darker shadow in the haze. 'There is the Dwarfie Stane. We can shelter there until the mist rises. The weather here changes as fast as a man's temper. We shouldn't be delayed for long.'

She didn't wait for Thork's decision, but left the track and headed towards the chambered cairn. The mist closed round her and she was out of sight when the others heard her voice. 'Come on, what are you scared of?'

'We'd better follow her,' Phalt said.

Marna calculated where Peria was by her

grunts, which expanded in the mist to sound like a beached whale. Alekander and Phalt lifted Nuttal to his feet and carried him between them.

The other prisoner was attached by his ropes and had to hurry to keep up with Alekander's long strides. They found Peria at the tomb. 'I don't like it, messing with giants,' the pirate grumbled.

'No-one cares what you like,' Ralfe answered.

Alekander and Phalt dropped Nuttal on the ground with less care than they gave to the supply sacks. Peria unpacked bannocks and water skins and handed out rations, ignoring the two enemies. Marna offered her water skin to Nuttal. He refused and she offered it to the other man, who grabbed it. While he was drinking, Marna found her sack.

'Let me look at your wounds,' she said to the young pirate. 'The dressing on your leg is dirty and my shawl has slipped from your shoulder. It is doing more harm than good.' She opened her sack and brought out a small covered pot of dried and ground leaves. The boy shifted away from her. 'It is horsetail,' she said, pouring three drops of water into the pot. She let the powder soak while she removed the old dressing. The wool had stuck onto clotted blood and she had to pull hard to remove it.

Nuttal groaned. 'I've got a knife. I can scrape it off.' She reached into the sack for Sylva's antler knife. 'You'd better not move or I could cut your leg as well as the dressing.'

The boy took her humorous comment as a threat and sat as if frozen while she ripped through the wool. He flinched when the wound was exposed. The edges had turned a yellowish colour and the discharge had a sour odour. Marna wiped the antler knife on her tunic before returning it to the top of her bag. She bathed the leg, applied the plant leaves and covered the wound.

'That will have to do,' she said. The boy didn't reply. Picking up her sack she moved across to where Peria was resting. The woman had removed her footwear and was examining her feet. Even through the mist, Marna could see to her horror that the woman's toenails were green.

'What is wrong?' she gasped. 'Is it serious? Will your toes fall off?'

Peria laughed. 'You won't catch it, if that is what you are worried about. Doesn't anyone at the Ness colour their nails? I use green kohl, ground from the rocks on the island of Burray. A wise priestess told me about it. There are other pigments.

I use galena to dye them black. It's this blister on my heel I'm concerned about.'

'I can help,' Marna said. 'I have dock leaves in my bag.'

'There are plenty growing wild I can pick.'

It was impossible to tell how long they waited. The mist thickened to a fog and Marna could no longer make out faces. The wind blew the fog into eerie shapes that fooled her into thinking Thork was ready to move off. She stood up to find him resting.

She lay on the heather and thought of her mother and step-father on their adventure. She thought of her friend Sempal and her dog, Pip. She was thinking about Thork's new baby when she felt a nudge on her arm and jumped.

'Time to go, sis,' Thork said.

The mist had risen above the hills. Marna rubbed her eyes and got to her feet. Alekander was shouting. 'What's wrong?' she asked Thork.

'I don't know.' He walked towards the men and Marna followed. Ralfe, Alekander and Phalt were standing where the prisoners had been. There was blood on Alekander's arm. Marna looked down and covered her mouth to dampen her scream.

Chapter 3

The older prisoner lay face up. His eyes were open, but they didn't see the band of blue sky. His throat had been slit.

'He's dead,' Ralfe said.

'Where's the lad?' Marna asked.

'Gone.' Ralfe demonstrated the cut rope. 'We should have killed him when we had the chance.'

Thork seized the rope from Ralfe and examined it. 'How did he manage it? Wasn't someone guarding him?'

Phalt bent to pick up a knife. 'He must have used this.'

'Oh!' Marna recognised the antler.

Peria came across to join them. 'What do you know about this?' she demanded.

'That's my knife. Well, it's Sylva's knife. I borrowed it.'

'And gave it to the lad,' Peria said. 'We all saw how you threw yourself on him.'

'That isn't true. I didn't give it to him. I used it to remove the dressing on his leg, but I returned it to my sack afterwards. I don't see how he could have got it.'

Peria gave a knowing look.

'Why would he kill Toomac?' Ralfe asked.

'Maybe they quarrelled or he thought the man would hold him back,' Peria answered.

'Wait, how do you know the dead man's name?' Thork asked.

'He told me,' Ralfe answered.

'He said he wasn't speaking to anyone except Quint. What else did he say?' Peria asked.

'Nothing although he might have loosened his tongue if his comrade hadn't cut his throat.'

'The lad couldn't have killed anyone,' Marna objected. 'Not with his arm hanging limp.'

'That was a trick,' Phalt said. 'He's a pirate – they know how to fool honest folk. Besides, even with one arm, it takes less than a heartbeat to run a knife through a man.'

'I saw them on the beach together,' Thork said. 'The lad was trying to help the older man get to his feet.'

'Look,' Marna broke in. She indicated a carved pin on the dead man's tunic. 'The lad had a similar pin. They must be from the same village or family.'

'It would be unusual for someone to kill a kinsman in cold blood,' Thork said.

'If the lad didn't kill him, who did?' Peria asked. She looked around the group, her eyes judging them.

'I was with you, after you finished talking to Marna,' Phalt said.

'Alekander and I were together,' Ralfe added.

Peria glared at Marna. 'That leaves you…and your brother.'

'We didn't kill anyone,' Thork asserted.

'So it must have been the lad. What do we do about it?' Phalt asked.

Thork ran his tongue round the inside of his mouth. It looked like he was thinking, but Marna knew it was to fool the others.

'The lad can't have gone far,' Alekander said.

'There are no footprints. He could be hiding anywhere on the hillside,' Ralfe said. 'The overgrowth is thick, the clouds are low and there are caves further up with linking passageways.'

'He will know where his pirate friends are and will try to reach them,' Phalt said.

'You mean, the pirates are hiding somewhere on Hoy?' Thork said.

'He didn't say that,' Peria snapped. Phalt looked at her and she softened her voice. 'The island has secret inlets in every bay, difficult to access by land. They didn't get what they came for, so they may regroup and try again.'

'They got my wife,' Alekander said.

Peria gave a snort. 'They got her jet ring. If she'd given it to them she would have been released.'

Thork stepped between Peria and Alekander to prevent a fight. 'I say we should report what has happened to the Ness.'

Ralfe and Alekander grumbled, but didn't object.

'We don't all need to go,' Phalt argued. 'Not now that we don't have prisoners to guard. Peria and I shall return to the village.'

'Marna, Alekander and I can go to the Ness,' Thork said. 'There is no need for you to come, Ralfe.'

'I have a mind to see the Ness and put questions to the priests there. The more voices petitioning from our island, the more likely they will be heard.'

'We are wasting time talking,' Alekander broke in. 'The mist has cleared. We can reach the boats at Moaness before the sun goes down. I can row by moonlight.'

'And wake the priests before dawn? Rather you than me,' Thork answered.

Marna guessed her brother was more concerned about crossing the unpredictable waters of the Flow in the dark, rather than disturbing the priests, but she held her tongue.

'We should see to the body first,' Thork said.

'Leave it here for the carrion birds,' Ralfe answered.

Thork bent to remove the pin from the man's tunic. The body was beginning to smell. He made a throaty noise and held his nose as he unfastened it. 'This might be needed at the Ness as proof,' he said, handing it to Marna. She wiped it and put it in her pouch. 'He was a warrior, there should be recognition of that.' Thork continued. He took his axe from his belt and positioned it on the dead man's chest, repeating words he had heard Patro announce when someone died.

'I am done here.' Alekander walked away. The others followed.

Phalt and Peria packed dried meat, bannocks and skins of water into one of the sacks and set off. The others collected the remaining sacks. They walked in silence to the bay at Moaness where there was mooring for boats. It was where Thork and Marna had left the small craft they had travelled over on. It belonged to their friend Sempal.

Marna was keen to talk with her brother in private, but he increased his pace whenever she was near enough to speak. The odd rolling of his eyes towards Alekander and Ralfe showed her he didn't want them to hear what she told him.

The weather brightened and when they emerged from the valley the sky was clear. The sun was fading behind one of the hills, to be replaced by the moon popping out from over the summit of the opposite one. Marna watched a pair of seals bob their heads above the surface. From their round faces she recognised them as common seals. They would be pupping soon. Thork raised his right arm and drew it back before realising he didn't have his spear with him.

'Instinct,' he muttered.

The seals dived under and swam off.

'There is a swell on the water,' Thork said.

'No worse than usual,' Ralfe said. He opened the sack he was carrying and nosed inside. Finding it to be empty apart from a cracked pot and an empty sealskin pouch he searched through the sack Alekander had. 'Peria and Phalt have taken the food with them,' he grumbled. 'If we stay here for the night, we will have no supper.' Thork looked to Marna to come up with a reason to wait until morning.

'We have to return Sempal's boat,' she said. 'It wasn't built for rough water and isn't strong enough to carry four people.'

'Why didn't you come over on a boat from the Ness?' Alekander asked. It was a reasonable question.

'Quint wouldn't let us borrow one,' Marna replied. 'I got the impression he didn't want us to come.'

'Don't be stupid. Why should Quint care what we do?' Thork said. 'The boats were simply needed for more important business.'

'Like what?' Marna challenged. Her brother didn't have an answer.

'Sempal lives in Skara Brae,' Alekander said, examining the craft. The willow frame was sturdy, but creaked when he pressed his weight on it. He lifted his fingers to his nose and sniffed. 'Pig fat?

How did he manage to get this raft round the western coast and into the bay of Ireland?'

'He didn't,' Thork said. 'He's at the Ness. He has friends working on the dyke near the new stone ring who gave him the wood to build a boat for us. We have been planning this trip for some time.'

'Alekander, Ralfe and I can take one of the Hoy boats and row over tonight,' Marna said to Thork. 'I can introduce them at the Ness. You remember the trouble Gerk and Olan had last year when they came over from Eynhallow to speak with Patro.' Thork looked bewildered. 'I told you about it. It isn't important. You can bring Sempal's boat back tomorrow, when the sea is calmer.'

'That way you won't have to face the priests or the sea gods,' Ralfe laughed.

Thork shrugged off the slur to his courage. 'Brains win against brawn. We will take Marna's advice although I doubt Quint will agree to see you before morning.'

Ralfe and Alekander went to prepare one of the island boats leaving Marna to speak with her brother.

'They are talking about us,' she said. 'They are suspicious.'

'We have nothing to hide.'

'Will you be safe here alone?' she asked.

'You sound like Caran. I don't need a wife or a sister to guard me. I can take care of myself.'

'I'll keep a watch on Alekander and Ralfe,' Marna said.

'What do you mean?'

'If the pirate lad didn't kill his friend, who did? Quint doesn't care about creating a new society. There are no tanners, rope makers or potters. No-one has the faintest idea how to separate salt from sea water. More able people have tried to start villages here before, but the land is not good for growing grain. The few families who have lived on Hoy for ages are hunters, not farmers. Quint wants stone workers, not settlers. Why would anybody come here willingly?'

'We know Alekander,' Thork argued. 'He stayed at Skara Brae with Sylva for months before they married. Sylva was never happy in Skara Brae after Jona spread those horrible rumours about her running off to have a child, which died. She wanted a new start.'

'What of Ralfe and the others?' Marna persisted. She heard Ralfe and Alekander nearby and lowered her voice.

The men had dragged the boat to the shore and there was a splash as it hit the water.

'Life on Hoy isn't about farming,' Thork said. 'It is about excitement.'

'People still need to eat,' Marna said.

'They can fish and hunt for seals or whales.'

'Patro says we have advanced from that type of dangerous work.'

'Patro has advanced from working at all,' Thork answered.

Marna laughed. Ralfe was in the boat and Alekander was waving from the shore. He had a hand on the prow, steadying it while they waited on her.

'Wishing to leave home doesn't make you a murderer,' Thork said.

'I know that. I'll be fine. See you tomorrow.' Marna gave her brother a peck on the cheek, took her sack and ran down to the boat. Alekander offered her a hand then swung his body in and picked up an oar. The boat wobbled, then righted.

'The journey should be smooth until we round Graemsay,' Ralfe said. 'It can get choppy before we head into the bay of Ireland.'

'I'm used to Sempal's rowing,' Marna said. 'I can cope with waves.'

A pod of porpoises leapt from the water as they rounded the smaller island between Hoy and the mainland. Marna smiled. Her companions' faces were taut from the exertion of rowing and they didn't react. She wished Sempal and his sister Henjar were with her. Sempal would bamboozle them with stories of how sea animals can hold their breaths underwater and Henjar would complain that it was made-up nonsense. She hadn't seen Henjar and her young son Boda since moving to the Ness the previous autumn and she made a note to visit Skara Brae as soon as her mother returned.

Alekander was in more of a hurry to get to the Ness than Ralfe, consequently his rowing was more energetic. The boat lurched. Marna had to grip the sides to stop falling over and despite her bravado her stomach was rolling in time to the boat. She was glad when she spotted the entrance to the bay.

Ralfe and Alekander pulled the boat onto the land and secured it beside two others. It was a fifteen minute walk from the landing site to the Ness, passing the ancient stones of Stenness and the village of Barnhouse, with the tomb of Maeshowe in the distance.

'It will be dark by the time we arrive at the Ness,' Alekander said.

'It never gets dark at the Ness,' Marna said. 'There are lights burning through the night.'

The Ness lookouts spotted them passing the Stenness Stones and as they crossed the stretch of land between the two lochs, they were stopped by a party of four priests. One of the priests raised his torch close to Ralfe's face and he shielded his eyes.

'They are with me.' Marna stepped forwards.

'Marna.' The man sounded surprised. 'It is a strange time to return. Where is Thork? Who are your companions?'

'Thork will be here tomorrow. Alekander and Ralfe are friends from Hoy,' Marna answered. 'They need help.'

'Aye, my wife has been snatched by pirates,' Alekander said. 'You need to send men and boats to search for her.'

The spokesman was above average height, but even he had to tilt his head to stare along his dyed beard at Alekander. 'Do we?' he sneered.

Marna reached for Alekander's arm to prevent him threatening the man. 'It is the duty of the Ness to protect the islands,' she said.

'I thought it was the duty of the Ness to educate them.'

'You thought wrong, Hunkel,' Marna countered.

Hunkel scowled, but knowing who Marna was, he didn't argue.

'We need to speak with Quint,' Marna continued. 'That is, unless Patro and my mother have returned in my absence.'

'There has been no news from them. Perhaps they are afraid of pirates in the Firth and have delayed their voyage home,' Hunkel said.

Following Patro's departure, Hunkel had been promoted to be one of Quint's senior advisors. Marna suspected he wouldn't care if Patro never returned. She would have a word with her mother about him when she came home. First she had to prevent Alekander pushing him into the loch.

'Patro is not afraid of pirates. He will be back before the full moon,' Marna said.

Hunkel smirked. 'Many things can happen before then.'

Ralfe took no part in the conversation. He changed his weight from one foot to the other and while Marna intervened between Hunkel and Alekander he wandered off towards the loch. He suddenly appeared behind Hunkel and put a hand on his shoulder. Hunkel jumped.

'What's the problem?' Ralfe asked, tightening his grip. 'Is Quint not at home?'

Hunkel tried to shake himself free, but Ralfe was strong. The other three priests were armed, but they waited for Hunkel's instructions before stepping in.

'He isn't worth wasting your energy on, Ralfe,' Marna said. 'He's no more than a watchman.'

Marna's words hit a raw spot. Hunkel puffed out his chest and managed to shrug Ralfe off. 'I am Quint's personal aide,' he declared.

'Then you can escort Ralfe and Alekander to the visitors' chambers and send for refreshments while you inform Quint of our arrival.' Marna put on the voice she had heard her mother use when she wanted to be obeyed.

Hunkel hesitated then said, 'I shall inform the head priest of your arrival.'

'The acting head priest,' Marna reminded him.

Two of the priests returned to their watch

duties, while Hunkel and a junior priest led Ralfe, Alekander and Marna to the Ness. Marna still hadn't got used to the imposing town with its boundary walls and monstrous buildings towering over the landscape. Ralfe had never seen it and although Alekander had walked past on several occasions he hadn't approached the gates. She wanted to show her friends the decorated halls and workshops stocked with advanced tools, but Hunkel gave her no time. Back inside the Ness he regained his officious nature. He ordered the junior priest to take Ralfe and Alekander to the guest quarters.

'Wait here while I inform Quint of your arrival,' he instructed Marna.

Marna had no intention of waiting in a cold corridor. She followed Hunkel to a meeting room. Quint was sitting on a cushion, covered by a deerskin, perched on top of a flat stone. He wasn't as tall as Patro and his feet didn't reach the ground. He squirmed to prevent his backside from falling off. A horn player was blasting out notes, two long followed by three short. Quint raised his hand at Hunkel as they entered, instructing him not to speak until the musician finished.

The musician stopped to gather his breath and Marna stepped in front of Hunkel. Quint sighed when he saw her.

'Bored with Hoy or have the islanders had enough of you?'

Marna suffered her step father making jokes about her, but she wasn't going to take insults from his jumped-up brother. 'I have come from Hoy with a ...delegation,' she said. She had heard Patro use the word. It rolled sweetly from her tongue. 'We claim the support that the Ness promised to provide.'

'We? Why is it that you always feel a need to meddle in other people's affairs?'

'The settlement was attacked. I could have been injured or killed. My friend Sylva was kidnapped. I consider that my business,' Marna retorted.

'Mmm.' Quint struggled to shift his well-fattened stomach from the chair and waddled to a side table where various delicacies were laid out. He picked up a roasted bird wing and snapped it in two. 'The village on Hoy is well supported. What more do the settlers want?'

'Men, weapons, boats,' Marna answered.

'We have no boats to spare, as I told you before you set out, but I don't intend discussing matters with you. Where is your brother?'

'He was delayed on Hoy. He will be here tomorrow morning.'

Quint made a show of eating the meat, using a bone to remove a sinew from between his front teeth. He gulped ale from a beaker and burped before addressing Hunkel. 'Has the delegation from Hoy brought any sacks of haematite?'

'I don't believe so,' Hunkel answered.

'We were more concerned with saving Sylva and the village from the pirates,' Marna answered.

Quint licked the fat from his fingers before answering. 'I will discuss the matter with your "delegation" of renegades when Thork returns,' he decided. He turned his back on Marna and signalled the horn player to resume. Hunkel took hold of her arm and pulled her away. She "accidentally" kicked his ankle as she was marched out.

Hunkel left her at the door of her mother and Patro's private dwelling, fuming at how easily Quint had put her down. The house was dank and gloomy. Marna didn't go in. She was reluctant to find Ralfe and Alekander to explain her failure to influence Quint and she decided to visit Sempal and see Pip. Her dog would cheer her up with a sloppy lick or a whack of his tail. Sempal was staying with friends in one of the houses built on the land outside the Ness, home to craftsmen and labourers.

The buildings were alike and Marna couldn't remember which one Sempal was in, but when she reached the first house she heard Pip barking, followed by Sempal's raised voice. Man and dog tumbled out, tangled together. Pip was on top of Sempal. He recognised his mistress and leapt from Sempal's chest to career towards her with his lop-sided gait. She bent to pick the dog up and gave him a kiss.

Sempal got to his feet and rubbed dirt from his tunic. 'What about me?' he asked.

'I can't kiss you, you stink of fish. Is that what we are having for supper?'

'There isn't any left. Pip stole the last morsel. That's why we were wrestling. Is Thork with you?' Sempal asked.

'Why is everyone worried about him?'

'Sorry. I'm guessing you didn't have a good time on Hoy. Did you argue?'

'The village was attacked by pirates. The men

49

were in the woods chopping trees when they landed. Sylva and I managed to warn them and they forced the pirates out.

Sylva was taken prisoner. It sounds like one of your tales, but I'm not making it up. Ask Alekander if you don't believe me. He and his friend Ralfe are here to ask the priests for help.'

'Slow down.' Sempal put a hand on Marna's shoulder, but removed it when Pip growled. 'I believe you,' he said. 'You said Sylva was taken prisoner. Do you know where the pirates have taken her? Did the men capture any of the pirates?'

'One died and some escaped. Two were wounded and couldn't flee to their boats. We were bringing them here when one escaped and the other was murdered.'

'Murdered? You must be in shock,' Sempal said. 'You'd better come inside. Kris and Tama can find space if you want to sleep here tonight.'

Marna was welcomed by a hearty fire and the aroma of the baked fish. Although it was early summer the evenings could be crisp when the sun went down, and winds swept across the island whatever the season. Kris had stuffed moss and heather into the gaps between the stones of the walls to keep out draughts. Marna drew near the fire to warm her hands. Kris was carving patterns on an antler and his wife was using a bone awl to punch holes in a seal skin.

'Hello Tama,' Marna greeted her. 'I don't know how many needles I've broken, trying to sew up seal skins without punching the holes first.'

'You should never try to cut corners,' Tama advised.

'We weren't expecting you back for days. There's nothing wrong, is there?' Kris asked, looking to Sempal.

'I'm afraid so,' Sempal said. 'Is there any ale left?'

Kris fetched Marna a beaker of ale flavoured with meadowsweet. Tama put aside her needlework and arranged skins for them to sit round the fire and hear Marna's tale. She was used to listening to Sempal and despite the horror of her story, she liked the fact that the attention was on her. She took her time to piece together the events.

'The mist came down from the hills,' she explained.

'Not from the sea?' Kris queried.

'We had travelled inland. We were forced to

stop at the Dwarfie Stane when the mist clung in the air and blocked our way ahead.'

'What is the Dwarfie Stane?' Tama asked.

'It's a stone tomb,' Sempal answered. Marna frowned at him and he allowed her to continue.

'It sits alone on a barren hillside, carved from a single boulder the length of five men and the breadth of two. It is sealed with a stone put there by giants.'

From their faces it was clear Kris and Tama found this hard to believe. Marna continued with her story. 'We need to find the lad,' she finished.

'Why is he important?' Tama asked.

'He can lead us to where the pirates have taken Sylva.'

'I don't know Hoy, but I have heard the land is a wilderness,' Kris said. 'Finding one lad will be impossible.

'We have to try,' Marna said. She sipped the remains of her ale.

'Sylva has friends here. We will help if we can,' Sempal re-assured her.

'Quint is preparing a fleet to rout the pirates, isn't that what you told me, Kris?' Tama looked to her husband.

'The boats are ready, but I haven't heard of any plans for them to set out,' Kris answered.

'When Patro returns, he won't delay the attack,' Tama said.

'That could be weeks yet,' Sempal said. 'Patro will send a messenger ahead to tell the Ness when to expect him. Nobody has come. The pirates could finish their business and return to wherever they came from before Patro gets here.'

Marna put her empty beaker down on Pip's tail as he crept closer to the fire. He let out a yelp and Marna gave him a hug, taking comfort from his soft fur.

'Quint has agreed to speak with Ralfe and Alekander when Thork returns tomorrow,' she said. 'They may be able to persuade him to send men to Hoy.'

'I wouldn't count on that,' Sempal said. 'Quint and the elders have been discussing when to take action for days. The only decision they made was when to have another meeting. '

'Then we will have to go to Hoy and find Nuttal,' Marna said.

'We? Nuttal?' Sempal spluttered the questions so that they seemed to merge.

'That is the name I gave to the lad. You have tracking skills, don't you?' Marna answered.

'No, and I have never been to Hoy. Thork has taught me how to recognise signs, but interpreting them is a different matter. You are tired and aren't thinking straight, Marna. You need to sleep.'

'Stay here,' Tama offered again. 'Things will look different in the morning.'

Marna accepted Tama's offer of a bed, but she didn't believe things would improve simply by a night's sleep. She woke early and strolled to the bay to wait on Thork's return.

Her brother had twisted his wrist rowing against the tide and his right hand was swollen larger than a lamb's head. Marna helped him pull the boat up the shore and offered to dress his arm when they got to the Ness.

'Thanks sister, but I need Jolty's skill.'

'Can't you wait? Alekander and Ralfe want to speak with Quint. He won't entertain them unless you are there too.'

'I'm in pain. I can't see Quint until my hand is sorted,' Thork answered. 'Besides, Quint always bathes in the loch at this time.'

Her brother strode off in search of the healer,

leaving Marna to explain the delay to Alekander and Ralfe. She found them in the outdoor pottery. One of the experienced potters was showing Ralfe how to stoke the fire and restrict the air during the process to give the darker ware that the priests preferred. While he explained the need for careful cooling to avoid cracks, there was a commotion at the gate.

'Come on,' Marna urged, taking Alekander's arm. 'You can learn how to be a potter later.'

Marna counted five priests and two lay workers gathered outside the Ness walls. They formed a half-moon around a newly arrived messenger. The man was leaning on a stout stick to stay upright, struggling to breathe. Despite his ragged clothes and tangled beard, Marna recognised him as Yarl, Patro's chief aide. He had been the first to volunteer for the expedition.

Marna rushed towards the group. 'What has happened?' she asked.

Yarl tried to answer. He coughed and there was blood at his mouth. One of the guards offered him water. He drank deeply, spilling half the contents of the skin in his haste. When he finished he wiped his mouth. His face was gaunt. When he caught Marna's eye, he looked away.

Marna felt as if she had been hit by a stone. 'Is it about my mother - where is she?'

Chapter 4

'She is well,' Yarl forced the words out. It seemed an age before he recovered breath to continue. 'She was taken to South Ronaldsay. I came to warn Quint and the elders.' He paused to swallow. 'I bring bad news.'

'Warn us of what? Why didn't my mother come here instead of South Ronaldsay?' Marna demanded.

'It wasn't safe,' Yarl answered.

'What bad news?' Ralfe asked.

'I must speak with Quint,' Yarl waved away their questions. 'He should be the first to know.'

'Know what? We are talking about *my* mother.'

'And *his* brother - I have news of Patro.'

The group of priests had moved closer, eager to ask their own questions. Yarl refused to say any more before seeing Quint. Marna was relieved to hear Jolty's voice. He was the oldest priest at the Ness and was well respected. He was also Quint and Patro's father. The others moved aside to let him through.

'Yarl? What is going on?' he asked. Marna saw a look of fear cross his face. 'Where is my son?'

Yarl bowed his head and looked at the ground. His voice was grave. 'We set off for home before the new moon. Patro wanted to arrive at the Ness for the feasting to mark the achievements of our new priests, but you must know this.'

'No.' Jolty shook his head. 'We weren't expecting them back until the full moon.'

'Patro sent Barnard ahead to advise Quint of his plans. I was there when he gave him his instructions.'

'Barnard? Alone? He hasn't arrived here. There must have been a delay.' Jolty rubbed his chin. 'This could be serious. We shall look into the matter. Go on.'

'We knew the journey would be slow, because one of our boats was laden with gifts from our travels. Mainly stones – chalk from the south of England and pitch stone from Arran, but also skins and polished mace heads from the Hebrides. Patro insisted that he travelled in the same boat as the gifts. He wanted to make sure nothing happened to them.' He paused and turned to Marna. 'Your mother preferred the comfort of one of the larger boats. The chalk gave off white dust that caught in her nose and throat.

We were made welcome wherever we stopped and given shelter, food and fresh water. With a fair wind, we rounded the tip of Scotland yesterday at noon. The weather was fine and we crossed the firth without problems, but as we crept up the coast off Hoy we spotted two boats that were floundering although the water wasn't rough. I was in the same boat as Patro. We were the nearest to the troubled crafts. Grateful for the hospitality we had ourselves received as strangers, Patro was keen to help. He could not have known they were pirates and their helplessness was a trick.

We were taken by surprise as we pulled up beside them. Patro is a strong fighter when needs be and he fended off the attack, but during the skirmish Gord and Rakso were dragged overboard. Gord was not a strong swimmer and was hit by a spear in the water. Rakso made it to your mother's boat and was picked up. He warned the rowers to flee. Your mother was anxious about Patro.'

'What of my son?' Jolty asked.

'He took an axe to the side of his skull, slicing his head from ear to beard. He toppled into the water and didn't rise to the surface.'

'What are you saying?' Jolty's face was pale.

'The pirates had hold of our boat, tying it with ropes to their own. I jumped into the water to search for Patro, but the current was strong. His staff was floating on the waves, but I couldn't find its owner. I dived under until my eyes became blurred, my skull pulsed and I was too weak to search further. Rakso pulled me into the second boat. The pirates' crafts were lighter than ours. Even dragging our boat between them, they had a head start and were faster. We couldn't follow them.'

'You mean my son is lost?' Jolty said.

'I have his staff.' Yarl shifted his weight and lifted the stick he had been leaning on. It was tangled with seaweed, but Marna could see it was the High Priest's staff. Patro attached it to his belt with leather throngs when he was unable to hold it. 'I saved it from the pirates,' Yarl said, 'I'm sorry I couldn't save its owner.'

Jolty accepted the staff. The gathering hushed as Yarl's words sank in. They stood looking at one another. No-one was willing to break the silence until Quint approached from the loch.

'Hasn't anybody got work to do?' he asked.

Nobody answered, or moved to return to their business. 'Yarl, what are you doing here? Has the Stonehenge expedition returned? I must welcome my brother and sister-in-law. Where are they?'

Quint looked around. His voice held a hint of something Marna couldn't grasp. It was as if he knew what had happened. Yarl's demeanour would tell him the situation was wrong, but Quint seemed to be mocking him.

Jolty took hold of his son's arm and led him aside. Marna didn't hear them speak. She saw Jolty raising the staff for Quint to examine and expected Quint's face to turn white as Jolty's had. Instead she glimpsed a smile, before he controlled his muscles and changed it to a frown. He grabbed the staff from Jolty and the two priests walked off. Marna moved to speak with Yarl.

'You said my mother was well?' she probed.

'She wasn't injured, but the shock of seeing her husband fall...'

'Ah.' Marna didn't need to hear the rest. Her father had fallen from a cliff and drowned and Wilmer, her mother's suitor before she married Patro, had drowned in the loch. To have a third partner die in a similar manner was more than bad luck. 'I have to go to her.'

'She will return to the Ness when she is ready,' Yarl said. His shoulders slouched. Marna prepared to let him go, but Thork was storming towards them.

'I can't find Jolty anywhere,' he complained to Marna then noticed the messenger. 'Yarl, what are you doing here?'

Thork insisted that Yarl repeat his tale. He interrupted with questions every time Yarl paused. Marna grew impatient.

'Patro is dead,' she said. 'Mother is in South Ronaldsay.'

Thork stood for a moment with his mouth open. 'What about the ceremony? South Ronaldsay, why there? She said she would be back to hear my drumming.'

Marna sighed. 'Patro is dead.' She spoke loudly and slowly. 'Can't you think of anything but your drum?'

'I wasn't thinking of that, it's just a shock,' Thork said. He straightened up. 'Mum needs support. She needs family with her. I'm going to fetch her.' He clenched his right knuckle and banged it into his left fist, forgetting about his injury. He grimaced and held his wrist.

'You can't row to South Ronaldsay with that hand,' Marna said.

'I've got another one. I'll get Sempal to come with me, if that pleases you.'

Marna could think of no objection. Thork strode towards the Ness to prepare for his journey, his pain forgotten.

So much for her idea of returning to Hoy, Marna thought.

The priests were dispersing in a hum of confusion. Marna returned her attention to Yarl. 'What happens now?' she asked him.

'I need to speak with Quint and the elders,' Yarl answered.

'You have given your account of events. You need to rest.'

'I know the coast round Hoy. There are inlets where pirates can hide, but with a boat load of stones their options are limited. I think I know where they would head to. We need to act swiftly. If you will excuse me...'

'You need to speak with Quint,' Marna finished his sentence.

Yarl turned and followed Thork towards the

buildings.

Alekander and Ralfe had moved out of hearing distance to discuss their own matters when Quint had appeared. They waited until Quint walked off with Jolty before approaching again, concerned that their meeting with Quint would be postponed. Thork, then Yarl, marched past without speaking and they feared Marna was about to abandon them too. They moved to stop her leaving.

'Were the pirates who attacked Patro the same ones who took Sylva?' Alekander asked.

'I don't know,' Marna answered.

'We haven't been bothered by pirates for years,' Ralfe said. 'It would be odd to have two groups of pirates now.'

'Patro made alliances with the people in Northern Scotland and Ireland,' Marna said. 'We trade, we don't rob one another.'

Alekander pulled his beard. 'They must have known Patro was away.'

'He's been away before,' Marna said.

'Not for this length of time,' Alekander said.

'Why did he have to take half the council with him?' Ralfe asked.

'There is safety in numbers and he wanted to

impress the Southerners.'

'He cares more about strangers in the South than us. My wife is a prisoner.' Alekander jabbed the air with a finger. Ralfe put a hand on his shoulder.

'Staying here will achieve nothing.'

They left Marna alone. She wasn't sure what to do. She could nag her brother to take her with him to South Ronaldsay or she could remain at the Ness and discover what Quint and the elders intended to do. It was unlikely she would be able to influence their actions and an inner voice told her she would find out more on Hoy.

She wanted to go back to the Dwarfie Stane and re-trace what had happened. How had Nuttal managed to steal her knife? The mist obscured a great deal, but his hands had been tied. She had replaced the knife in the sack, she remembered doing so and she had been watching his every movement. Why had he killed his friend? Despite what the others thought, it didn't make sense.

Her feet began walking while she thought. They took her back inside the Ness walls, to be jostled by priests and craftsmen who should have been working. Yarl's arrival had brought about a myriad of unexpected activity. Quint had called a meeting of senior priests and advisors. They couldn't have any sort of gathering at the Ness, Marna had discovered, without a feast to match.

Fires were lit in every building and food was prepared. Meat was chopped, sprinkled with herbs and roasted. The heat and smell, mixed with her unsettled emotions, made Marna feel faint. Quint had given word for dried aromatic roots to be burnt to help Patro's spirit pass over between worlds and Marna choked on the smoky scent. She wiped a tear from her eye and as she did she thought of Patro. It had taken her a while to get used to her step-father, and she couldn't honestly say that she liked him, but she knew her mother would be devastated by his loss – which meant living with her would be difficult. Once Thork brought her home, leaving to go to Hoy would be impossible.

Unless...

An idea came to Marna and she punched the air. Her mother liked having people she knew around her – people she could talk sense to. She enjoyed the comforts of living at the Ness, but never ceased to complain about the priests who classed star-gazing as serious business. One of the reasons she had accompanied Patro on his latest trip was to see for herself the standing stones, dolmans, dykes and circles they enthused about, and decide if they were worth it.

Marna's idea was to send a message to Skara Brae, where they used to live, and ask their old neighbours to visit and keep her mother company. Lin would come, with her daughter Henjar and little Boda, who was now walking and getting into all sorts of mischief.

Two of the Ness herdsmen were taking a young bull from the Ness herd to Skara Brae. The village only kept one old bull and needed new blood to freshen their breeding stock. The herdsmen were happy to take Marna's message.

'Tell Henjar I have new dyes she will like,' Marna said. 'Light green and orange.'

'Henjar, is she the pretty one with the little blonde boy?' one of the men asked.

'Yes, and also a husband,' Marna answered.

She left the herdsmen and went in search of Sempal and Thork. They were arguing when she found them, but stopped as she approached. Thork had his drum slung round his neck and Sempal was struggling under the weight of two sacks. When he spotted Marna, Thork took hold of one of the sacks.

'We're ready to set off for South Ronaldsay,' he said.

'You won't need your drum,' Marna said.

'Mother will want to be cheered up,' Thork answered. 'I can play my new tunes for her. I've composed one about her and Patro's wedding. Do you want to hear it?'

Marna turned to roll her eyes at Sempal, which her brother didn't notice. 'I'm afraid there isn't time.' She gave them both a kiss on the cheeks. 'Take care. There may be pirates in the Flow.'

'I'm not afraid of pirates,' Thork answered. 'Let them try to mess with me.' He moved his cloak to show a mace stuck in his belt.'

'One mace won't help against a boat full of marauders,' Marna said.

'The drumming might,' Sempal teased.

'Or Thork could bore them to death with his story of how the jadeite travelled from the Alps to Ireland then over here, to be made into his mace head,' Marna said.

'Ha, ha. Why don't you do something girly like stringing beads, while we men do the work?'

'I shall be filling beds with fresh heather and

straw, adding sprigs of bog myrtle to repel fleas.'

'Why?'

'I have invited your mother and sister to stay here, Sempal.'

'What – they get to sleep inside the Ness?' Sempal said. 'And feast on fresh beef.'

'They will be special guests of my mother,' Marna answered, feeling smug. She didn't admit that apart from feasts, their normal diet was no different from anyone else's.

She watched the men head towards the Brig O' Wraith where Thork had moored Sempal's boat. If he hadn't taken care to cover it against the weather, Sempal would show his disapproval. Despite what she told Thork, there was no need to arrange beds straight away. Her friends wouldn't arrive until at least the following afternoon. The sun had risen above Wideford hill and was shining over the water of the lochs. There was a light breeze to freshen the air, perfect for a stroll to gather herbs. She would take Pip. They both needed to stretch their legs.

She collected her dog and borrowed a sealskin pouch from Tama to collect the plants in. She headed towards the bank of Stenness loch, at the back of the new stone circle being built at Brodgar.

It was too early for the meadowsweet to be flowering, but she could pick leaves and there were reeds and plenty of comfrey plants, which could have helped Thork's wrist if he had allowed her to treat him. She took care to protect her fingers gathering the prickly leaves.

Pip amused himself by barking at his reflection in the water although Marna supposed he may have seen a seal. It wasn't uncommon for one to make its way into the loch across the narrow land barrier from the sea. When the bark became a howl she looked up in time to hear a splash. Her heart jumped. Pip hated water. He wouldn't go into the loch unless he was thrown.

'Pip,' she called, dropping her pouch and hurrying to where her dog had left muddy paw prints. 'Oh no.' He was in the water, frantically doggy paddling a few feet from the bank. The water wasn't deep and Marna was able to wade in. She grabbed his scruff before his head disappeared under. He struggled in her arms, soaking her tunic. 'What's wrong Pip?'

Pip wouldn't stop barking. There was something in the water, floating a little way out. Reeds had tangled round it and it was attracting flies. It wasn't alive and it wasn't a seal.

Marna felt the life drain from her face. Her stomach contents gurgled and she tasted bile. Her feet sank into the mud of the loch bottom as she stood in the water gazing at the body. It was face down with arms outstretched and a mace lodged between the shoulder blades.

Chapter 5

'Marna, what are you doing in the loch?' She heard a voice and swivelled round to see Jolty coming towards her. The water rippling against her ankles felt heavy, but the words stirred her into motion. She dragged herself to the bank with Pip squirming in her arms. She was crying when she met Jolty.

'He thought it was Wilmer,' she said absently.

Jolty took Pip from her, put him on the ground and took hold of Marna's hands. 'What is this talk of the drowned jeweller? Are you all right?' he asked.

'Animals don't forget. Wilmer was his old master.' She looked towards the body and Jolty's eyes followed hers. He gasped. 'I don't know who that is,' she said. 'He's dead.'

'Stay here. I'll take a look.' Jolty removed his cloak and handed it to her before wading into the water. He took hold of the dead man's belt. Although he was strong for his age, he struggled to drag the body to the bank. Marna stood shaking, unable to believe what she saw.

Another body in a loch. It couldn't be true.

Jolty managed to edge the corpse near the bank and she reached to help him. Together they succeeded in pulling the body out of the loch. There was a thud as Jolty rolled the corpse over. Marna looked away.

'It's Yarl,' Jolty said.

Marna faced Jolty rather than look at the bloated features. 'It can't be. He has only recently arrived. You saw him,' she said.

'I saw that he was exhausted,' Jolty answered. 'If he tumbled into the loch, he wouldn't have had the strength to get out.'

'He wasn't going to the loch,' Marna's mind was clearing. 'He went inside to find Quint and the elders. He said he knew Hoy and had an idea where the pirates were hiding.'

Jolty shook his head. 'Quint called the elders. We gathered, a beef stew was served, Quint was keen to start eating, but Yarl did not appear. That is why I am here – I came to look for him and I heard your dog howl.'

Marna forced herself to look at the dead man. 'Where has it gone?'

'Where has what gone?'

'He had a mace in his back. I saw it. Did you remove it when you turned him?'

'I didn't see anything.' Jolty bent to force the

body onto its side.

'It was there.' Marna pointed at a dark area on Yarl's shoulder. 'Beneath that green stain on his neck.'

Marna grimaced as Jolty poked his knife into the wound. 'There is no evidence of a broken mace head,' he said.

'It could have fallen in the water when you shifted him. He was attacked,' Marna said. 'He must have been waylaid before he reached the meeting room by somebody who didn't want him to talk with Quint.'

'You are racing ahead. Your mind is unsettled. I can understand why.' Jolty laid Yarl onto his back. He stood up, stretched his spine and gave it a rub. 'We need to find strong men to shift the body. Quint shall have to be informed at once.'

'What can I do?' Marna asked.

'You have done enough. You have had a tiring few days. You should rest.'

'I can't. I need to do something,' Marna protested. 'I could search for the missing mace.'

Jolty sighed. 'And get yourself drowned too.' He raised a hand to brush aside Marna's protests. 'I bumped into Thork while he was searching for his drum. He said he was going to fetch your mother. You could help by making the house welcoming for her return. Coming home without...Pat...' He faltered as he spoke his son's name. '...Under these terrible circumstances, won't be easy.'

'I'm sorry,' Marna said.

'The worst part is that it happened at home, after all his travels, but life goes on.' Jolty glanced at Yarl's body. 'For some,' he added softly.

They stood in silence for a moment.

'Quint intends holding a feast in Patro's honour for the nearby villagers,' Jolty continued. 'There is talk of erecting a standing stone on the path leading to the Ness.'

'Patro's stone,' Marna said. 'He would like that. I'll attend to the house. I'll light a fire to warm the stone and gather sweet flowers to make it smell fresh.'

Jolty left her inside the gate and went to inform the elders of Yarl's death. Marna made her way to her parents' house. It was unusual to have individual houses in the Ness, but Patro had instructed it to be built. It sat next to the main celebratory chamber, and Patro had it painted as brightly. He liked colour; on the walls, the dresser, the beds. Her mother liked wall hangings and dyed woollen cushions and rugs. Despite this, when she entered the house, she was met by a chilly draught. The stone numbed her hands. She feared if she left them for long, her fingers would turn to icicles. The skins on the beds were damp, with mildew creeping round the edges. The ochre on the walls had faded and a grey dust covered the floor and dresser.

When her parents left on their journey, she had thought it would be fun to have the space to herself, but after a day she wanted company and moved into a communal dormitory. She ran a finger along the dresser the way her mother did. Her first task would be to clean the surfaces. The water cist was empty. Being Patro's step daughter had its advantages. She was able to call on two of the older children, whose duty it was to fetch water from the loch, and instruct them to fill the cist.

She set about cleaning, beating ash from the skins before airing them. Afterwards she went to the storeroom for fresh ochre and yellow clay to redo the patterns on the wall. Norra was in the neighbouring workshop grinding malachite. She was happy to take a break to help, bringing along deer hair brushes and spatulas.

Norra wasn't a member of the senior enclave, but she had been at the Ness for as long as Patro, studying the properties of different types of earth. She was able to advise farmers on what to plant, where and when and was helping Marna with her studies. Norra had an ear for gossip and Marna bombarded her with questions while they worked.

'I would have thought an attack on Patro and his party would have Quint rushing to send a force to rout the pirates,' Marna said. 'I haven't seen anyone sharpening weapons or gathering supplies.'

'Quint is not like his brother,' Norra answered. 'He likes to have every detail thought through before committing to a plan.'

'You mean Patro is hot-headed,' Marna said with a laugh, before remembering the situation. 'Was,' she corrected in a grave voice. 'I didn't mean...'

Norra looked away. 'That's the walls done, what about the floor?'

'My mother has a rug,' Marna answered. 'I put it aside while we were using the ochre.'

'One moth-eaten, old rug?' Norra scoffed. 'Not much of a homecoming. Your mother likes coloured pebbles. Why don't we collect stones from the shores of the lochs? Patro was fascinated by the different textures and shapes. He was keen to know why some were a certain colour and others a combination of different tones. He told me, when he was younger, it was a source of wonder to him that certain stones could be broken open to reveal crystals, while others held the shapes of insects or bones of fish. It will be strange not having him here, forever questioning things. Really interested, not criticising, like Quint.'

'I know.' Marna took the other woman's hand and rubbed it between her palms. 'Collecting pebbles is an excellent idea. We can polish them and make them shine.'

Norra wiped a tear from her eye and looked round the room. The walls were bright, but the space still felt lifeless.

'It will be cosier after I light a fire,' Marna said. 'There's no point doing that yet. The smoke will undo the cleaning.'

'You need more skins,' Norra decided. 'I know where the best ones are stored. We can lay out the deer skins in that corner to match the red wall. The seal skins will sit snugly over the stones in the corner and once we've renewed the heather on the bed we can cover it with tinted sheep skins.'

'I wish I had your eye for colour,' Marna said.

'It is so dark in here,' Norra said. 'We need lights, lots of them, twinkling like the stars.'

'That will remind my mother of Patro,' Marna said.

'You think it is bad idea?'

'No. Sometimes it is good to remember. Let's go for the pebbles while the day is warm.'

Marna hadn't told Norra about her gruesome find in the loch. Her nerves were raw and she wasn't ready to speak of the event. When Norra suggested they search for pebbles near the spot, Marna felt a lump in her throat and had to think of an excuse to avoid the area. 'Mother loves the red and yellow pebbles on the beach at Skaill that are sought after for making jewellery. We don't have time to go there, but I have seen similar pebbles at the Brig O' Wraith. We can find pretty shells too.'

They made their way south to where the Stenness loch reached its fingers to touch the sea. A small strip of land separated the two.

Norra took time to pick individual stones while Marna filled her pouch with handfuls of pebbles without being choosy. They returned to the Ness and Marna polished the stones while Norra prepared a meal with barley and eggs collected from the loch the previous day.

A messenger came to tell them that Quint had called a meeting of the community that evening. They met in the building near the south wall. It was large enough for everyone with room to spare, which allowed Quint to take his place at the head of the gathering. He held Patro's staff, which had been scrubbed and repainted.

News had travelled and most of the folk inside the Ness and in the surrounding huts knew of Patro's death. Quint made an elaborate show of his grief as he outlined his plan to hold a feast and erect a standing stone in his brother's honour. There were tears in his eyes, but Marna suspected if they were real the skin round his eyes would be red and puffy.

Quint made no mention of Yarl's death and if he had expected the meeting to pass quietly, he was mistaken. The people registered their horror and sadness at the death of their leader. Those who were close to Patro took their places at the front and spoke well of him. Marna considered adding words on behalf of her mother, but decided not to. After the speeches, the mood changed and people wanted answers and action. Alekander was the first to step forward. He pulled at his cloak as he spoke, but his impatience and anger countered his nerves.

'We on Hoy are sad to learn of Patro's death,' he began, 'But the Ness is not the only place to suffer at the hands of these pirates. My wife...' There was a mumbling among those gathered. Everyone knew of Sylva's plight. 'My wife is alive,' Alekander declared. 'At least, she was when I left Hoy.'

'I am aware of the situation,' Quint snapped, but hurriedly revised his tone. 'We are working on the matter.'

'The pirates must be stopped. Now!' Alekander raised his voice. 'It is time to fight, not to talk, feast or raise stones.'

The potters, rope makers and masons clustered in one of the corners cheered. The priests quietened them with sour looks, annoyed by Alekander's disrespect for their traditions.

'The Ness is doing everything we can,' Quint replied glibly. Alekander made a noise through his teeth that showed he didn't believe him. Quint raised his staff. 'Boats are ready to set out once we have the information we need to inflict maximum damage to the pirates. Random attacks on small groups will weaken our force and hinder victory. It must be added that the raiders are not our only concern. We have other affairs of equal importance to deal with.'

'Like what?' Alekander challenged.

'The Ness is a major centre. A trade delegation from the Northern isles will arrive here when the full moon brings favourable tides. We need to prepare beds, bread and meats for them and have ample cisterns of fresh water. There are ceremonies to be organised. A party of drummers intend visiting from Ireland to share their music and we have young priests to initiate. As you are aware, the solstice is not too distant.'

'Traders, drummers, the solstice – what of them? My wife's life is in danger.'

'Would you have us deny hospitality and anger the gods?' Quint said.

Flemeer, one of the senior priests stood forward to speak 'Before we can consider our plans, we need to decide on a leader.'

'We need time to consider how we wish our community to advance,' the priest, Vill, said.

'We know what your ideas are,' Flemeer turned on him. 'You would turn our place of study into a training camp for thugs to take over the island.'

Flemeer and Vill both had followers and arguments broke out.

'The news of Patro's death only reached us this morning,' Norra spoke with a quiver in her voice. 'We cannot think about a replacement before we mourn our loss.'

'Aye, where is Yarl?' Flemeer asked. 'Shouldn't he be here?'

Marna wondered why Jolty did not rise to clarify matters. When he had left her, he had gone to inform the elders of Yarl's death. It seemed odd that Flemeer had not heard the news. Looking round, she couldn't see Jolty among the gathering. Quint banged his staff on a flagstone.

'After his recent experiences, Yarl is in no state to address a meeting such as this. My father is currently attending to him.'

'That isn't right,' Marna said, but her voice was drowned by Quint's. No-one else contradicted him.

'It will not be easy for anyone to take over

from my brother.' The reminder of Patro brought a sense of order to the room, allowing Quint to continue. 'Deliberations will take time. I am happy to stand in until a worthy successor is chosen. As our friends from Hoy have said, we need to re-evaluate our response to the pirate raids. Men, weapons and supplies are not granted simply by calling to the gods.'

'Or by calling to the Ness,' Alekander retorted. His supporters laughed, but the priests rallied together.

'Quint should lead us,' Hunkel called from the back of the room. He strode forwards with three friends and stood next to Quint, pushing Alekander and Flemeer out of the way. Ralfe was about to get to his feet, but he was pulled back by the priest beside him. Intimidated by the hostile atmosphere growing among the gathering, Marna decided to hold her tongue about Yarl.

Having Hunkel at his side bolstered Quint's confidence. He began speaking again. 'I have a vision of a raised altar to the gods housed in a stone hall with decorated walls. We must reconsider our priorities. The plans to build workshops and dormitories for visiting students must be halted. We need to please the gods, not probe their heavens.'

'Aye,' one of the men beside Hunkel agreed with his fist raised.

Quint hadn't said 'Patro's plans to build workshops and dormitories', but that is what he meant. Marna had heard her mother and step-father discuss future developments at the Ness. Patro was keen to build on their reputation as a place of learning and discovery. Her mother was supportive, but also practical. There were skilled potters at the Ness and those with the knowledge to control firing processes. She wanted to expand the pottery production to produce quality ware that would entice traders from different lands, who in turn would share their cultures, know how and produce.

'Arrangements will be made to re-allocate Patro's property,' Quint said.

'What!' This was going too far for Marna. She jumped up. The elders were shocked by her interruption, but she wasn't deterred. 'Thork has left for South Ronaldsay to fetch my mother. They will be back tomorrow. She should have a say in what she keeps and what she feels would be of more value to others.'

'Your mother,' Quint sneered. He hesitated,

judging the mood of the room. Hunkel snorted and wiped his nose on the back of his hand. Quint chuckled. 'I never understood what my brother saw in her. She may have amused him on Eynhallow, but marriage? Seriously? It wouldn't surprise me if she weds again and you have a new father before the winter is upon us.'

Marna's face blazed like a well stoked fire. She wished Thork was there to bloody Quint's nose. 'You never liked my mother,' she hissed. 'You don't even know her name.'

'I have nothing against...her,' Quint answered. 'She is pleasing to look at, but a farmer's widow from a coastal village is unfit to be the head priest's wife, but enough of this,' Quint sensed he had gone too far and was in danger of losing ground. 'I shall speak to your mother when she arrives. There is no further business.' He turned to leave and was surrounded by Hunkel and his guards who fended off protests.

Marna sat down in a huff with her elbows on her knees. Once Quint had gone, the room emptied. Alekander moved to sit beside her.

'Quint shouldn't speak about your mother like that,' he said.

'Wait til she does come back. She'll put him in his place,' Marna said defiantly.

'Your mother is a wise woman. I'm sorry I will miss seeing her. I intend returning to Hoy tomorrow morning. Ralfe and I have spoken. He will stay here and keep nagging the council, but I see no point in talking. I need action. I'm going to search every valley, hill, cave and bay on Hoy until I find the pirates or that boy who escaped.'

'You won't manage that alone. Why don't you wait until Thork gets back?'

'He is more interested in his drumming and priestly duties in Orphir,' Alekander said.

'That is unfair,' Marna argued.

Alekander thought for a moment. 'If I wait on Thork, are you sure he will come with me? He has a wife and child to consider.'

'Yes. Caran would want him to help Sylva. Sempal will go too.'

'We'll need someone to tell us stories to raise our spirits,' Alekander said.

'He may have been born with a crooked leg, but Sempal can fight if he has to.'

Alekander looked wary, but he didn't argue. He got up and helped Marna to her feet. She was about to confide in him that Yarl had been killed, but he bade her goodnight and left.

Late the following morning, Sempal's boat was spotted approaching the bay, with Thork and Marna's mother on board. Marna had prepared a fire and coaxed it to heat the house. Despite the new skins, coloured stones and twinkling oil lights, she felt the room was cold. It needed something lighter, to lift the chill in the air.

Flowers, she thought. Both her mother and Patro loved flowers. Patro liked the bright colours and her mother appreciated their scents. There was time to pick a handful before her mother arrived. She made her way towards the gate, pausing when she heard raised voices inside the woodworkers' workshop. The door was ajar and although she couldn't see anyone, she recognised Quint's nasal voice.

Pressing against the wall to make sure she wasn't seen, Marna listened to the conversation. She couldn't work out who Quint was speaking to, which made it difficult to follow the flow.

'Fool,' Quint shouted. Marna pictured the dribble spurting from his mouth.

'It wasn't my fault,' the other person replied.

88

The voice was higher pitched than Quint's, but it could have been a man or a woman. 'Besides, the problem is solved.'

They carried on in quieter tones. Marna strained her ears, but she couldn't make out words. Finally a third voice said, 'Yarl was a good man.'

'He was Patro's man,' Quint answered coldly.

Marna was desperate to hear the rest of the conversation, but she heard footsteps getting louder as they came along the passageway towards her. She stepped away from the door and pretended to adjust her belt as Jolty appeared.

'Marna, what are you doing here?' he asked.

'I'm on my way to pick fresh flowers for my mother's return.'

'She'll appreciate that,' Jolty agreed, glancing towards the workshop door. 'She and Patro both love daisies. Patro would spend hours as a little boy weaving them into chains.'

'I can't imagine Patro as a child,' Marna said.

'He has…had…a lot of responsibility here, but your mother made him feel young. It was one of the things that drew him to her. It's hard to believe he is no longer with us. Things will change, but I hope you will continue with your work. Patro was intrigued by it.'

'I don't see why. I'm not getting anywhere. The climate here isn't suitable for early food plants, not even the kale I've been testing.'

'I wouldn't give up,' Jolty said. 'But I was referring to your other work.'

'I'll always continue with my dyes,' Marna assured him.

Jolty touched the side of his nose with a finger. 'I meant your sleuthing.' He tilted his head towards the door. Quint's voice could be heard, but he was speaking about mundane matters. The word 'cattle' was repeated.

'I wasn't eavesdropping,' Marna said. The lie sounded feeble.

'Of course not, but I know you are keen to find out who killed Yarl. I'm surprised that you haven't weighed me down with questions. Don't you trust me?'

'What do you mean?' Marna said.

'You saw a mace in Yarl's body, which wasn't there when we pulled the body onto the bank,' Jolty said.

'I don't blame you for losing it.'

Jolty moved closer and spoke in a low voice.

90

'There are things going on that you don't understand.' He scratched his head and said more jovially, 'I'm not sure I do either.'

He walked off before Marna remembered the questions she wanted to ask him.

He hadn't told the elders of Yarl's death when he said he would. Who had prevented him and why?

Chapter 6

Marna saw the boat with Thork and her mother while she was in the meadow. She had already picked enough flowers to decorate the house and ran back to lay them on the dresser before returning. Thork was a stronger rower than she gave him credit for and she met the party as they made their way past the Stenness Stones. A crowd of well-wishers from Barnhouse and the Ness had already gathered. Marna squeezed in front of them.

'I thought you would have come to meet us at the bay,' Thork complained.

They were accompanied by the remaining priests and aides who had been on the expedition with Patro, bringing the remaining gifts that the pirates hadn't pilfered to the Ness. Marna didn't see Sempal among the party and imagined he was tending to his boat.

The priests cleared a path for her mother. Marna barely recognised her and might not have if Thork hadn't put a hand on her shoulder. She had caught the sun on her visit south and her complexion was ruddy, but her hair looked greyer and her face was lined with worry. It was at odd times like this that Marna remembered how old her mother was.

Marna could only see her mother's head above the well-furred body of an enormous animal. She knew it was a skin, but it belonged to no beast she had seen or dreamt of.

She pushed through a bunch of gossips to give her mother a huge hug. The fur she was wearing was soft and deep and her face was buried in it as her mother returned the embrace. When she was released she couldn't help stroking the pelt.

'It's from a bear,' her mother said. 'The elders in a place called Aylesbury presented it to me.'

'A bear?' Marna said. 'What is that?'

'Bears are beasts that are bigger than a grown man when they stand on their hindquarters and more than twice the weight.'

'Did you see a live one?'

'Thankfully not. Bears are extremely dangerous, stronger than Thork and more hot-headed than you are.'

Marna laughed at the joke. She put an arm round her mother's waist and walked with her and her brother towards the entrance to the Ness, stroking the luxurious fur when no-one was watching. She felt a little red-faced about the inferior skins she had lain out for her mother's return.

'Where is Quint?' her mother demanded of the men at the gate. One of them scurried off to find him and report the return of the party. Quint did not arrive himself. He sent one of his junior priests to pass on a message. He would speak with Marna's mother in good time, once she had rested.

'There is no time to rest,' her mother insisted. 'A party should already have been sent to Hoy.'

'Why, what is the immediate danger?' the messenger asked.

'There is the danger of not finding my husband before the sea has consumed him. He must be brought back to the Ness and prepared for burial with full honours.'

'Patro's body could be anywhere,' the priest countered. 'It may have washed up on Hoy. The currents may have taken it towards South Ronaldsay or Scotland. It could have been caught by the seaweeds and snared below the waves.' He stopped short of suggesting it could have been eaten by large fish, but Marna sensed it was on his tongue.

'I don't care if fifty men and women have to

scourge every island from now until the winter solstice. Patro will be found and please stop referring to him as "it".'

Marna admired her mother's determination, but she couldn't see Quint agreeing to her demand. The young priest was embarrassed. He had nothing to say, but her mother held him with her gaze.

'I've prepared your room,' Marna said. 'Norra helped me. We collected pebbles and I picked daisies to decorate the dresser.' Her mother didn't look as pleased about it as Marna hoped, but she understood why. 'Lin, Henjar and little Boda are coming to visit,' she added.

'From Skara Brae? When?'

'I sent a message to the village yesterday morning.'

'Let them come,' her mother said. 'I imagine with the news of Patro they will try to persuade me to return with them to Skara Brae. They may succeed. There is nothing for me here now.'

'You mean you would go back to live there?' Marna asked. 'What will happen to your work with the healing herbs?'

'I can continue that in Skara Brae, if I have a mind to. Jolty can teach the younger priests here.'

'He doesn't try out new mixtures and plants. Besides, Jolty is old,' Marna said. 'He won't be around for ever.'

'Neither will I,' her mother replied.

Marna could tell her mother was in one of her awkward moods. She stepped away from Marna to link arms with Thork and allowed him to lead her to her house. Marna followed a little way behind. As she reached the door she heard her mother scream.

'What is it?' She rushed up. 'Oh.' She had left the hut open to let in fresh air. It had also allowed Pip to sneak in. The dog was lying across one of the cots licking his tail. All the pretty flowers had been knocked from the dresser and beheaded, the coloured pebbles she had gathered were scattered across the floor and the skins were covered in hair.

'That animal had better not come anywhere near my bearskin,' her mother yelled. 'Get it out of here.'

Thork tried to grab Pip, but he squirmed free and scurried between her mother's legs to reach Marna.

'Bad boy,' Marna scolded, lifting him in her arms. 'You know you aren't meant to be in the house.'

Her mother slumped onto the second cot. She looked exhausted and there were tears in her eyes.

'I'll clean up the mess,' Marna said. She put Pip down and bent to pick up the flower heads.

'Don't worry, mum,' Thork said. 'Whatever Quint decides, I'll gather a group of my friends together and we'll set out for Hoy as soon as we can. We will find Patro's body.'

'What about the drumming ceremony?' his mother asked.

'Quint and the elders have postponed it while the community is in mourning for Patro,' Marna answered.

'I'll find one of the helpers and tell them to fetch you food and hot ale,' Thork said. 'Then I'll find Stu and the lads I hunt with. Sempal should have finished attending to his precious boat too.'

'Alekander and Ralfe are here,' Marna said. 'Alekander has worn his nails down waiting to return to Hoy although Ralfe intends staying at the Ness for a while.'

'We'll need people who know the island,' Thork agreed.

'Yarl is from Hoy,' Marna's mother put in.

'He knows the bays and inlets. He was pointing them out when we spotted the pirate boats. If he has recovered from the attack, he will be able to help you.' Marna's mouth dropped open. 'He has returned, hasn't he?' her mother queried.

'Emm, yes.'

'His injuries were not serious, I hope,' her mother said.

'Not from the pirate attack, but...' Marna wasn't sure how to tell her mother the news. She was saved by the entrance of Jolty. Marna's mother sat up. He embraced her and she returned the greeting. Marna put the flower heads on the dresser then touched Thork on the shoulder.

'We should leave them to talk,' she whispered.

Marna and Thork made their way out, with Pip following. Marna agreed to arrange for her mother's food and drink while Thork went to speak with his friends. She was itching to volunteer to go with him, but she had a duty to stay with her mother, at least until Lin and Henjar arrived. She tried to work out when that would be. Boda could walk at home without support, but he would have to be carried from Skara Brae and he was growing into a stout lad. She couldn't delay Thork's departure for more than a day.

When Thork reported back, he hadn't had the success he anticipated. His fellow drummers were preparing for the mourning ceremonies and they weren't keen to go anywhere without permission from the council. The hunters had reports of a herd of boars foraging in the Orphir hills that they were anxious to track. He returned to the house in a state of frustration, upsetting the pots of food that had been brought for Marna and her mother. He swore curses between stuffed mouthfuls of cured fish and strips of smoked ham.

'When you have finished eating, you can come with me to find Quint,' his mother said. 'He won't come here to talk. He made some ridiculous excuse of feeling sick.'

'The woman who brought the food told us,' Marna explained.

Marna cleared the pots while Thork went with his mother in search of Quint. They didn't find him.

'He wasn't in the Ness,' Thork said. 'Jolty thought he had gone to Barnhouse, but the people there swore a fisherman had taken him out on his boat in Harray Loch.'

'We kept missing him,' her mother said.

The atmosphere in the house that evening was as cold as a winter wind. Marna wished Sempal would appear to tell a tale or two. Her mother wasn't ready to speak about her adventures in the south. Instead, Marna began to tell her mother about the new village on Hoy. She was explaining how the settlers were making use of local materials, chopping trees and gathering seaweed, when Thork took over to boast how he had fought off nine pirates single-handedly. Her mother made the right noises, but she didn't seem to be intent on the account until Thork assured her that the store of haematite in the village had been saved.

'You are saying that a pile of grubby stones is more important than poor Sylva,' her mother said.

'I didn't mean that,' Thork said.

'I know, but...' Her mother perked up. 'But you have a point. Quint may be reluctant to search for Patro's body, but the council will want the chalk and pitchstone that the pirates stole returned. It is a tool I can use, if I ever get to speak with him.'

****

Lin and Henjar arrived the next day, with

100

Henjar's husband Albar carrying a heavy sealskin bag and dragging another on a sled. A lookout spotted their arrival coming down the hill from the Ring of Bookan. Marna went to greet them. She was about to ask why they needed so much stuff when she realised the 'bag' Albar was carrying was Boda, wrapped tightly in the skin.

'It stops him struggling,' Henjar explained.

'And kicking,' Albar added.

'Let me see how he's grown,' Marna said.

Henjar un-wrapped the skins while Boda tried to escape, making his mother's task twice as difficult.

'Let me go. I can walk,' Boda told Henjar.

Marna's mother had come from the house. She waited for them a short distance from the entrance to the Ness. 'Why, it is little Boda,' she said.

'I'm not little. I'm a man,' he answered.

'He's just like his father,' Marna's mother said. Henjar looked away. 'I'm sorry I didn't mean to remind you of the... accident.'

Marna stared at her mother. Joel's death had not been an accident, but a wilful killing. Her mother knew that, but the killer, Wilmer, had been a close friend of her mother's and she denied his involvement in the crime.

Henjar overlooked the matter. 'Albar is his father now,' she said. She put a hand on her stomach. 'We have good news.'

'Not now,' Lin chided. 'Marna's mother doesn't want to hear about you.'

'I'll show you the house,' Marna said. 'It isn't like our old one in Skara Brae, but it is the only proper house within the walls of the Ness. Patro had it built specially for mother.'

'It isn't exactly as I would like yet, but I have done my best,' Marna's mother added. 'We don't have a proper dresser. Patro was having the stoneworkers make one…'

'I decorated it with coloured stones,' Marna said to ease her mother's distress. 'Pip messed them up, though.'

'Where is Pip?' Henjar asked.

'In the dog house,' Marna's mother answered.

'I could do with resting my feet,' Lin said. 'I want to look my best when we meet the priests. A beaker or two of good ale wouldn't go amiss.'

'Is Thork here?' Albar asked.

'He said something about hunting boar,' Marna replied. 'He will be back before evening.'

'I can't stay long,' Albar said. 'I only came to carry Boda and the bag.'

'Don't be silly, you'll need rest, food and drink before you set off again,' Marna's mother insisted.

Boda was bored of the adult talk. He wriggled from his mother's grip and ran unsteadily towards the side of Harray loch. 'Water,' he pointed. 'I want to swim.'

Henjar gave a shiver, remembering the washed up body of her first husband, Joel, but once an idea lodged in Boda's head it was as immoveable as one of the standing stones.

'I want to swim,' he repeated. He was a three year old with hearty lungs and his voice carried.

'You and your mother go inside and rest,' Marna said. 'I'll take care of Boda.'

'You won't let him go in the water, will you?' Henjar said.

'No. We'll find Pip and play with him.'

Henjar, Albar and Lin followed Marna's mother into the Ness. Marna took hold of Boda's hand.

'Where has mum gone?' Boda demanded.

'She needs to rest. Do you want to play with my dog, Pip?'

Boda started barking in a high-pitched squeak and Marna regretted her decision. Pip would have to endure his ears and tail being pulled, but he liked the attention. Patro was fond of animals and allowed Pip to stay in the Ness with Marna. While he was gone Quint was in charge and he pretended that dogs made him ill. Pip had been confined to the yard with the other hounds until Sempal arrived and persuaded his friends Kris and Tama to let him stay with them.

Boda still wanted to swim. Marna held his hand with a firm grasp. He gave a squeal, and dragged his feet, but she managed to lead him towards the group of workers' huts. Sempal was outdoors, talking to Kris.

'Uncle Sempal,' Boda called and squirmed to get free. Marna let go of the boy. He ran towards the men, but in his excitement he tripped over a stone. Kris caught him before he fell to the ground.

'I take it my sister has arrived,' Sempal said to Marna.

'Henjar, Albar and your mother. They are indoors resting. We are looking for Pip,' Marna answered.

'I'd better go and welcome them,' Sempal

said.

Kris returned to his work. Sempal was about to head towards the Ness when they heard Thork calling. He waited with Marna until her brother approached.

'I thought you were hunting boar?' Marna said.

'The herd had moved on and I didn't have time to follow them. I caught a couple of ducks, which I've left with Tama to prepare for our journey. We're leaving for Hoy this afternoon.'

'Today?' Marna said.

'That's what I said, stone-ears.'

Boda found this amusing and repeated the word several times, until Sempal told him to stop.

'Can't you wait a day?' Marna asked.

'I promised mother I would leave as soon as I could.'

'I want to come too,' Marna said. 'But I want some time with mother.'

'Mother needs you here for more than a day,' Thork argued.

'No she doesn't. I'll get under her feet in the house. She'll moan if I make my dyes and get annoyed if I'm idle. She has been picking on everything I say. Now that Lin and Henjar have arrived, she can talk to them and she'll enjoy playing with Boda and teaching him manners. I can be of help on Hoy.'

'How?'

'I can climb, better than you can. I'm not afraid of heights. If we spot something unusual at the bottom of a cliff I can scale down and investigate.'

'That's how she was able to reach the dead Irishman's body when there was the trouble at Skara Brae,' Sempal said.

She had been looking for birds' eggs and finding a body had been a shock. Her brother hadn't liked her mentioning his fear of heights, but her argument was convincing him.

'If we let you come, you must promise to do what you are told,' Thork said.

'Great, I'll let mum know and collect my stuff.'

'What stuff?' Thork asked.

Marna scurried off without replying. When she entered her mother's house, Lin and Henjar were far from resting. They were giggling as they applied her mother's face colouring powders to each other's cheeks. Henjar had a steadier hand and the powder she applied to Lin brought out her strong cheekbones, while covering up the blemishes of age. Lin did not have her daughter's skills and Henjar's face looked like she had been crawling backwards through ripe bramble bushes on a windy day.

'How do I look?' Henjar asked. Marna hesitated.

'Wow, I love your coloured nails. How did you get them like that?'

'It's ground malachite,' Henjar answered. 'Your mum said that Norra gets the powder from Burray. I've used a thin layer of oil to get the powder to stick on the nails.'

'There isn't much left. I shall have to ask Norra for some,' Marna said.

'No, your hands wouldn't suit green nails,' Henjar said. 'Your fingers are too long. They would have to be red. I have seen soft stones on Skaill Bay you could grind down.'

Marna pictured her hands with red nails. 'I would think they were bleeding,' she said.

'Where is Boda?' Marna's mother interrupted the beauty talk. Marna hadn't noticed her mother standing in the shadow beside the dresser. She had rescued a few flowers Pip hadn't destroyed and arranged them in a pot with water to release their scents.

'Oh,' Marna looked behind her. She had forgotten about the boy. 'I must have left him with Sempal.'

'Idiot.' Henjar jumped up. 'Sempal is bound to let him go in the water.' She made for the door.

'I wouldn't… I mean…' Marna lifted a finger towards Henjar's face, but decided not to say anything.

'Where is Albar?' Marna asked.

'He went in search of Sempal,' Lin replied. 'Didn't you meet him?'

'No.'

'The boy has no sense of direction,' Lin complained. 'In fact, he has little sense at all. Just as well he has his strength and looks.'

'Albar is a good man,' Marna's mother objected. 'His daughter will be beautiful and wise.'

Lin gaped in astonishment before answering, 'It is obvious to see Henjar is expecting, but how can you tell it will be a girl?'

'Little signs, like the way she carries the baby,'

Marna's mother explained. Marna wasn't convinced.

'I wouldn't mind finding a good man,' Lin said, running a hand through her thinning hair. 'I won't if my hair falls out every time I comb it.' She demonstrated the greying strands wound round her fingers.

'Seaweed will help,' Marna's mother said. 'I use dried powder mixed in the ale.'

Marna liked listening to the gossip and her mother's advice was worth remembering, but Thork wouldn't wait for her. 'Have you seen my yarrow leaves?' she asked.

'*MY* yarrow leaves,' her mother reminded her. 'What do you need them for? Have you toothache? Is it Boda?'

'No, you told me they were good for stopping bleeding if the skin gets cut or scratched.'

'Has he tripped or scrambled through gorse?'

'It isn't for Boda,' Marna repeated.

'What have you done?'

Marna gave an exasperated sigh. 'Nothing, it's not for me. You know what Sempal is like.'

'He always was a careless lad,' Lin agreed. 'He is as much use as Albar. You are so lucky to have Thork.'

'It is not luck, it is upbringing…' Marna's mother began.

Marna took the opportunity, while the older women were comparing their sons, to lift the yarrow from the dresser and secure it in her bag. She was reaching for dried dock leaves when Sempal, Thork and Albar arrived. Albar was carrying Boda.

'You didn't tell me Thork was back,' Marna's mother chided. Marna gave her brother a dark look.

'I see you found Thork and Sempal,' Lin said to her son-in-law.

'I also found the biggest cattle shed in the world.' His wide eyes reflected the excitement in his voice.

'Patro likes a draught-free shelter for the beasts, especially in winter when the wilder winds blow across the island,' Marna's mother explained. 'No doubt Quint will assign a new use to the building. He seems set on wiping out everything Patro has done.'

'The building would make a grand meeting hall,' Thork said. He lifted one of the pots beside the fire.

'More space for everyone to listen to Quint,' Marna said. Nobody responded.

Thork scraped round the side of the pot with a wooden spoon. Getting little from it, he poked his face in and licked the rim with his tongue.

'Manners,' Marna said.

'The boy is hungry,' her mother said.

'Starving,' Thork agreed. 'I can't be expected to row to Hoy on an empty stomach.'

'The fire is going out. See to it please, Marna,' her mother instructed. She began fussing around with pots and sacks of grain. Lin put aside the coloured powders and gave her a hand. They spilt more grain than they got into a pot and Thork finished the job for them.

'Where is Henjar?' Albar asked.

'She went to find Sempal and Boda,' Marna answered. 'She must have got lost. She doesn't know the lay-out of the Ness.'

'Nobody knows it,' Thork said. 'It changes every season.'

'I'll look for her,' Marna offered. She was wiping the hearth ash from her hands when Henjar returned.

'Look who I have found.' Henjar said.

Alekander was beside her and she had linked arms with him. Albar gave her a disapproving look.

'What are you cooking?' Henjar asked, poking her nose into the pot. She was skilled at preparing meals and she took over from Lin and Marna's mother. It wasn't long before a delicious aroma of bread and stew wafted through the house. Marna fetched water so that they could wash their hands then she helped Henjar serve. They sat round the hearth while they ate.

'You are lucky to have so much space here,' Henjar said. 'When we have people eating with us, our house is crammed. There is never anywhere to put the pots.'

'It is a matter of organisation,' Marna's mother said. She began to lecture Henjar on tidiness, but Henjar turned to Alekander.

'How is Sylva?' she asked. 'Did she come over to the mainland with you? Has she gone to Skara Brae?'

Marna had spoken with her mother about the attack on Hoy, but news hadn't reached Henjar and Lin. She glanced at Alekander to see how he would react.

'You don't know?' Alekander said, looking at

Thork. Thork glanced at Marna, who recounted the story.

'Oh, I am sorry,' Henjar said.

'Sempal and I are going to Hoy to find her,' Thork said. He saw his mother look at him. 'After we find Patro's body. Will you come with us, Alekander?'

'Aye, I'll come,' Alekander answered. 'I've spoken to Ralfe. He does not intend returning to Hoy yet.'

'Why not?' Marna's mother asked. 'What keeps him here?'

Alekander shrugged. 'He intends to demand support from the Ness. He feels the leaders are using the settlers without giving enough back. It is nigh impossible to farm the land and we are not fishermen. The waters are seething with dangers. There are deer on the hills, but if we spend our time hunting and gathering berries like our ancestors, we won't have time to gather the haematite the priests want. Several families speak about leaving if things haven't improved by the autumn. I agree with them, it will be a struggle to feed our families in winter, but Sylva was keen to persevere. She has faith in Ralfe. He is the one determined to make the community work.'

'The new settlement wasn't one of Quint's better ideas,' Marna's mother answered. 'He has never set foot on Hoy. Patro had advice from Yarl and was aware of the nature of the land. He saw no reason why working parties couldn't row out on a regular basis during the summer to collect the stone. He argued with his brother, but Jolty sided with Quint. Patro wouldn't go against his father. '

'I didn't say the idea was a bad one,' Alekander said. 'The Ness has other concerns and we are a burden, but we could make a settlement work. Quint has to realise it will take eight to ten years for the land to be made rich enough to sustain crops and to build a sustainable herd of cattle.'

'If the village looks like it's going to fail, Quint won't give you eight months. He will forget you ever existed,' Thork said.

'And no doubt blame the whole fiasco on Patro,' his mother added.

'Forgetting about the settlement isn't the same as allowing pirates to attack you,' Marna argued. 'Quint can't be happy that Sylva was kidnapped.'

'Quint cares nothing for Sylva. He is relieved they didn't get the gathered haematite. I bet he had

114

to let them take the precious chalk and pitchstone as reward for attacking our party,' her mother said bitterly.

'What do you mean, mother?' Thork said.

'The pirates knew where we were. Someone told them we were returning.'

'You don't mean Quint?' Thork said.

'That is going too far,' Lin said. 'You don't like your brother-in-law. That doesn't mean he's rotten.'

'Through and through,' Marna's mother grumbled. She had expected her guests to side with her and she gave a grunt in annoyance. No more was spoken on the subject. Boda was toddling round the house, lifting anything he could grasp. Marna had to move fast to prevent a mishap.

Albar left when he finished eating. Henjar gave him a list of jobs to do at home before kissing him goodbye. Thork, Alekander and Sempal finished their ale and rose to leave. Marna stood up and fetched her bag.

'Where are you going?' Henjar asked.

'Hoy.'

'When?' Her mother overheard.

'You can't leave your mother,' Lin objected.

'I'm sorry mother, I have to go to Hoy. I have a killer to catch.'

Chapter 7

'A killer?' Lin gasped. 'You must let the men go.'

Henjar wasn't impressed. 'She's not after a murderer, she's after a man.' She made a face at her brother. 'You had better watch out, Sempal. You have a rival.'

Marna didn't rise to Henjar's taunting. 'The young pirate lad knows who killed his companion and he can help us find Sylva.'

'He's a sly one,' Alekander said. 'The sooner we leave the better.'

Marna gave her mother a kiss on the cheek. 'Don't worry I'll have Thork to protect me.'

'Nobody ever worries about me,' her mother grumbled. 'Go, both of you, but make sure you find my husband.'

Marna followed the men out.

Sempal's boat wasn't built for four people plus their supplies. Alekander suggested they take the island boat they had come over on.

'What about Ralfe?' Marna asked. 'Won't he need it, if he changes his mind about staying?'

'How long will we be away?' Sempal asked. 'I thought this was to be a short trip.'

'It will be,' Thork answered. 'If you prefer

though, we can borrow one of the Ness boats. There are plenty now that the expedition boats are back.'

'You know what Quint is like,' Marna said. 'He didn't sanction this trip. He will tell the council that we have stolen the boat.'

'He might send men after us,' Sempal said. 'We could use their help.'

'They will have us tied up and returned to the Ness before we reach the settlement.'

'We don't have a choice then, so why are we standing here arguing?' Alekander said. 'We take the island boat.'

They packed the boat and dragged it to the water. Marna sat at the stern next to Thork. He had persuaded Alekander and Sempal to do the rowing, because of his sprained wrist.

'You managed to row to South Ronaldsay with it,' Sempal complained.

'That it made it worse,' Thork answered.

They made their way out of the bay, with Thork shouting navigation instructions.

'We know what we are doing,' Sempal said.

'Bear left to miss the seal,' Marna yelled.

'A seal, where?' Thork reached for the spear

that was lying along the bottom of the boat. By the time he had recovered it from between Marna's legs the seal had dived underwater.

'You're wobbling the boat,' Sempal warned as Thork positioned the spear, ready for the animal to re-surface.

Thork grudgingly put the weapon down. 'Mind the rocks,' he said.

There were no rocks at that part of the sound, the water was too deep, but Marna said nothing. Sempal enjoyed being on the water. He and Alekander were seasoned rowers. The water was calm and they reached Hoy without incident, landing in the small bay at Moaness. Sempal rubbed his fingers, examining them for blisters. Alekander ushered him and the others out of the boat and drew it up the shingled beach.

'You should keep your strength for other battles,' Thork advised Alekander, but didn't move to assist him.

Marna looked around to get her bearings. A puffed up cloud barred her view of the hill tops, but her keen eyes spotted movement. 'What's that?' She pointed.

'It's a bird,' Thork said.

'A large bird,' Sempal added.

'Like the fire birds in your tales?' Alekander joined in once he had secured the boat. 'It is a sea eagle. They nest in crags in the hills. If you don't disturb them, they will do no harm.'

Thork had hold of his spear and was running the shaft between his thumb and forefinger. The bird flew too high in the sky to take aim. He relaxed his hold.

'We should eat and drink,' Sempal said. He opened his bag and brought out a skin of ale, nuts, bannocks and slices of the duck Thork had caught.

'We ate before we left,' Alekander said, keen to get moving.

Sempal stuffed a slice of duck into his mouth. He kept a bannock in his hand and returned the rest of the food to his sack. Marna and Thork collected their belongings from the boat. Alekander had walked ahead and they jogged to catch up with him.

'That isn't the way to the village,' Marna said. 'Shouldn't we report to the elders there?'

'We are here to search for Patro,' Thork reminded her. 'A body will wash ashore onto a beach. We need to look around the coast.'

'There are cliffs in the way,' Sempal said. 'I

suggest we try to find the boy Marna spoke about. He knows what is going on.' He scanned the surroundings in the dimming light. 'If I were him, I would hide in those woods.'

'There are plenty more trees inland,' Alekander said. 'The caves in the hillsides would provide better shelter.'

'If we head through the valley, we'll reach the village where there is a track up to the top of the cliffs.' Marna tried to appease everyone. 'It isn't as steep as trying to climb from this side. We'll be able to explore the valley, reach the coast and talk to the villagers.'

'You go that way if you wish. I can't return to the village without Sylva,' Alekander said.

Marna wanted to ask him why not, but the others understood. She decided it must be a 'man thing'.

'We should stick together,' Thork said. 'My mother told me to protect Marna.'

'She shouldn't have come if she needs to be looked after like a child,' Alekander argued.

'I don't need protection,' Marna said.

'I might,' Sempal said, trying to lighten the mood.

121

They couldn't agree, and were wasting time arguing. It was decided that Alekander and Thork would head round the coast to inspect the bays, while Sempal and Marna would take the safer path between the hills to the village.

'Will we see the Dwarfie Stane?' Sempal asked.

'No, you need to take the path round the side of Ward Hill,' Thork answered. 'The route is longer.'

Sempal chewed his bottom lip. 'I wouldn't mind seeing the tomb, while I'm here.'

'There isn't time for sight-seeing,' Alekander reprimanded.

'We could walk fast,' Sempal argued. 'Besides, Marna will want to re-examine the scene of the pirate's murder. The last time you were there, the stone was shrouded in mist. Seeing it in the light will reveal clues to what happened.'

'The murder was days ago, what can she find now?' Alekander asked

'Won't the body still be there?' Sempal asked.

Marna shivered, thinking about Sylva's knife next to the man when they found him. What was scarier was the warrior's axe Thork had left with the body. Dead men couldn't fight, could they?

She remembered the tunic pin Thork had removed and given to her for safe keeping. She had intended to show it to Jolty. He knew most of the tribes in Caithness and could have identified where the man came from. With Yarl's death it had slipped from her mind.

'Yes,' she answered Sempal's question.

'We need to think about where we can rest overnight,' Sempal said. 'I don't fancy sleeping beside a corpse.'

'We didn't come here to sleep,' Alekander said.

'We have had a strenuous day. We will be useless if we are half asleep - worse than useless if we fall in with pirates while we are tired.'

'Nuttal could be hiding in the hills,' Marna agreed.

'Nuttal?' Sempal queried. 'What's that?'

'The pirate boy. That's not his real name. It's what I call him.'

'I've got other names' Alekander said. 'You can rest if you want. I need to go. Are you coming Thork?'

Thork took a drink of water. 'Take care, sis,'

he said then walked after Alekander. Marna watched them go. They both strove to show they could walk faster than the other, barging into one another to take the lead. 'They should cover a distance at that pace,' she said.

'It won't matter how much if they are going the wrong way,' Sempal replied.

'We should be going too,' Marna said.

'What is the rush?' Sempal stretched his weak leg. 'This Nut lad has likely rejoined his friends. They could be home in Wick by now.'

'It sounds like Alekander was right. You did come to see the sights. What if the pirates are planning another raid on the village?' Marna argued. Her tone challenged Sempal to come up with a good answer or do as she bid. He decided to do as she said.

The path rose uphill from the shore and they took it at a steady pace. It had been a hot day and the air was still warm, tempting them to rest. Marna didn't stop and Sempal knew better than to suggest it. They bore left when they reached the mud-cracked bed of a winter stream and followed the track as it circled inland, running round the side of the highest hill. The sheer slopes cast a shadow that blocked the sun and a light breeze blew through the valley onto their backs. When they came across a bank of berries Marna stopped to pick them. The dark berries weren't ripe, but the strawberries were fit to eat. They ate a handful and stored the remainder for later.

'This could be a pleasant trip,' Sempal ventured.

Marna frowned. 'A village was attacked. Men were injured and Sylva was kidnapped. Patro is dead, my mother has weird ideas about Quint not caring and somehow being involved and the Ness won't spare any men because the proper rituals haven't been performed.'

'I do understand…' Sempal began.

'No you don't,' Marna snapped back. 'You don't know the hardships of life here on Hoy and you don't live at the Ness. You don't have to deal with the power games. If Patro hadn't been killed, Quint would have found something else – the beginning of summer, the end of spring, the new moon, the full moon - anything instead of helping. What annoys me most is that he is celebrating. You can see him jumping in delight at being in charge of the Ness. Things are changing – and not for the better.'

'Quint is a stand in leader. He won't take over as a matter of course. You know that. The elders will meet and ask the gods for a sign.'

Marna stared at him as if a passing bird had dropped him on their island for the first time. 'I thought your friendship with that Irish woman would have shown you that anyone can say they receive messages from gods or faerie folk.'

'Gods and faeries are not the same and I don't know why you keep bringing Erin up. She was a stranger. I was trying to make her welcome.'

'You didn't have to try so hard,' Marna huffed.

'Who else might be considered for Patro's position?' Sempal asked, directing the conversation away from his friendship with Erin.

Marna poked her tongue against her cheek lining as she thought. 'Yarl would have been a possibility. He was popular, he knew about the running of the Ness and he had an even temper.'

'Do you think that was why he was murdered?'

'I hadn't thought of that,' Marna admitted. 'It may have been. He was Patro's man, but I don't think he would have been a serious threat to Quint.

He didn't have the same ambition and no great vision to build on the reputation the Ness has achieved. Flemeer would be more of a rival, or Tia Famel.'

Sempal laughed at the mention of Tia Famel. 'The elders wouldn't elect a woman as their leader,' he said.

'It has nothing to do with being a man or a woman,' Marna answered. 'The gods don't care. They want the best person in charge. Tia Famel is the cleverest at recognising the movement of the sky. She knows how to cure cattle ailments and she can sing the ancient songs in the old dialect.'

'She is strong in her opinions. The gods will not want a representative they have to argue with to get their way,' Sempal said, trying to rouse Marna.

'She does have a temper when others disagree with her, though no worse than Quint. She is consistent in her views. Quint changes his views faster than a storm can surge from the west.'

They were walking as they discussed political matters at the Ness. The sky was darkening and Sempal was slowing when Marna pointed up the hillside on their left. 'There it is – the Dwarfie Stane.'

'Wow!' Sempal stopped to admire the massive stone from a distance. The blurred outline merged with the heather, giving it a mystical appearance of having sprouted from the earth. 'It is said it was thrown there by a giant. It must have been an enormous one to lift that.'

'That is why they are called "giants",' Marna mocked. 'I thought it fell from the hillside.'

'Haven't I told you the tale of the giant god-men who used to live in the hills?' Sempal tried to keep his tone serious. When it appeared Marna believed him, he couldn't stop himself chuckling.

'No, you haven't,' she answered. 'Toomac, the pirate who died, spoke of giants living inside the stone. The entrance is sealed by a massive boulder. Do you think they are still inside?'

'They could be. It's a long story, one for a large fire, good company and a hearty feast.'

'You mean you aren't going to tell me,' Marna complained.

Sempal increased his pace as he walked towards the sandstone monolith. The vegetation round it was rough and the ground boggy. Marna found it difficult to keep up. When she reached the stone, Sempal was tramping round it. He circled three times then walked round in the opposite direction. Marna waited until he finished. 'It's a pity we can't move the entrance stone,' he said. 'If we had Alekander and Thork's strength...'

'...And that of a couple of oxen,' Marna added. She stopped abruptly. A long, mournful cry seeped out from the stone. Sempal jumped back towards her.

'What was that?' he said in a whisper. The notes lingered in the air like a wailing mother whose child had died. 'There's someone inside.'

'A giant god-man,' Marna mocked.

'Don't make jokes.' Sempal was shaking.

'It will be a bird or small animal trapped in the chambers,' Marna said. 'We can't get in, but mice and voles can burrow underneath or squeeze through cracks.'

'It didn't sound like a vole.' Sempal said. He inspected the stone again, tapping the walls and looking for cracks. There was a gap of a finger width between the entrance stone and the edge of the tomb. 'I suppose you're right,' he conceded. 'Is this where you rested in the mist?'

'Yes.'

'There doesn't appear to be any evidence of

129

you being here.'

'We didn't light a fire. We ate, but the crumbs will have been scooped up by gulls,' Marna answered.

'What about the dead body?' Sempal said. 'Where did you leave that?'

Marna walked to the spot. 'Here, I think.' She searched for an impression in the shrubs.

'It can't have decomposed in three days,' Sempal said. 'Are you sure you remember the spot?'

'It was here.' Marna bent to push the heather aside. She spotted something a few feet away. 'Look, here is part of the woollen dressing I removed from the boy's leg.'

Sempal screwed up his nose. 'If his wound is as bad as that dressing suggests, he can't have gone far. My guess is he would have found a cave with a fresh water supply nearby and rested there until his leg healed.'

The hills on Hoy were the highest Marna had seen. The rocks were covered in small pebbles that would shift and slide if a foot was put on them. Nuttal would have been a fool to risk climbing with his injured shoulder as well as his leg.

'He may not have had the time to rest,' she countered. 'If his friends planned to return to Wick, he wouldn't want to be abandoned on a hostile island.'

'Thork and Alekander are searching the coast. If he's there, they will find him,' Sempal said. He began scouring the area around the Dwarfie Stane and didn't answer when Marna asked him what he was looking for. 'There,' he said at last, pointing at a shadow in the near distance. Marna turned to look.

'What is it?' she asked.

'A cairn – was it there three days ago?'

'It was too misty to see that far ahead,' Marna said.

'It could be where your friend Nuttal moved his comrade. He could have piled the rocks so that the bones could be found later.'

Sempal's idea made sense, but Marna wasn't keen on climbing the hill to see if the dead man's horrified face confirmed his suspicions. 'The sun has gone down. Let's find somewhere to rest,' she suggested.

'Not here. The skuas have started to arrive,' Sempal said. 'If they are nesting, not even a band of warriors would venture into their territory.'

Marna inspected the hillside, glad to have Sempal as company. 'It looks like something has,' she said. There was a small clump of thick bushes about half way up the hillside on their left. Three adult skuas rose in the air above it then dived to a few feet above the top of the gorse before pulling out. The noise sounded as loud as thirty birds.

'It could be a hen harrier after their eggs,' Sempal said.

'Three skuas against one hen harrier, I don't think so. Come on.' Marna wasn't taking excuses. She grabbed Sempal's arm and pulled him towards the bushes.

'Are you mad?' Sempal protested, struggling behind her. She released his arm.

'It could be Nuttal,' she answered. 'You said he could be recovering here.'

'If it is, he will have seen and heard us coming from the Dwarfie Stane,' Sempal said. 'Making his presence known could be a trap.'

'When could he have made it and why would Nuttal want to trap us?'

'It might not be him,' Sempal said. 'People say there are still tribes of wild hunters in the hills.'

132

'You told me that was a story to scare children. Anyhow what sort of a trap could somebody make here?'

Marna took lengthy strides forward. As she reached the edge of the bushes the undergrowth gave way. With a sharp gasp, she lost her footing and tumbled into a murky ditch of peat and water. Sempal was a few steps behind. He pulled up when he saw her fall.

'Are you injured?'

Marna rubbed her elbow. 'I don't think so,' she said, then yelped as a spasm ran up her arm.

Sempal leant towards her and held out a hand as a net was thrown from behind the bushes. It landed over him and he fell on top of Marna. They both lay, limbs tangled, in the ditch covered by the netting. A figure stepped out from the bushes to stand over them. Sempal's body blocked her view, but Marna could see the sharpened tip of a spear hovering above them.

Chapter 8

Thork was used to keeping an even pace, necessary for stalking the deer and boars he hunted over long distances, but Alekander strode ahead, unhindered by the rough shrubs and boggy terrain.

'We should slow down,' Thork argued. 'We could miss what we are looking for.'

'I can use my feet and my eyes at the same time,' Alekander answered.

'What about your brain?' Thork asked. Alekander paused. 'I take it you did notice that dead seal,' Thork continued. 'It has been killed by a spear and ripped open to remove the best meat.'

Alekander made a face. He glanced over the edge of the cliff towards the rocky bay. 'People come out in boats to hunt seals here.'

'Exactly. Their purpose is to hunt and they take the whole carcase.'

'Perhaps they had a small boat, like your friend Sempal's. If they killed a number of animals, they could have taken some back to their village and left this one, meaning to return for it.'

'Perhaps pigs can sing. No hunter would come unprepared or kill more than they could handle. Only a fool would slash at a kill, leaving the bones

134

and a good skin lying unconcealed on a beach.'

'Perhaps they didn't have time to skin it.' Alekander was struggling, but he was unwilling to admit his lack of hunting knowledge.

'Use your head.' Thork gave him a thump on his back. 'There is still light. Why wouldn't they have had time?'

Alekander thought about it, but didn't answer.

'I believe they were interrupted by pirates,' Thork said.

Alekander rubbed his beard. 'In that case, why didn't the pirates take the skin?'

It was Thork's turn to consider the problem. After a pause he snapped his fingers. 'What would you do if you found a dead seal?'

Alekander opened his mouth, but nothing came out. Thork encouraged him to answer. 'I don't know. I'm a farmer.'

'And the pirates are raiders. They are used to stealing cleaned bones, distilled oil and skins that have been removed and cured, not smelling of the sea and dead flesh.'

'Whatever the reason, it is a waste of a good animal.' Alekander bemoaned the loss.

Thork sat on a rock to rest while Alekander

was still. 'I think they will come back for it, probably at dusk. We should wait here until they return then follow them round the coast. Their boats won't be able to travel fast in these waters. We can keep up with them on foot – if we rest now.'

'That is the real reason you are spouting this nonsense about dead seals. You want to slack off.' Alekander's feet were itching to keep moving and he wasn't convinced. A dead seal was a dead seal, but he sat next to Thork and drank from his water skin then offered it to Thork. 'Do you often get weird ideas like this?'

While they waited they played games, throwing rocks to see who could toss the heaviest and the furthest until it was too dark to see where the stones landed. They told tales, or rather Thork told his tale about the journey of his mace head from the Alps to Orkney while Alekander whittled a piece of driftwood with his stone knife. The story was long-winded and despite denying he was tired, Alekander's eyes closed.

'Are you listening?' Thork shook his companion.

Alekander woke with a start. 'Yes, it was

traded in Ireland for three flint heads and the chief's daughter.'

'That was ages ago, but that's not what I mean. Can you hear it?'

Alekander listened. 'No, what?'

'Come on.' Thork took the lead, insisting they bent their backs low to keep out of sight as they crept to the edge of the cliff. 'Someone could be looking up,' he warned.

When they reached the cliff edge he had them lie on their bellies, hidden by the long grass and shrubs, to look down the sheer face. A four-man boat was bobbing on the water.

'I knew I heard voices and oars,' Thork said. 'It's the pirates.'

'They don't look like pirates,' Alekander said. 'They could be hunters or fishermen.'

'No, I recognise the man at the front. My axe gave his right hand a hefty blow during the attack on the village. His fingers were sliced to the bones. I'd be surprised if he hadn't lost one or two.'

Alekander wriggled back from the edge and stood up. He gave his back muscles a rub. Thork waited until the boat moved further from the shore before getting to his feet. He moved to stand next to

Alekander. 'They don't seem interested in the seal,' he said.

'The seal was most likely attacked by a killer whale,' Alekander answered. 'I have seen pods of them in these waters, especially when the seals are near the shore.'

Thork wasn't interested in explanations. 'For pirates, they don't seem to be seasoned boatmen. They are heading south along the coast, close to the rocks.'

'I am ready to test if they are better at fighting than rowing,' Alekander answered. He began to run. Thork followed at a jog. He stayed close to the edge of the cliff, keeping track of the boat. There was a breeze and he was wary of his footing. The boat didn't move quickly and Alekander was forced to reduce his pace. He muttered to himself. Thork made out the words 'throat' and 'guts' and he imagined Alekander was planning what to do with the pirates once he had rescued his wife.

They trod across the moorland on top of the cliffs for several miles, with the boat in sight on the water, outlined by the moonlight. On occasions they would glance over and think it had disappeared, to find that a wave had obscured the

138

view. There were inlets and bays which Thork and Alekander had to make wide detours inland to skirt. Both men were tired, but when they came to a rocky stretch of land where their footing was steadier, Alekander insisted they jogged to get ahead of the boat at the far side of the bay.

'My arrows can reach them from there,' he said.

'You can't fire arrows in this light,' Thork answered. Alekander made a face, suggesting he could fire arrows blindfolded.

The cliff face sloped at an angle that hid their view of the shore. When they circled round and were able to see it again Alekander peered along the coast. There was no sign of a boat.

'Where are they?' he asked. He glared at Thork. 'We've lost them.'

'We can't have. They weren't rowing fast enough to clear the bay. Perhaps their boat has sunk.'

'There is no-one swimming in the water, or drowning.'

Thork sucked on his lower lip. 'They could have found a cave with an entrance in the bay.'

'Great,' Alekander fell to his knees. 'What will

happen to Sylva now? "Perhaps", "maybe", "could have" – you have no idea, do you?' He tugged at his beard.

'I have a plan,' Thork answered. 'We head down to the bay and search.'

Alekander lacked Thork's optimism, but any plan was better than giving up hope. He got to his feet. A clump of dead kelp had blown up from the beach onto his tunic and leggings. He rubbed it off as he headed towards the edge of the cliffs.

'We can make our way down over there.' Alekander pointed to a track where a stream rippled into the bay. You take that side, I'll take this one.'

'We should stick together,' Thork said.

'Why must we always listen to you?' Alekander grumbled.

'Because I am right. If one of us has an accident, the other will be needed to help.'

Thork chose his steps carefully. At the bottom, he surveyed the cliff edge, paying attention to where it met the tide line. 'That shadow in the cliff face looks promising.'

He had barely got the words out before Alekander was on the move. The pebbles crunched beneath his feet. The sound echoed against the rocks and Thork gestured to him to make less noise. Alekander didn't notice. Thork followed, keeping to the sheltered side of the bay, keeping out of sight. When they reached the spot, Thork was as surprised as Alekander to discover that his instincts were sound. The cliff face split into an opening, wide enough for a boat to enter at high water.

'See,' Thork boasted, tapping the side of his nose. The tide was going out and there was no more than a string of rock pools along the entrance to the cave. 'They must have had to drag their boat in. Look, those could be marks in the sand.'

'Doesn't look like that to me,' Alekander said. He splashed his way in through the pools of water without looking.

'Hold on, the pirates will still be unloading the boat,' Thork called after him.

'Then we'll take them by surprise,' Alekander answered.

Thork followed him. 'I wish we had more light,' he grumbled. His voice grew and altered in the surrounds of the cave and for a moment he thought someone was laughing at him. He reached for the knife that he kept tucked in his belt. Alekander kept moving. Thork listened to the

141

sound of the footsteps, keeping a hand on the side wall for guidance. The rays from the early morning sun were focussed in a beam that shone into the cave. It produced sufficient light for the first steps. As they ventured further in it took time for their eyes to become accustomed to the dark. Thork's fingers were still on the handle of his stone knife. He had spent dark winter nights chipping and smoothing the flint to fit his grip and he was ready to pull it from his belt if danger sounded.

The roof of the passageway sloped downwards. Alekander was the first to bend his neck, then his back. Thork took four steps. On the fifth, he bumped his head and stopped.

'They can't be here,' he said, making an effort to keep his voice soft. 'There is no torchlight or noise. Wait, what is that?'

His voice trailed as his eyes adapted to make out a shadowy object ahead of him that wasn't Alekander's backside. It was the stern of a boat. Thork crept up to it, feeling the side. The design felt familiar. A thrill rose along his spine as he imagined the pirates nearby.

'Alek, where are you?' he whispered. His friend had vanished although Thork could smell the reek of seaweed from his clothing. It filled the enclosed space making it impossible to place the source.

The men couldn't have dragged the boat up, unloaded it and disappeared in the short time it had taken Alekander and himself to scramble down the river bed to the shore. Thork moved to the prow of the boat and leaned over. The floor was covered in skins and balanced on both sides were blocks of light coloured stone.

It wasn't the same boat. They were in the wrong cave.

Thork fumbled to find the damp wall of the cave to regain his bearings. His hand disappeared into the stone and it took a moment for him to realise there was a gap in the tunnel wall. It was an opening to a side tunnel. The smell of seaweed was stronger and he guessed Alekander had turned down it. He turned to investigate. The roof was lower than the entrance passageway. Wary of another thud to his head, he lifted his arm to protect his skull.

The air was choked with smoke. Thork's eyes smarted and he released his grip on his knife to rub them. Taking a blind step forward he bumped into

Alekander.

Thork let out an exclamation. Alekander shook his arm, warning him to be silent. Through the tears clouding his eyes, Thork saw that the passage opened into a semi-circular cavern. A fire was burning on a hearth and as there was no chimney the smoke was making its way along the tunnel. Peering through it Thork managed to count three pirates sitting round the fire. Their backs were turned and Thork didn't recognise any of them from their hair or clothing.

'There's Sylva,' Thork said, immediately regretting it as he was forced to grasp his friend's tunic to stop him leaping into the room.

Sylva was seated with her knees pulled up in front of her. Her hands were behind her and she was tied back-to-back with a man. She squirmed to get comfortable

'We have to rescue Sylva,' Alekander protested, forgetting his warning of keeping silent.

'We can't rush in. We need a plan,' Thork whispered, pulling Alekander further from the entrance. They crawled backwards into the main tunnel and stood beside the boat.

'We can't fight the pirates here. There are too

many of them,' Thork said.

'I'm not afraid,' Alekander replied, but his head was cooling and his senses were returning. What's your great plan?'

'We need to know how many pirates we are up against. I didn't get a good look, did you?' Thork asked.

'I was looking at Sylva. I didn't recognise the man she was tied to.'

'Stay here. I'll go back and take a closer look,' Thork said.

Thork returned along the side tunnel to inspect the cave. Gazing in, his jaw fell.

'Patro,' he said aloud.

'Aren't you the clever one,' a woman's voice echoed across the wall behind them. Thork felt a spearhead in his back. He raised his arms and turned slowly.

'You thought we were stupid, didn't you?' Peria said.

'Like we would allow strangers here without having people on watch?' Phalt jeered. He was standing behind Alekander, holding a sharpened, stone knife to his throat.

'Peria, Phalt…' Thork was speechless. He

lunged towards Peria in an attempt to disarm her. She was quick to respond and jerked her spear into his tunic, ripping the fabric.

'I'm not afraid to use this,' she said.

'I would do as she says,' Phalt advised. His voice had lost the amiability they had come to expect in the village.

'Move,' Peria ordered. She didn't allow Thork to turn and he was prodded backwards into the cave. Phalt forced Alekander to join him. The three men round the fire jumped to their feet, clutching their weapons.

'Look what we found in your doorway,' Peria said. 'Where are your guards?'

Sylva looked up and gave a gasp. Alekander ducked away from Phalt's knife and stepped towards her. One of the pirates, annoyed at being criticised by Peria, aimed the blunt end of his axe at Alekander's face. There was dull thud and he staggered and fell.

'Are they alone?' another of the pirates asked.

'Seems so,' Phalt answered.

'What should we do with them?' the third pirate asked.

'Kill them now,' the first man said.

'No,' Peria disagreed. 'Lional will want to know what information they have about us and who they have told.'

The second man kicked Alekander's legs. 'He is from the settlement. The other one has the brooch of a Ness priest.' He pointed at the bone ornament on Thork's cloak.

'He was in the village when Toomac and the Camster lad were taken,' Peria said.

The pirates grumbled. 'Who made a mess of that business?' the first man accused Peria.

'Would you have murdered Kennet's son in cold blood?' Phalt waved his knife at the man.

'The Ness would have taken the blame,' the man answered.

'Enough. We can't fight among ourselves,' Peria said.

The first pirate spat on the blade of his axe and rubbed it against his tunic, testing its sharpness before replying. 'Very well, we'll keep them here until Lional and the others come. Make sure you tie them up well,' he instructed. Phalt had a line of rope wound round his belt, which he began to untie. 'Search them for weapons first, fool.'

Phalt did not appreciate being called a fool in

front of the others. He responded by pushing and prodding Thork and Alekander. Alekander had already been stripped of his bow and arrows. Thork's knife was grabbed from his belt and Alekander's axe was removed. The prisoners' hands and feet were tied and they were forced to their knees. Phalt bound them together and they were shoved towards the back wall, next to Sylva and Patro. Alekander tried to reach his fingers to touch Sylva's, but only succeeded in tightening the rope around Thork's wrist. Peria spotted him and laughed. The other pirates goaded them until they lost interest and returned to drinking ale and throwing dice by the fire.

The alcohol and warmth sent the men to sleep. Phalt and Peria moved to sit at the entrance, talking to one another. Thork was happy they couldn't see or hear him. He made a hissing sound to gain Sylva and Patro's attention. 'Don't worry,' he whispered, 'Marna and Sempal are on the island. Once they realise we aren't where we should be, they will rush to rescue us.'

Patro groaned. 'And I thought things couldn't get any worse.'

Chapter 9

Marna thrashed her arms against the netting, becoming entangled as she tried to free herself. She heard sniggers and aimed a kick in the direction of the sound, thinking it was Sempal. 'You think this is funny?' she snapped.

'Aye,' a voice answered. It wasn't Sempal's. Marna stopped struggling and twisted her neck to see who was speaking. Nuttal was standing over the net, holding a hazel branch with a crude stone blade attached to the end.

Sempal intended to say, 'If you hurt Marna, I'll rip your brains out,' but he had fallen beside Marna and her foot had knocked his jaw. The jabbering that came out sounded like baby talk. Nuttal laughed louder.

'If you would remain still, I could free you,' he said, once his laughter died. He bent to cut the rope. Marna pushed the end over her head and Nuttal offered her a hand to help her up. She refused, getting to her feet unaided and spending a moment brushing down her tunic while her temper cooled. Sempal stood up and scrambled to stand in front of Marna. He felt for his knife, but his belt was empty.

Nuttal gathered up his net. 'Is this what you

149

are looking for?' He untangled the handle of the knife from the meshing. Sempal grabbed at it, but the boy swept his hand away. He held it up to admire the bone handle then ran a finger across the blade.

'Give it back,' Sempal said.

'Useful as well as ornate,' Nuttal said. 'Was it a gift from your friend?'

Sempal didn't answer, but his look towards Marna told Nuttal that it was. Nuttal held out the weapon again, this time allowing Sempal to take it. Sempal snatched it and examined the blade for damage before replacing it in his belt.

'Are you finished with your game?' Marna asked. 'Good, then you can tell us the meaning of your trap.'

'I have to eat,' Nuttal answered. 'There are plenty of birds and small creatures in the moorland, but they are faster than I am. I found this natural crack in the land, dug it a little deeper and camouflaged it with heather stems.'

'You could see we weren't rats or hares,' Marna objected.

'There are people searching the hills for me. I didn't know it was you. I couldn't take a risk.'

'If the settlers are searching for you, why do you trust us?' Sempal asked.

'I don't know you, but she is Patro's step-daughter and I trust Patro.'

Sempal was about to declare that Patro was dead, but a glare from Marna stopped him. The lad seemed not to notice. 'There are others looking for me,' he continued.

'Pirates?' Sempal asked.

Nuttal didn't elaborate. He turned to stride up the hill. Marna gave Sempal a nudge, urging him to follow. He had bruised his ankle in the ditch and was slow to respond.

'Wait,' she called after the lad. 'We need to talk.'

Nuttal either didn't hear or didn't wish to talk. He continued his march and although he hobbled on his injured leg, he made greater headway than Marna and Sempal.

'I guess his wound isn't bothering him,' Sempal muttered as he puffed behind Marna. 'His shoulder is fine for throwing.'

'I was sure it was out of joint,' Marna said. 'How could he have fooled me?'

Sempal moved his neck and shoulder to feign

an injury. 'Like this?'

Annoyed, Marna gave him a light shove.

'Watch my shoulder,' he said in a high voice, pretending to be hurt.

'What are you doing?' While they were arguing, Nuttal had come back towards them.

'Nothing,' Sempal said, his face reddening.

'I went ahead to make sure you were alone,' Nuttal explained before Marna could ask. 'I have questions for you too. I want to know why you are here and what news there is at the Ness. I can't keep watch out here in this fading light. I'll take you to my den.'

'It could be another trap,' Sempal whispered over-loudly to Marna.

'Why would I need another one?' Nuttal answered. 'The first one worked pretty well.'

Sempal smarted. He took hold of Marna's hand. Marna wanted to shake free, but knowing that would demean Sempal in front of Nuttal, she allowed herself to be led. Nuttal kept a steady pace, giving them the chance to keep up. He stopped half way up the hill. 'We're here,' he said proudly.

They were standing next to a clump of gorse bushes. 'Will it keep out the rain?' Marna asked sarcastically.

Nuttal drew aside a clump of the gorse to reveal the concealed entrance to a small cave. He grinned as Sempal admired his handiwork.

'I keep it hidden as a precaution, but nobody dares come up here because of those,' Nuttal said. High above them was the soaring silhouette of a sea eagle. 'A pair is nesting in the crags higher up. I don't bother them and they don't disturb me.'

'Why are you still here?' Sempal asked. 'Why haven't you rejoined your comrades?'

'You know they are still on the island?' Nuttal sounded surprised. 'We can't talk here. Go inside.'

Nuttal stepped back to allow his guests to enter. Marna made a face at Sempal, implying he should lead the way.

'Do you have a torch?' Sempal asked.

'You won't need one. The fading sun will guide you.'

'I thought that would be your answer.' Sempal bent double to crawl through the narrow opening. Following behind, Marna heard him give a cry as he knocked against the cave wall.

An ember was glowing in the hearth. Nuttal had arranged dry wood, grasses and peat at the side, ready to be used as fuel. Marna took it upon herself to get a fire going, blowing gently until the flame took hold. The smoke swirled and rose to find an escape through a gap at the top of the cave, leaving an earthy aroma. With the increased light Marna could make out the crude furnishings in the cave. The space was barely large enough for the three of them to stand upright. Nuttal had arranged dried heather and grass around the domed edges.

'Not quite like home, but it suits me,' Nuttal said. He set aside his knife and handed them berries he had gathered and stored in a clay pot near the hearth.

'Where did you get the pot?' Marna asked.

'There are disused huts further along the valley. They don't have roofs or doors, but I found pots and tools.'

Marna accepted a berry and put it on her tongue to taste it.

'It isn't poisonous,' Nuttal said. 'I found the strawberries in the valley near the stream.' He took a handful and ate them before continuing. 'You think I killed my comrade Toomac, don't you?'

'You know who did,' Marna replied.

'I don't know his name. The fair man with the

belly that looks like he is about to give birth,' Nuttal said. 'He would have killed me too if he hadn't toppled over Toomac's legs and caused a commotion.'

'Phalt,' Marna said. 'Why would he kill you when we had agreed to hand you over to the priests?'

'He feared Toomac would have talked, giving the names of those on Hoy who are helping the pirates. Don't look shocked. Did you think it was by chance they attacked when the men-folk were absent? We were told the women would be unprotected.'

'You are saying that Phalt is a traitor,' Marna said. 'Are there others?'

'I suspect the woman he was with is too.'

'You said "the pirates" and "they" as if you weren't one of them,' Marna said.

'My father is chief of our village in Camster. He and the other leaders in the area met with Patro of the Ness and came to an agreement. Our people would come and go, trading with one another freely and sharing ideas. There would be no hostilities between us. The situation worked for several years, but a few months ago my father discovered that one of the other chiefs, Lional, had been disregarding this pact and had got together a band of raiders. My father deems friendship and bonds of agreement to be of great worth. He also fears retaliation from the Ness. I chose to join the raiders to find out what was happening. That is where I learned that Patro has been away from the Ness for several months. In his absence, other influences are at work.'

'You joined the pirates as a spy. You could have been killed,' Marna said.

'I don't fear death.'

'What else did you discover?' Sempal asked.

'Lional had assurances from an important priest in the Ness that there would be no resistance to the raids, if they made adequate payment.'

'A traitor at the Ness, never!' Marna declared. Her mind flicked through the faces she knew. She could think of no-one who would betray their own folk. 'Who?'

'I don't know, but Toomac did. He was a messenger, sent from the Ness with information for Lional. Phalt feared that he would reveal names to save himself.'

'I didn't see Toomac at the Ness,' Marna said.

'He wasn't there long, besides his presence

would have been a secret.'

Marna smarted. She liked to think she knew everything that was going on.

'Why didn't Toomac tell you what he knew?' Sempal asked.

'He didn't trust me.'

'You have the same design on your pin as Toomac. Aren't you a kinsman?'

'He was from our village,' Nuttal said. 'But we are not related.'

Marna was silent. She sensed Nuttal was hiding something. She prodded the fire with a stick. 'What about Sylva?' she asked. 'Do you know what has happened to her?'

'Yes. She is still on the island,' Nuttal replied. 'The raiders are hiding in a series of interlinked caves. The tides around the island's coast make it hard to navigate and Lional is no seaman. He must have been told where to find safe havens. The men and supplies are split between three caves. I didn't re-join them when I saw the man you call Phalt among them. The girl was there, with another prisoner – an older man.'

'Can you show us the cave?' Marna asked.

'You won't be able to rescue them without

help.'

'We can get that from the settlement,' Sempal said.

'The raiders would have no qualms about killing their prisoners if they suspected an attack. They are brutal men.'

'We know. They attacked Patro's party as they returned home from the south. My mother was among them. Luckily she escaped, but Patro was killed.'

'Oh, that is bad. It changes things.' Nuttal paused. He scratched his head and made to say something then closed his mouth and scratched his head again.

'What is it?' Sempal asked. 'Head lice?'

'How did you hear of the attack?'

'A messenger came to the Ness. He was murdered before he could give his full report to the elders,' Marna replied.

'Convenient,' Nuttal observed. 'That confirms there is an enemy at the Ness. Lional must have been told of Patro's return.'

'Nobody at the Ness knew,' Marna said.

'I think somebody did.' Nuttal rubbed the hairs on his chin. 'What does Patro look like?'

'You said he had visited your family,' Sempal said. His mind was alert to inconsistencies in the lad's account.

'I wasn't at home.'

Marna was about to repeat the reply of 'convenient', but she felt Nuttal was telling the truth and she wanted to trust him. She described her step-father, with Sempal adding unhelpful comments. Nuttal wasn't interested in Patro's deep set eyes that pierced through people like arrows when he disagreed with them or his dry wit that her mother found irresistible.

'I didn't see his eyes or hear him speak. Does he have a scar on the back of his neck?' Nuttal indicated the area.

'Yes,' Marna said. 'It is a birth mark, not an injury. Have you found his body?'

'I think he could be the prisoner I saw in the cave.'

'You mean he's alive?' Marna jumped to her feet, banging her head on the low roof of the cave. She rubbed a hand across her hair to check for blood. Realising she wasn't injured, Nuttal laughed.

Sempal scrambled to his feet. 'I'm with Marna,' he said.

'You can't fight them all. There were five men in the cave when I saw them and others are within distance to help if warned. The full pirate force is twenty men and ten women. Not everyone was sent to attack your village.'

'Oh!' Marna sat down and helped herself to the last of the berries.

Sempal remained standing. 'We need to get the pirates out of the caves,' he said. 'If we fight them there, we could be trapped.'

'We could lay siege to them,' Marna suggested.

'This isn't a story where the good folk win,' Sempal said. 'We would need enough people to surround three caves for several days, if they have access to fresh water.'

'It could be done,' Marna insisted.

'No it couldn't,' Nuttal answered. 'Each cave has several passageways leading to secret parts of the island. If the settlers blocked one exit, they would use another.'

Marna accepted defeat. She stared at the smouldering wood on the fire, preparing to add another branch, when she had an idea. 'I've got it. We lure them out with news of another village the

Ness is setting up. One that has no protection. If we add in supplies from the mainland and quarried stones, they won't be able to resist such easy pickings.'

'How do they find out about an imaginary village?' Sempal asked.

Marna looked up at Nuttal. 'You're one of them. You could go back and tell them you found it here in the hills. The pirates haven't ventured inland. They won't know any better.'

'Phalt tried to kill me. He murdered Toomac. It won't be easy to convince Lional to trust me. Even if he did, you would need men and women armed with strong, sharp weapons who know how to fight, not quarry stones.'

'We can get fighters from the Ness,' Sempal answered. 'There are priests who specialise in weapons as well as workers on the dyke who can wield axes and picks. Patro is a popular leader. If he is in danger, there will be no shortage of folk willing to rescue him.'

'Sempal is right,' Marna said. 'Patro's brother Quint was the only person who appeared unmoved by the news of his death.'

'The area around the Dwarfie Stane would be

perfect for a fight,' Sempal offered. 'The heather is deep and there are crags in the hillside we can use as traps.'

'It will make a fair site for a skirmish – as long as we don't wake the sleeping giants. The raiders are wary of the place because of its reputation,' Nuttal agreed. 'They are a superstitious bunch. That might work to our advantage.'

'*Our* advantage? Does that mean you are with us?' Marna asked.

Nuttal pushed out his bottom lip with his tongue. 'Aye. It won't be easy, though. The raiders have lookouts along the coast. Your people will have to get here without being seen.'

'We should let Thork and Alekander know of our plan,' Sempal said.

'We arranged to meet in the settlement village at the top of Rackwick Bay, tomorrow,' Marna explained.

'The raiders won't linger on Hoy for long,' Nuttal said. 'They will leave when the injured men have recovered. Lional will be anxious to return home with his spoils.'

'They have one of Patro's boats, laden with chalk and skins,' Marna said. 'We need to split up.

Sempal can go to Rackwick, while I return to the Ness with news of Patro.'

'Will you be able to row over the Flow on your own?' Sempal asked cautiously. It wasn't wise to tell Marna what she couldn't do.

'I can do anything you can,' Marna declared. She thought for a moment then decided, 'Nuttal can come with me.'

'If the raiders spy me with you, they won't trust me.'

'You could tie Marna up and pretend she is your prisoner,' Sempal suggested.

'Why would I take a prisoner to the Ness and not to Lional?' Nuttal asked. Sempal looked embarrassed.

'You will have to change roles,' Marna said. Sempal can come with me while you go to the settlement to find Thork and Alekander.'

'Easy, except they will kill me before I have time to speak.'

'You could take a token,' Sempal said. 'That worked for Lull in the story of the sea monsters.'

Marna groaned, but with no other suggestion she searched in her bag for something useful. Her hand felt the edge of an object tucked in the seam and she pulled it out. 'Here, this might do.'

'What is it?' Nuttal took the finger length strip of willow bark she offered and turned it over in his hand. 'What are these slits for?'

'It's the whistle I use to call my dog.'

Sempal chuckled. Marna glared at him. 'You have to admit, no manner of whistles or calls does a speck of good. He comes when he wants to, or doesn't.'

Nuttal held it to his mouth and blew. Nothing happened. He forced his lips into a circle with his tongue in the centre and blew again. The bark gave a burp.

'You don't need to use it,' Marna said. 'Show it to Thork. My brother knows I would only give it to someone I trusted.'

'What if he thinks I killed you for it?'

Sempal found it difficult to control his giggling. 'Who would kill for that?'

Nuttal secured the whistle under his belt. 'I've explored the area. I know a short cut that should get me to the bay ahead of your brother and his friend. If I find them before they reach the settlement, I might have a chance of winning them over.'

'We need to set off at once for the Ness,'

164

Marna said to Sempal. 'The darkness will hide us from lookouts. Movement in the water will be put down to the tides.

'It is too dangerous to go the same way back,' Nuttal over-ruled her. 'Fishermen keep boats on the east side of the island. There is a track between the hills. You could travel to the Mainland from there.

'It would be a full morning's walk from where we land in Orphir to the Ness,' Marna said.

'Thork's wife and her family live in Orphir,' Sempal said, for Nuttal's benefit. 'We could rest and eat there.'

'If you know folk there it is well, but you can't set off tonight.' Nuttal wasn't cowered by Marna's protests. 'There is no way you will make it between the hills. The sun will rise tomorrow. An early start will get you safely to your friends.'

'You are saying we should stay here tonight,' Marna said.

'It isn't much, I know,' Nuttal said.

'We accept,' Marna said gallantly.

'Make yourself comfortable while I fetch fresh water from the stream.'

Nuttal took the skins to replenish their supply. Marna arranged heather and bracken into cots away

165

from the draught. Sempal hunched near the fire and brought out a knife. He looked around the cave for a stone to sharpen the flint blade. He was busy whittling the edge when Nuttal returned.

'I had luck at the stream. I found this napping. We can have supper tonight.' He laid a fish beside the fire. It wasn't big enough to bake, but they were able to cut chunks and skewer them, cooking the flesh over the embers of the fire until the cave smelt of trout. Marna and Sempal were tired and Nuttal promised to wake them when it was light.

It hardly seemed a moment after Marna lay down until Nuttal was pulling on her arm to wake her. Sempal wasn't in the cave. He returned with his hair and light beard wet.

'Do I have time to wash?' Marna asked. 'I don't want Caran to see me looking a mess.' Nuttal and Sempal knew it wasn't a question she expected an answer to. 'What can we give the fisher-folk for the use of their boat?'

Sempal rummaged in his sack. 'I've got one mouldy bere bannock in my bag and a world full of tales in here.' He tapped the side of his head.

Marna smiled. 'That should suffice.'

Chapter 10

Thork and Alekander spent a sleepless night shifting their weight from side to side to avoid cramp. Alekander tried to reach Sylva's hand, but whenever he did, Thork's shoulder was wrenched. Different pirates came and went, bringing food or fresh water. The increased activity and movement of goods suggested that the pirates were planning a move. Despite listening in to their conversations, Thork couldn't make out what it was.

No sunlight found its way into the chamber. Thork guessed it was morning when their captors drew lots to decide who would stay and guard them while the others went about whatever business they had planned. Two men and a woman were chosen. They offered the prisoners water, held to their mouths in fired pottery beakers, and lumps of hard bread. When they finished, they spent their time throwing pebbles on the ground in a game of skill. Thork was intrigued, wishing he could join in. The woman was practised at the game and beat the men. Amid their groans and complaints, the men conspired to cheat.

'Are you listening?' Alekander whispered to Thork.

'Sorry.' Thork pulled his attention back to his companion.

'If I speak any louder the guards will hear,' Alekander said. He made gestures with his hands, rubbing them against his back and twiddling with his fingers. Eventually Thork realised Alekander wanted him to slide their hands together to loosen the ropes and undo the knots. They tried until their fingers tingled and their wrists throbbed. The knots were tied tight. Thork's shoulders slumped and he sat still.

'Are you two finished whatever it is you are doing?' Patro grumbled.

'We are trying to free ourselves,' Thork said.

'You are going about it in the wrong way. You've tightened the knots and added an extra throw. Here, allow me.' Patro glanced over to make sure the guards were occupied, arguing about the rules of their new game. He shuffled nearer to Thork. When he was beside him he revealed that although a rope was visible round his hand, he was not bound by it. He fiddled with the rope tying Thork and Alekander's hands together and they were released.

'Why didn't you say you were free?' Thork

168

accused, rubbing his reddened arms. Patro signalled for him to lower his voice and to stop moving.

'Until we can find a way out, it is wiser to keep this a secret from the guards.'

Wise as Patro's advice was, Alekander was in no mood to wait. He tore at the bonds on his legs. Before the guards noticed and could react, he was on his feet, holding a stone he had lifted from the floor of the cave. He let out a yell and grabbed the nearest pirate, locking his strong right forearm round the man's neck. The other two guards hesitated, giving Thork the chance to reach for a hot stone beside the hearth.

He stood beside Alekander, juggling the stone between palms. The second man seized his axe. Thork tossed the stone as the man jumped towards him, wielding the axe. In his rage the man didn't notice Patro's leg, stuck out in his path. He tripped, dropping his axe as he lost his balance. It bounced from his reach. Sylva was first to grab it. Her limbs were numb from being tied awkwardly, but she lurched towards the female guard. The woman saw her two companions on the floor and made her decision. It was fight or flight and she chose to run.

Sylva rushed after her. Her legs wobbled and

169

she was weak from lack of proper food. The woman was too far along the shore to catch by the time she reached the cave entrance. Thork and Alekander heard her oaths as they tied the guards with the ropes. When Sylva returned, Alekander rushed to embrace her.

'Did they hurt you?' he asked, combing his fingers through the tangles in her hair and removing a frond of seaweed.

'I'm not injured,' she replied.

Alekander aimed a kick at the nearest prisoner.

'The other pirates will arrive soon,' Patro said. 'The woman will warn them.' He struggled to his feet. A deep, purple bruise starting on his forehead had spread to his eyes. The tissue round the sockets was swollen, forcing the right eye to close. A wound ran down one cheek from his ear to his beard. The skin had started to knit together round blisters of clotted blood. He coughed as if trying to expel sea water from his chest and clenched his fists to prevent his hands shaking.

'Wait a moment,' Sylva said. She hurried from the cave and returned with a drift wood branch which she handed to Patro. It reached from the ground to his waist. He thumped it on the stone floor to test its strength then nodded his appreciation. With its aid, he shuffled towards the cave entrance. Thork went ahead to guide the way.

'My boat,' Patro muttered as they turned into the main passageway.

There was no time to stop. Outside, they stood on the beach, dazzled by the sunlight, soaking up the warm rays and breathing in the tingling air.

'We can't stay here,' Thork said.

Sylva was the first to have her vision restored. She pointed towards a bank where the overgrowth was dense. They could remain hidden until they recovered. Thork and Alekander strode ahead, while she linked arms with Patro to help him climb the rocky slope.

'What do we do now?' Alekander asked once they were out of sight.

Thork looked to Patro. The priest lay sprawled in the tall, sea grass.

'If no-one says otherwise, Sylva and I will return to the settlement,' Alekander said. 'What about you, Thork?'

'I told Marna and Sempal we would meet them at the settlement, but Patro needs to get to the Ness. He won't make it on his own.'

Alekander glanced at Patro, who was oblivious to the conversation. He put a hand on Thork's shoulder. 'We'll split up. I will meet your sister and her friend and tell them the good news while you escort Patro home. I'll wish you strong arms and a fair wind for your journey.'

Alekander and Sylva didn't linger. They took a path inland towards the wooded valley, assuming the pirates would stick to the coast. Thork watched them leave, Alekander with an arm around Sylva's shoulder, before approaching Patro. He bent to tug his sleeve.

'We have to move on,' he said.

Patro rose in stages, his joints creaking like a falling tree. He rested sitting with his knees up in front of his body and rocked.

'That is where we were attacked.' He pointed at a spot on the horizon then turned to Thork. 'Was my wife's boat attacked? Where is she? Is she safe?'

'My mother escaped the pirates and was escorted by your aides to South Ronaldsay. I fetched her home. She is with friends at the Ness, unharmed, but in shock and mourning.'

'Mourning?'

'She saw you take a blow and fall into the sea. Your party believed you to be dead. She sent me here to recover your body for the proper rituals.'

Patro gave a snort, which turned into a cough. 'Dead?' He repeated the word several times then gave a croak that may have been intended as a laugh. 'I wouldn't put it past my beloved brother to carry out the rituals on my live body.' He pulled at his unkempt beard and strands of the dyed hair fell out in his hand. He looked at it in dismay. It seemed to bring him to his senses. Thork was staring at him, as if he believed what the head priest said was true. Patro gave a sigh. 'Is that a pirate boat dipping in the waves?'

'Yes, I think so,' Thork agreed. He had been watching it since Patro began speaking.

'Help me up. We need to make haste. I take it you have a boat. Where is it moored?'

'At Moaness,' Thork answered.

Patro shook his head. He reached for his stick. Thork steadied him until he was on his feet. 'We can't go to Moaness,' he said, swaying as he regained his balance. 'That will be the first place the pirates will search for us – and they will come after us. They have men bringing reports from all the landing sites this side of the island. The settlement village will be the next place they look. Sylva and her husband will need speed and caution.'

'Alekander is a good man,' Thork re-assured him.

'I remember, from the reports we had when we were planning the settlement, that there are boats kept to the east of the island, overlooking Orphir,' Patro said. 'The pirates won't venture there in fear of the Orphir fishermen.'

'I can understand that,' Thork said. Patro frowned, not appreciating his humour.

'There must be a pass between the hills we can travel through to reach the boats without taking the coastal route,' Patro continued.

'You mean the way that runs near the Dwarfie Stane?' Thork asked.

'Does it?' Patro's eyes shone. 'I have a mind to see that, if it isn't far out of our way. It holds secrets that I have long wished to discover.'

Thork suspected Patro knew exactly where the stone was. He wasn't inclined to hang around a weird relic waiting for Patro to receive answers to the question of the stars and tides. It didn't seem a

174

good idea to mention this, though. 'We will certainly see it,' he answered.

The way was clear and they began their walk. Thork feared it would be a slow one and was grateful that they had an early start, but either the thought of returning home to his wife or of seeing the Dwarfie Stane enlivened Patro. He increased his speed and there was little need for the stick, although he kept it with him. As Head Priest he was used to wielding his staff and Thork supposed he felt he was missing a limb without it in his grasp.

For a short while after Jona, the head priest of Skara Brae, was murdered, Thork had had possession of his staff. His mother had nagged him into returning it to Jona's son Kali, but while he owned it, he found it difficult to put down, such was the power of a priestly staff.

Thork found ways of keeping out of the open, crawling through thickets and taking detours into woods. Patro allowed him to show off his skills at camouflage, complaining only once when he refused to slither along a shallow stream like an eel. Emerging from a birch and hazel grove, Patro was about to cross a heather moor when Thork pulled at his stick to hold him back.

'Look, there,' he said in a voice that could be heard over the heather and towards the hills.

'Keep your voice down,' Patro whispered. A shadow darted behind a stunted willow tree. Patro freed himself from Thork's grip and stepped out.

'Show yourself. We know you are there,' he called towards the willow tree.

Thork reached for his axe, before remembering it had been taken from him. In the thrill of the escape, he hadn't thought to reclaim it.

'We come in peace,' Patro said, holding his arms out to show all he carried was his walking stick, cum staff. Thork pushed him to the side in time to see an arrow fly past the spot where he had been standing. 'Do you know who I am?' Patro called indignantly. 'I am Patro of the...' Before he could finish, Thork pulled him towards the protection of the hazel trees.

Nuttal stepped from behind the gorse bush holding a roughly made bow. He had an arrow nocked and ready to strike. 'Did you say Patro of the Ness?' he called.

'It's a trick,' Thork warned.

Patro shrugged him off. He brushed down his tunic, straightened his beard and stepped out.

Chapter 11

'I am Patro,' he said boldly.

Nuttal lowered his bow to waist height and walked towards him. 'You know my father, Kennet of Camster.'

'Indeed, I do young man,' Patro said. 'You must be Caordhu. You've grown since I last saw you.'

'Caordhu is my brother. I am Fergeas.'

'Don't trust him,' Thork said, moving to stand in front of Patro. 'He is one of the pirates who attacked the village and kidnapped Sylva. We captured him and were taking him to the Ness when the mist came down and he escaped. He murdered his friend.'

Fergeas laughed. 'I told Marna you wouldn't trust me.'

'Marna!' Thork and Patro said together.

'She gave me this, to prove to you I can be trusted.' He reached for the whistle and held it out to show them.

'What is it?' Patro said.

'A dog whistle, I think.'

'What have you done to my sister?' Thork lunged towards Fergeas, who skipped aside. With nothing to barge into, Thork sprawled headlong onto the heather. Fergeas was standing over him when he swivelled onto his back. 'Marna wouldn't have given you that freely,' he spat.

'I don't see why not,' Patro said. He had taken the whistle from Fergeas and was examining it. 'It is useless. Even if it worked – which it doesn't because the slits are too far apart - there is no way that goose-brained dog of hers would obey it.'

Fergeas handed Patro his bow and offered Thork a hand up. 'I was heading to the settlement to find you,' he said. 'Marna and Sempal are on their way to the Ness to fetch warriors to fight the pirates and rescue you ...' He tilted his head at Patro, '...and the woman who was taken. Marna has thought of a plan.'

Thork got to his feet. He tried to copy Patro's action of rubbing down his tunic, but it failed to give him the same dignity and spread dirt from his hands over his cloak. 'How did they know Patro was a prisoner?' he asked.

'I told them.'

'See, I said he was one of the pirates.' Thork spoke to Patro then advanced towards Fergeas. 'What is your plan, to lure us into your trap?'

178

'Boys, we can sort this out without a fight,' Patro interrupted. 'Which way did Marna go?'

'Did you advise them to go to Moaness?' Thork prodded a finger into Fergeas' chest.

'No, I told them the bay was being watched. They are travelling east.'

'When did they leave? We may be able to catch them,' Thork said.

'There is no need for that,' Patro said. He was fingering the whistle, which helped him concentrate. 'You can return home if you wish, but I don't have the strength for an exhausting trek. I will stay here until the fighters arrive. Sylva is safe, but we still need to end these raids. I can study the Dwarfie Stane and its alignment while I wait.'

'Won't you be needed at the Ness?' Thork objected. 'My mother believes you are dead. She will jump like a young goat when she sees you.'

'I wouldn't refer to your mother as a goat,' Patro said with the hint of a smile. Fergeas gave a chuckle and Patro cleared his throat before continuing. 'It seems pointless going to the Ness, simply to lead the men back here.'

'You intend to lead the fighting?' Thork asked in disbelief.

179

'Why wouldn't I?'

Thork could think of at least five reasons, beginning with Patro's age and physical condition. 'What about my mother?' he repeated.

'That is another reason to remain here. There is the danger your mother would not allow me to return.'

Thork let the matter rest, hoping that once the fighting started, Patro would stay out of the way. 'Someone should return and let my mother know you are well,' he said. 'I'll try to find Marna. If I don't I'll row to Orphir, re-assure my wife that I haven't abandoned her then go on to the Ness.'

The suggestion met with Patro's approval.

'You will need food and drink before you go,' Fergeas said. 'You are welcome to share mine, if you trust me not to poison you. Marna and Sempal finished the berries I picked, but I trapped a curlew this morning. Since there is no need for me to go on to the settlement, we can return to my cave and I'll prepare it for us.'

'Splendid,' Patro answered before Thork could object.

On the way to the hideout, Patro and Fergeas spoke about Fergeas' community near Wick. The talk was about standing stones and chambered cairns rather than what animals they hunted. Thork felt left out and hung back, until there was a break in the conversation. Patro had discovered a patch of edible mushrooms poking from the top layer of peat and stopped to pick them. Thork jumped in with a question about deer and wild boars. Fergeas was a keen hunter and was happy to discuss tracking, breeding grounds and arrowheads.

Patro paused along the path to pick burdock, marsh thistle, lovage and sow thistle. 'Whoever said there was nothing to eat here…' he muttered as he gathered handfuls of dandelion leaves.

When they reached the cave, Fergeas prepared the bird, but Patro took it upon himself to tend the fire and do the cooking. A mouth-watering aroma of the cooked meat and plants filled the cave. Fergeas and Thork went outside to allow Patro space to work. They returned when a wind blew up and a cumbersome cloud threatened a downpour. They huddled round the fire, listening as the first drops of rain changed to hail.

'Do you really want to travel in this?' Fergeas asked.

'I can wait until the weather brightens.'

'The sea will be angry for the rest of the day,' Fergeas said.

During the meal, Patro regaled them with tales from his journey to Stonehenge.

'You saw a giant eel that slithers on the land?' Thork was incredulous. 'Wouldn't it die out of the water?'

'It lives in long grass. The people call it a snake. One bite from its fangs could kill a grown man,' Patro answered.

The weather didn't relent until evening and by that time Thork had decided to stay on Hoy with Fergeas and Patro.

'What about your wife?' Patro asked. 'And your mother?'

'Marna can see to them. She is better at that sort of thing.'

* * * * * * *

Marna and Sempal travelled with more haste than Fergeas had thought necessary and made good progress on their way to the mainland. Sempal's sense of direction was as honed as the geese that flew to the island every winter from their summer homes in the north. They found the fishermen's huts and boats. In exchange for Sempal's sea tales two brothers agreed to row them across to Orphir in their boat. The men were squat and well-muscled. Used to rowing together, they made short work of the waves. They arrived in Orphir as Sempal finished his tale of the Selkie's treasure while around the same time on Hoy Patro was stuffing the curlew with mushrooms. The brothers dropped Sempal and Marna off and returned at once, despite Marna inviting them to stay for a meal with Caran.

'There is a storm brewing,' the elder brother explained.

The sun was up, but it was dark thanks to the clouds. The villagers were alerted to their arrival by the dogs barking. Marna had visited before and was recognised by the watchman.

'Your brother is not here,' he said. 'Caran will be glad to see you.'

'I am eager to see my little niece,' Marna agreed. 'We can't stay long, though. There is trouble on Hoy. The Ness must be warned.'

'Trouble on Hoy is trouble for us,' the watchman said. 'I will inform our village elders while you see your family.'

Caran was tending to her baby when Marna and Sempal entered the house. She had a haggard look, as if she had been awake all night. She looked up, but didn't immediately recognise Sempal, who was first through the door. A smile appeared when she saw Marna. She settled the baby in her basket and insisted on taking Marna's bag and making her sit down. Her smile suddenly vanished.

'Is Thork in trouble?' she asked.

'No,' Marna answered. 'At least, he wasn't when I left him. He is on Hoy, searching for Patro's body.'

'Patro's body?' Caran raised a palm to her mouth. 'Why, what has happened? You don't mean..?'

'I thought you must have heard. Didn't Thork send someone to tell you?'

'We've had no news from anyone in days,' Caran admitted. 'There have been rumours from passers-by of changes at the Ness. The elders have talked about sending a messenger to find out.'

'Quint has matters under control,' Sempal said.

'His control,' Marna said scornfully.

'Do you know when Thork will be home?' Caran asked.

Marna pretended not to hear. Sempal was busy investigating a pot of left-overs.

'I'm a poor host,' Caran said, without conviction. 'I'm afraid I have little for you to eat after your journey. If I'd known you were coming…' The sentence was left unfinished as a mild rebuke. She moved around fetching bannocks and scraping the last of the stew from the previous evening's supper pot. 'Will you be staying long?'

'No,' Marna answered. 'Once we have rested and spoken with the elders, we need to get to the Ness. We have heard news that Patro is alive.'

'I thought you said a moment ago… is he dead or not?'

'A messenger reported him dead, but a…friend…of Marna's believes he has seen Patro alive,' Sempal answered, emphasising the word "friend" in a way that left Caran confused. The baby began crying and Caran tried to soothe her by rocking the basket.

'I could do with a nap,' Sempal said. 'We had an early start and the Flow was rougher than it should be at this time of year.'

'I'm afraid the bed isn't made up,' Caran said. There is heather at the bottom of the dresser.' She

185

indicated the pile of dried shrubs.

Marna filled the cot with handfuls of heather and pressed it down with her knuckles while Sempal finished eating the stew. Caran took the baby, in its basket, outside for air to stop her crying.

'Do you know where the spare skins are?' Sempal asked.

'Caran didn't say,' Marna answered.

The fire was at an ember and the room was gloomy. Neither Sempal nor Marna could find them.

'We'd better not disturb the room,' Marna said, as Sempal moved a reed basket and two large pots.

Sempal lay down and pulled his cloak around him. Marna had hoped to rest by the fire, but when Sempal began snoring she decided to go outside and talk to Caran.

Her sister-in-law was keen to hear about the Ness and whether Marna's mother was safe. While they were speaking three elders came over.

'You have news for us about Hoy?' the chief elder asked.

Marna explained everything that had

186

happened, painting Nuttal's role in a better light so that the Orphir folk would believe his story. Sempal emerged from Caran's hut and made his way towards them. He listened to Marna's account. She could tell that he wanted to interrupt her, so she spoke rapidly, not allowing time for him to get a word in. Other inhabitants of the village had gathered to hear what was being said. This led to doors being opened and folk coming out until most of the village were circling round.

'That's why we need to get to the Ness, to raise a party of fighters,' Marna concluded, appealing to the crowd.

'You say Patro has been taken captive?' one of the elders said.

'I believe so,' Marna answered.

'You trust this strange boy?' the leader asked. He turned to Sempal. 'You were there too. What do you have to say?'

Sempal looked at Marna and recognised the furrowed brows. He didn't dare disagree.

The elders signalled to one another and moved aside to speak in private.

'Why waste time heading to the Ness?' a woman asked while the elders were conferring.

187

'They won't offer support. We have men and women here who will row over and fight.'

'Why would you get involved?' Sempal questioned. 'You have no reason to risk your lives for Patro's sake.'

'Maybe not, but pirates are everybody's problem, especially to villages on the coast,' another man answered.

'We'd rather have Patro in charge at the Ness than his brother.' The chief elder overheard the conversation from where he stood and gave his opinion. The others made noises of approval. 'We know where we are with Patro. We pay our dues to the Ness and in return the priests supplicate the gods on our behalf. They fore-warn of evil weather, tell us about healing plants and store food which they supply in times of need. We have no complaints.'

'Quint would double the amount of grain the Ness demands,' one woman said.

'I have heard he would have one of his men stay here, feeding off our hard work and giving orders to our council,' another added.

'Thork is our priest.' A young woman spoke up, glancing at Caran.

'He has not finished his study,' Caran answered, but it was clear she was proud of her husband.

Marna feared the talk was becoming side-tracked onto a discussion about the Ness. She raised her voice to make herself heard over the chatter. 'Thank you for the offer of aid. Any help is appreciated. Now though, I have to return to my mother.'

Her words didn't reach far. Caran was standing next to her. She shook a wooden rattle she had for the baby and the noise quietened. 'The Ness needs to be told about Patro,' she repeated.

'We will ready folk willing and able to fight,' the chief said. 'And sharpen weapons for them.'

'Marna and Sempal must set off before the weather changes,' Caran said, hustling her guests towards her hut to collect their belongings.

Before they left, the villagers brought nuts, berries and roots they could chew on, which Marna stuffed into their bags. The clouds that had gathered while they talked let their rain fall and they hadn't gone far before they were soaked. The thong bindings holding the soles of Marna's shoes came loose from the upper seal hide and flapped as she walked.

'I don't suppose there will be time for Kustan to make me a new pair of boots?' she asked Sempal.

'Time before what?' Sempal said.

'Before we return to Hoy to challenge the pirates.'

'You don't need to come with us. Nobody expects you to fight.'

'Why not?' Marna objected.

Sempal gave her a look which she knew meant "don't be silly". She continued her protest. 'I can fight, better than some of the men.'

'No, you can't,' Sempal answered.

'Well, I can help in other ways. I don't mind sleeping outdoors or getting soaked.'

Sempal wasn't in the mood to argue. The heavy rain gave him the excuse of not being able to hear her and they walked on without talking. The wind eased as they travelled between the hills. The sky remained dark and the shadows from the heather gave Marna the feeling of eyes, fixed on the stems, watching their journey. She couldn't bear Sempal's silence any longer. 'You must know tales about people who dwell in the hills,' she said.

Sempal's face lit up. 'Have I ever told you about the three-headed mountain monster?'

'I don't think so,' Marna answered. She had heard it several times, but Sempal had a way of changing bits of the story, making it fresh at every telling. The mountain monster could be scary, funny, a good friend or even a god. 'As long as it doesn't live on Hoy,' she added.

As usual with Sempal's tales, one led into another. When he neared the end of the mountain monster story, he introduced the loch kelpie and the vanishing island of the moon. Marna urged him to keep going. They were through the Orphir hills and could see the Stone Circle of Stenness in the distance before his throat became too dry to continue. The rain had stopped, but they were both drenched. Sempal suggested they stop for a break at the village of Barnhouse. Marna didn't see the point.

'The Ness is no distance from here and the sun will dry us. Mother will want to know about Patro.'

Sempal hadn't given up on a beaker of warm ale at Barnhouse when they spotted Henjar approaching them with her son, Boda. She was trying to hold his hand, while the young boy was struggling to free himself. They could hear his shrieks.

'You would think my sister was killing Boda,' Sempal said with a laugh.

The boy spotted Sempal and stopped wailing. He pointed and said something to his mother, who looked towards them and waved. She started speaking to them before they were within hearing distance. Marna could see her lips move, but couldn't grasp the words.

'One of you has to do something,' Henjar said. She put her hands on her hips, waiting for a reply.

'Of course,' Sempal said. Marna wasn't convinced he knew what he was agreeing to.

'What are you waiting for?' Henjar demanded.

'Marna will see to it,' Sempal said. 'She's better at that sort of stuff.'

'I have to speak with Quint,' Marna answered. 'At once.'

Henjar nodded. 'That's what I was thinking. Quint is a pig-headed buffoon. He won't listen to me, but I knew I could rely on you. Come on Boda, let's find granny and tell her the news.' She took a few steps then stopped and turned back to Marna. 'By the way, do you know your shoes are broken?'

Marna made a face. 'Just being helpful.' Henjar squeezed her son's hand and they walked off.

'Do you know what she was talking about?' Sempal said once his sister departed.

'I've no idea,' Marna admitted.

'I'm sure we'll find out. I'd better go after her.'

'Wait for me.' Marna stayed with Sempal as they entered the settlement. The workshops were alive with the chiselling of stone and the firing of pots. Hot, noisy and stinking of men at work. Fires burnt in buildings set aside for discussions. Marna smelt charred meat and aromatic plants. When she heard horns droning and drums beating from the main celebration chamber she knew Quint and his elders were enjoying a feast. It wouldn't be the best time to speak to him – or perhaps it would be. She could address a larger gathering.

'Let's disturb their meal,' she said to Sempal.

'What about Henjar?'

Marna took hold of his hand and dragged him towards the door of the main chamber. Two of Quint's men stood guard outside.

'They must be expecting trouble,' Sempal whispered.

'Only senior priests allowed,' one of the guards informed them.

'I have to speak with Quint,' Marna argued. 'I have vital news about Patro.'

The man was unmoved. 'It will have to wait,' he said.

'Weren't you listening?' Sempal said. 'Or don't you care about your chief priest?'

'Patro is no longer with us. Quint is in charge and he has pressing business to deal with.'

'What can be more pressing than finding his brother?' Sempal said. Marna nudged him to be quiet.

'Has this business to do with the pirates on Hoy?' she asked. 'We have a plan that the council needs to hear.'

'It concerns the murder of our friend and colleague Yarl,' the second man said. 'The culprit has been captured.'

'Who is it?' Marna asked.

'That is not for you to know,' the first guard spoke before his companion could answer. 'Move on.'

Marna lingered nearby. Voices were raised and for a moment she thought she heard Ralfe's voice. The door was ajar and she tried to peek around the guards to see inside. The first guard pulled the door shut. Sempal dragged Marna away.

'We'll learn nothing if we annoy the guards,' he said. 'Let's go to your mother and tell her the news. She will find a way to get Quint's ear.'

Marna was reluctant to move, but she knew Sempal was right. She raised her voice to make sure the guards heard her as she left. 'I was the person who found the body. You would think I'd be asked what I saw.' The guards weren't swayed.

As they reached Marna's house they could hear squabbling. The voices stopped when Marna and Sempal entered. Henjar's mother Lin was sitting next to Marna's mother and from their faces Marna could tell they were having a disagreement, which was being carried on in silence.

'Did you have a nice time on Hoy?' Lin asked her son. Her voice was light and Marna wondered if she understood their reason for going. Her own mother raised and lowered her eyebrows in disbelief.

Sempal didn't answer. He was staring at his mother and exclaimed, 'What is that on your head?'

'Do you like it?' Lin smiled and touched the

clump of soil and plants balanced on her hair. She stood up and twirled round. 'Quint thinks it is wonderful.'

'Quint thinks it is ridiculous.' Henjar had appeared at the door and answered her mother. 'He was laughing at you.'

'He said he liked elderflower.'

'To drink, not to parade around in.'

Lin's face fell. 'I think it looks good,' Marna said to cheer her. 'It is different.'

'See,' Lin said, her smile returning. 'Someone appreciates fashion. I'm going to find Kra. She makes the most delicious honey cakes. Quint will need something to sweeten him after listening to details of that hideous murder. I hope he thinks of a suitable punishment for the killer.' Lin twirled again before leaving the house.

'My mother thinks she can woo Quint,' Henjar explained to Marna. 'I have to go after her and make sure she doesn't do anything stupid.' She departed as quickly as she arrived, with Boda in her arms chanting 'Stupid nana'.

Once their visitors had gone, Marna closed the door. She rounded on her mother. 'Tell me about the trial,' she demanded.

196

'There is little to say. The priests have their man. A witness saw him. You tell me what happened on Hoy. Where is Thork? Has he found Patro's body?' She grabbed at Marna's hands as she spoke. Marna struggled to decide which question to answer first, when she had many of her own. Sempal answered for her.

'There is news,' he said. 'We don't want to get your hopes up, but...'

'But what?' Marna's mother let go of her daughter and leant close to Sempal, her nose an inch away from his. For a moment he was tongue-tied.

'Patro may be alive,' Marna blurted out.

Her mother's mouth opened. Nothing came out and she staggered into the hearth before jumping back. Marna saw tears in her eyes. 'Alive, you say? How? Where? You wouldn't tease me like this?'

Marna put an arm round her mother's shoulder.

'We didn't see him ourselves,' Sempal said.

'Someone we trust did,' Marna said.

'Someone? Who? One of the settlers? Is Patro well?'

'The person who saw him didn't get a clear

view.' Sempal said.

'From his description, it could only have been Patro,' Marna added. 'Who else looks like him? He may be injured, which is why we need fighters to row to Hoy to rescue him.'

'Rescue him,' her mother croaked. 'From what?'

'He is a prisoner of the pirates,' Sempal answered.

Marna's mother gave a gasp and raised her hands to her head. Her legs shook. Marna helped her to sit down and knelt beside her. 'Patro is a strong man – a survivor. Remember on Eynhallow when he was attacked and left to drown? You nursed him back to health.'

'That was a year ago. He is older now and suffers pains in his chest from the effects.'

'Your knowledge of medicines has grown since you have been studying here,' Marna said. She looked to Sempal to help.

'There is no time to waste,' he said. 'We must speak with Quint. His guards prevented us. We thought you would have influence.'

'When did the high priest need men to guard him in the Ness?' Marna's mother complained. She pursed her lips. 'I'm not sure I can help. The guards will listen to Jolty. You should fetch him.'

'He will be with the other senior priests at the trial,' Sempal said.

Marna's mother shook her head. 'No. Quint is Jolty's favourite son, but they do not always see matters in the same light. While you were away, Jolty spoke against making rash decisions on Yarl's death. He has followers who agree with him. Quint was fuming and has forbidden Jolty from taking part in discussions.'

'I'll find him,' Sempal said. 'You stay with your mother.'

'He likes to stroll in the meadows near the Stones of Stenness,' Marna's mother said. 'I have heard him talk to the Stones and ask for advice.'

Marna feared that an old man who talked to stones would be more of a hindrance than a help, but he had been present when she found Yarl's body. Quint was trying to silence them both and she wanted to know why.

She and her mother were heating ale and discussing Caran's baby when Sempal and Jolty returned.

'Does my granddaughter have a name yet? I

should visit at once.'

'Visit who?' Jolty interrupted the talk. He caught his breath then presented his daughter-in-law with the flowers he had been gathering. 'Foxgloves – you can use them in your medicines,' he said.

Jolty's eyesight was going. Marna didn't recognise the flowers. They weren't foxgloves. He should have known it was too early in the year for those. Her mother took them and handed Jolty a beaker of ale.

Marna offered Sempal a beaker then filled one for herself and one for her mother. Sempal had tried to explain the situation to Jolty on their way to the house, but from what he said it was clear he had misheard.

'Sempal tells me the people on Hoy have found my son's body and are unwilling to return it to the Ness. What do they want in exchange?'

'Not his body,' Marna corrected. 'Patro himself.'

Jolty shook and ale spilt from his beaker. Marna's mother took it from him and ushered him to sit by the fire. 'My son is alive?'

Marna recounted what had happened on Hoy,

expanding on their plan to draw the pirates to the Dwarfie Stane. Jolty sat with wide eyes, a milky film reflecting the flames. It was difficult to know if he was listening. 'Can you help us?' she asked. Jolty took back his beaker and finished the ale before answering.

'I can help you speak to Quint, but I am too old to fight. You must find a strong man with a brain in his head who knows Hoy and the people there. You will need their support if you are to fight in the hills.'

'We have Ralfe,' Marna said. 'He knows Hoy and the settlers.'

'Ralfe! Haven't you heard?' Jolty answered. 'He is the man accused of murdering Yarl.'

'Never,' Marna spluttered. 'I do not believe that and neither will the council. I thought he was there as a witness. Why would Ralfe kill Yarl? He didn't know him.'

'There is a belief that Ralfe is working with the pirates,' Jolty explained. 'His accusers argue that Ralfe feared Yarl would give the elders information to purge the raiders for good.'

'That is ridiculous,' Marna said.

'Quint believes the man who killed Yarl also

killed Toomac.'

'Toomac was murdered on Hoy,' Sempal said.

'While Ralfe was guarding him,' Jolty said.

'I was there too,' Marna said.

'And you saw what happened?'

'No, but…' Marna hesitated. She wanted to tell Jolty that Phalt had killed Toomac, but she had glossed over the part of her tale involving Nuttal and wasn't sure how much to tell Jolty. 'If Ralfe is a traitor, why would he kill a fellow pirate?'

'Perhaps Ralfe didn't trust Toomac to keep his mouth shut,' Jolty continued. 'Ralfe wouldn't want to risk being named as a pirate informer. Besides, there is a witness who claims he saw Ralfe flee from the loch side at the time of Yarl's disappearance.'

'Who?' Marna demanded.

'A visitor to the Ness, I know his family. He is a man of honour and integrity, with no reason to lie. Fergeas of Camster.'

Chapter 12

'Your friend may have seen Ralfe near the loch, but that doesn't mean he killed Yarl,' Marna said. 'I know he didn't kill Toomac. Phalt did.'

'What proof do you have?' Jolty asked.

Marna bit her bottom lip. 'There was a witness on Hoy,' she answered.

'Alekander?' Marna's mother said.

'Nooo.' Marna dragged out the word.

'The person who told us Patro is alive,' Sempal said.

'You mean the pirate lad who escaped?' Jolty said. 'Ralfe spoke of him.'

Marna saw her mother's face drop. 'Don't worry, mum, I trust him,' she said.

'I see.' Jolty stood up and walked to the door. He stopped and turned to Sempal. 'And what of you? Do you trust this "friend" of Marna's?'

'I trust Marna's judgement,' Sempal replied without hesitation.

Jolty's face was severe, but his lips began to stretch across in a smile. 'Then so do I,' he decided. 'You must speak with Quint at once. I shall get you an audience.'

'And if Quint isn't convinced?' Marna's

mother asked.

'I have friends I can speak to who have sons willing to fight. We shall raise a band of warriors one way or another.'

Marna's mother rose to thank him, placing a kiss on his cheek. Once he had left, Marna began pacing the room. She paused to lift trinkets, wiped specks of dust from them then shifted them along her mother's shelf.

'Would you stop that,' her mother said. Marna put down the whale bone doll that Wilmer the jeweller had carved for her.

'I can't help thinking about Ralfe. What if the council don't believe he is innocent?'

'He will be found guilty of murder,' Sempal answered.

'And then…?'

'The elders will consider a punishment. It is likely he will be banished to one of the barren, northern isles,' Sempal said.

'Quint is eager to demand blood for blood,' her mother said. 'The coastal villages have been stirred up by the news of pirates. Their deeds have been built upon with every telling, but the threat is real and people are terrified. Quint knows that action has to be taken.'

'I don't see how blaming the wrong man will help,' Marna said. 'If he would send his men to Hoy…'

'Yes, we know,' Sempal tried to calm her.

'What if Ralfe is a spy?' her mother asked. 'You don't know him. He and this Phalt may have been working together. It is a pity Alekander isn't here. I trust him.'

'I wouldn't put it past Quint and his council to accuse him too, despite Sylva being taken prisoner,' Marna moaned. 'They could say he wanted rid of her.'

'You are getting worked up,' Sempal said.

Marna lifted the doll again and gripped it tight. 'Ralfe is a friend. Wilmer used to say that friends should stick up for one another.'

'The same Wilmer, who murdered three of his friends and tried to kill you,' Sempal reminded her.

Marna's mother's face turned red. She looked away for a moment then gently took the doll from Marna's hand and replaced it on the shelf. 'Marna is right,' she said. 'I can't rely on Jolty speaking to Quint. I shall go to him. He cannot continue to refuse to speak to me, although if there is no evidence that Phalt killed the man on Hoy, it will be difficult to alter his opinion.' Marna was about to interrupt, but her mother stopped her. 'The verdict may be postponed if the elders can be persuaded that Patro lives. Do you have nothing I can show to sway them?'

Marna shook her head. Sempal was silent for a moment then snapped his fingers. 'Marna's friend on Hoy knows where Patro is being kept prisoner. It would take less than a day for the priests to send a spy to Hoy to see for himself.'

Marna's mother frowned. 'The priests do not have "spies".'

'I meant an envoy,' Sempal corrected.

'That's better,' Marna's mother said. 'I shall suggest that to Quint. Every hour is precious. If Patro has wounds, they will start to fester.' She strode to the door.

'Quint won't listen if you barge your way in to his meeting,' Marna said.

'It will be late when they finish, if the amount of food is anything to go by,' Sempal added.

Marna's mother halted. 'Tomorrow then, I shall go first thing.'

'I would like to speak to the witness, Fergeas

206

of wherever,' Marna said. 'Do you know him?'

'I have heard Patro speak of his friend, Kennet of Camster,' her mother answered. 'I believe Fergeas is his eldest son. Strange, I haven't seen him here. I would have thought he should have visited.'

'You could ask him to dine with us,' Marna said.

'I could,' her mother answered, 'But with Lin, Henjar and Boda here, you wouldn't get to question him.'

Marna was lazing in her cot the following morning, listening to Henjar's snoring, when she heard her mother bustle around, preparing to leave the house.

She remembered her mother's intention to speak with Quint and pushed aside the skins covering her. 'Wait for me,' she said.

'I will speak to Quint alone,' her mother affirmed.

Marna rose from the cot, grabbed a shawl and tried to follow her mother out.

'You certainly can't meet Quint looking like you've slept in a hedge.' Her mother sent her back.

She waited until her mother had turned a

corner before sneaking after her, keeping a distance behind. Sempal passed her mother, going in the opposite direction. They greeted one another, but her mother didn't stop to chat. Sempal hobbled towards Marna.

'What are you up to?' he asked. She flapped her hand, signalling him to make less noise and keep in the shadows.

'Against the wall,' she whispered. 'I'm following mother. She doesn't know.'

Sempal accompanied her to the council chamber. It was empty and the guards had gone. Her mother carried on to Quint's private chamber. Marna couldn't enter, but she found an alcove outside the room. There was space for a child and while Marna squeezed sideways to conceal herself, Sempal tried to look inconspicuous, pretending to examine a painted wall.

'What are you doing here?' Marna heard her mother ask in a loud voice. She jumped, thinking her mother had discovered her eavesdropping, but she had been speaking to Lin, who was scurrying backwards from the room. Marna crushed against the wall, out of sight, as Lin banged into Sempal.

'She's got a nerve,' Lin said, adjusting a loose

lock of hair that had fallen over her eyes. 'She thinks she is the only woman from our village who can bag a priest.' She took hold of her son's hands. 'I was laying out flowers to make the room bright and fresh.'

Sempal looked beyond his mother to see Marna mouthing instructions. He knew what she meant. 'That is a great idea. Why don't you show me where to pick sweet smelling flowers for Marna? After that we can visit my friend Tama for ale and bannocks,' he suggested to Lin.

'I know a shaded spot where there are bluebells…' Lin began, her good humour restored. Her voice tailed off as Sempal escorted her away.

Marna continued to wait outside Quint's room. She couldn't feel her foot because of cramp and she feared she was about to experience the awful tingling sensation that followed. She put a foot out and circled her ankle to stretch her leg when she spotted Quint returning along the passageway. He was accompanied by Tia Famel or rather she was several paces behind him trying to get his attention. Like many of the older folk, she was deaf and she spoke with a loud voice that Marna had no difficulty hearing.

'Ralfe is the obvious suspect, but some of the council believe things fit too well,' she said to Quint.

'What do you mean?' Quint replied without turning towards her. 'He was seen at the loch, or do you doubt the word of Fergeas of Camster?'

'I do not,' Tia Famel answered, 'But Flemeer and Vill are keen to know what he was doing at the loch side. The elders have been given one account of the murder. Folk from outside the walls believe another. They claim Ralfe and his friend Alekander were with them when Yarl was last seen.'

'Who says that?' Quint demanded. He didn't wait for Tia Famel's answer before shrugging off her objection. 'Their testimonies will not agree. One man will say they ate together, another that they went hunting.'

'True,' Tia Famel argued. 'Nevertheless, we should be wary of forcing a decision on the council. I suggest we hold our final verdict until we have heard from Jolty.'

Quint stopped a step from where Marna was hiding. She could smell the fish he had eaten on his tunic, where he had wiped his hands. She held her breath and tried to make herself tiny. He turned his back on Marna to face Tia Famel and gave a forced laugh. 'My father is as hard of seeing as you are of hearing.'

'What about Alekander?' Tia Famel persisted.

'The same Alekander who has conveniently legged it back to Hoy?'

'With Marna and Thork to watch him,' Tia Famel answered.

Quint made a noise like a hunted hog, implying he had been unaware of this news. 'Marna is of no importance,' he said. 'The question is why Thork would go to Hoy.' He thought for a moment then answered. 'He intends to raise a band of supporters. With Patro gone, he wants to stake a claim to leadership here.'

'Against you?' Tia Famel snorted.

'The boy has ideas above himself, fed to him by his power hungry mother. I have heard that the people of Orphir are stirring. He is their drummer and pretends to be their priestly advisor.'

The idea that Thork could plan a boys' game of arm wrestling, let alone an assault on the Ness was ridiculous. Marna laughed. The chuckle echoed against the stone. She slapped a hand against her mouth, but it was too late. Quint whipped round and spotted her. His face turned purple. Before he could splutter a reply, Marna's mother appeared at the doorway.

'What is that you were saying about Thork?' she demanded of Quint then turned to her daughter. 'Marna, what by all things sensible are you doing here?'

Marna squeezed out of her hiding space and rubbed her tunic. 'I saw a rat. You know how I hate them with their beady eyes and scaly tails.'

'Don't be silly. Go and do something useful like searching for reeds, or find that dog of yours and take it hunting.'

Marna furrowed her eyebrows. Her mother knew that the only thing Pip had 'hunted' was a dead goose with an arrow through it. As she squeezed past Quint and Tia Famel she saw her mother give a wink. She had no idea what it meant.

Her mother had emphasised the words 'searching' and 'hunting'. That was something to ponder. They had birds, trout and hunks of meat hanging to dry from the roof of their house, more than enough for one family. She had tried using a bow and arrow, but gave up when the string flew back against her wrist, removing the skin and

212

leaving a painful sore. Thork could throw maces and axes, but she didn't have the strength to send them far or the accuracy to hit a moving target.

Her house was empty when she returned, although a small stone ball was lying on the floor, which she guessed Boda had been playing with. Her mother grew pots of herbs indoors and she set about checking them. The mint was growing well, the sage had withered and the pile of green powder may once have been chives. She separated out the mint and poured water on the sage.

When she finished she re-arranged her pots of dyes. They had been neglected while she was on Hoy. The paste she had made from dried nettles had left a blob of sticky material in the pot. She would need to clean it before preparing a new dye. Why hadn't her mother told her to do that, rather than go hunting? Even grinding seeds into flour, which she hated, would have made more sense. Searching for reeds was stupid. She knew where to find the growing plants and there were stacks of dried reeds in the store room.

She was busy crushing ochre when Sempal arrived. He had escorted his mother to Kris and Tama's house, where she was enjoying elderflower ale. Henjar and Boda had joined them and he had come looking for Marna. Tama was cooking a midday meal. Her sister was there, with her daughter. Both played the pipes and they planned a time of music and story-telling.

'Haven't your friends got work to do?' Marna asked.

'Quint has called a halt to the building work on the dyke until after the mourning period for Patro. It isn't suitable for outdoor digging and lifting. You don't notice the wind behind the walls here, but it is uprooting bushes and tossing them across the loch towards Stenness. It is raining as well.'

Marna could hear the pounding of the rain on the slate roof. 'My mother told me I should go hunting in this weather,' she confided to her friend.

'Hunting?'

'Or searching for reeds. She must have lost her senses, as well as her husband,' Marna said.

'That is harsh,' Sempal said. He paused and licked his lip. 'Quint could be right, you know.'

Marna stared at him. She thought about tipping the pot of ochre she was holding over his head, but that would have been a waste. It didn't stop her threatening him with it.

214

'Ralfe didn't kill Toomac or Yarl,' she protested. 'Phalt killed Toomac. He couldn't have killed Yarl.'

'I'm not stupid. Hear me out. Phalt was recruited by someone from Orkney, not by Lional. I don't believe he was the only one. The same person could be behind both murders, with agents doing the actual killings. Your mother was telling you to search for clues and hunt for the truth. We need to find out who killed Yarl and get them to talk.'

Marna put her pot down. 'This could be big,' she said.

That is what I was trying to say,' Sempal protested.

'We need to question Ralfe. He could have suspected someone from the settlement was working against them. Perhaps that is why he allowed Phalt to go with them to the Ness. It could have been a test.' Marna stopped. 'I'm getting ahead of myself, amn't I?'

'Yes, but we can speak to Ralfe. I know where the priests have taken him,' Sempal answered. 'He is being held in the old building that leans against the wall at the edge of the settlement. Quint had the carpenters fix holders to bar the door from the outside. To make extra sure Ralfe doesn't escape he has left a guard outside.'

'Do you know who?'

'The men will take shifts. When I passed on my way here, it was Hunkel.'

Marna screwed up her nose until she could see the end with cross eyes. 'He hates me. He won't allow us to speak with Ralfe.'

'You don't need his permission,' Sempal said, looking pleased. 'Last autumn, Patro asked Kris and his brother to do repair work on the older buildings. They removed fallen stones and cut back the overgrowth to find a disused tunnel. It led from the back of the building under the perimeter wall to exit outside the Ness. Kris asked Patro if he should fill it in, but you know what Patro is like. He loves secret passageways and hidden chambers. He was thrilled by the discovery, especially when crumbling pieces of pottery and rotten animal bones were found among the rubble. He told Kris to steady up the walls and make the passage safe for use. He kept the entrance and exit hidden from view. He and Patro are the only people who know how to get into the passage.'

'If Kris hasn't told anyone, why would he tell

us?' Marna said.

'We should be able to persuade him. Patro is your father.'

'My step-father,' Marna answered.

'Who is in grave danger. Talking to Ralfe could save Patro. Kris will understand that.'

Marna stroked a finger across her chin. 'We can get in to Ralfe's prison without Hunkel seeing us,' she mused, rubbing at a spot. 'That means we could get him out, beyond the wall. We could smuggle in a disguise and get Ralfe to Hoy during the night.'

'We could,' Sempal agreed. 'But he would be a fugitive. The council believe what they have been told – that he murdered Yarl.'

'Not all of them,' Marna argued.

'It would be difficult to keep him hidden. There would be the risk of someone reporting him, either a visitor to the island or one of the settlers he has a disagreement with. It would be better if we could convince the elders of his innocence.'

'We don't have time. My mother said that Quint wants Yarl's killer sacrificed – blood for blood.'

'Quint may want that, but the council won't

allow it,' Sempal said.

Marna scoffed. 'The council are like scared crows, flying into one another. The one thing that keeps them united is their fear of the pirates. Quint is happy to stir this up in order to keep control. He has named Yarl's killer and will deal with him swiftly, ensuring the ceremony to mark Patro's passing is also the one that starts his leadership.'

'Patro isn't dead,' Sempal reminded her.

'We know that, and so does Quint because Jolty told him. The trouble is, Quint intends to stop anyone else finding out.'

'He could be in shock,' Sempal said. 'To hear your brother is dead is terrible news. To learn he is alive…I mean, he may not want his hopes raised, to have them dashed again.'

'It would be a greater disappointment to him if he wasn't appointed leader,' Marna knocked back Sempal's suggestion. 'He had the gall to accuse Thork of raising men against him, because the people of Orphir are gathering to fight.'

'How does he know that?' Sempal asked. 'They made the decision this morning, when we were there.'

'Quint's spies will have reported back.'

218

'Envoys,' Sempal reminded her.

'No, spies,' Marna said firmly. 'Let's go and find Kris.'

'That is why I came for you, remember – the story telling lunch?'

'My head is all over the place at the moment,' Marna admitted. 'How long will it last for?'

'Until the weather improves. We can't go burrowing in tunnels before then anyhow.'

Marna gathered sealskins to cover their tunics and protect them from the rain. She laced new patches of deer skin round her shoddy sandals before making her way out of the house with Sempal. The path between the buildings was paved, but once outside the walls, her feet squelched in the mud. A fierce wind drove them forwards. Kris's door was shut tight and they had to bang hard before Tama opened it. They were blown inside. Tama ushered them towards the hearth, pushing the door closed before the flames were extinguished. Kris was sitting on a stone polishing a mace head. Marna sensed that such intricate work bored him and he would rather have been outside flexing his muscles. He got up when they entered. Lin and Henjar were sitting near the fire. Boda was pulling

Pip's ears. An older woman and a girl about Marna's age were standing in the corner, blowing through pipes.

The girl stopped playing. 'I thought you were on Hoy, Marna,' she said.

'I was, Jool,' Marna answered.

'What a journey it turned out to be,' Sempal added in his story-telling voice. Marna knew he was about to elevate their trip to an adventure worthy of a fire-side saga. The woman with the pipes sat down to listen. He had reached the point where Thork and Alekander went off towards the coast when Tama offered him a warm drink and he paused to accept. The musicians began playing again and Marna took the opportunity to lead Sempal across the room to speak with Kris.

'I heard your friend had been detained,' Kris said, 'Has he been accused of Yarl's murder?'

'Accused and found guilty,' Marna said. 'No-one is permitted to speak to him. He is being kept prisoner in the old building, guarded by Quint's men.' She lowered her voice. 'We need to know the secret way in so we can question him.'

'What good will it do to question him again?' Kris asked.

Marna and Sempal began speaking at once. Kris didn't wait until they decided who would speak. 'I trust you know what you are doing. We can't talk now. Wait until Ghea and Jool have gone, and Lin and Henjar have returned to the Ness.'

Marna helped Tama serve the food and Sempal continued his tale while they ate. Marna didn't remember the trolls they had outwitted at the Dwarfie Stane or the ferocious clawed birds twice the size of swans that had tried to seize them in their beaks, but she pretended she did.

'Sempal threw a rock and hit one of the monsters on the head,' she added.

'Did he hurt the poor thing?' Henjar asked. Her voice was serious and Marna couldn't tell if she was joking or not.

'It had two others, with sharp beaks,' Sempal said.

Once the meal was finished, Jool and Ghea played again. Marna moved closer to the door, trying to hear if the wind had died.

'I think the rain has stopped,' she said, when the music ended and the women paused to regain their breath. Kris lifted a stone hammer from the dresser.

'Quint will want us back at work if it has,' he said. 'We can't work on the dyke, but he wants foundations for another stone to match the one for Patro.'

'We should find Marna's mother,' Henjar said to Lin. 'Boda, stop biting Pip's tail.'

'He bit mine,' Boda protested.

'You don't have a tail,' Henjar said.

Boda wagged his thumb at his mother. She picked her son up and examined the finger. There was no evidence of a bite wound.

'Pip does like sucking fingers,' Marna said. She spoke to Boda. 'Tell my mother to give you a honey cake to make it better.'

The thought of honey cakes was sufficient to persuade Boda and Lin to return to the Ness. Ghea and Jool wrapped their pipes in skins and followed them out, leaving Sempal and Marna alone with Tama and Kris.

'Do you have time to show us the tunnel entrance before you go?' Marna asked Kris.

'Aye.' Kris moved to find his sealskins and Sempal gulped down the remainder of his drink. 'I can show you the tunnel entrance, but I won't go in with you. If one of the guards saw me...'

222

Sempal put a hand on his shoulder. 'Yes, I heard about the trouble you had with Hunkel last spring over the fish you caught in the loch. It would be better if you kept your head low.'

Marna was curious to know what the problem with the fish was, but it wasn't the time or place to ask. Sempal returned his beaker to Tama and they followed Kris out, shielding their faces against the wind. Kris insisted on keeping close to the walls of the houses, hiding in the shadows. Marna and Sempal did the same. Kris slipped between the workers' houses and it was difficult to follow him.

'There.' Sempal pointed as Kris darted across the open moorland towards the perimeter wall of the Ness. He raised an arm for them to join him. Marna rolled her eyes at Sempal.

'There is nobody here, why the secrecy?' She made a point of walking at a steady pace across the heather. Kris crept ahead and when they caught up with him he parted a gorse bush and searched among the loose rocks around the roots.

'Are you sure you know where the entrance is?' Marna asked.

'Patro may have altered it,' Kris said.

'Not with his own hands he didn't.' Marna was

sure of that.

Kris searched the next bush. 'Here,' he whispered.

'That is a tunnel?' Marna tilted her head to get a better view. The entrance sloped into the earth like an animal's burrow.

'It widens once you get in,' Kris promised.

'I'll go first,' Sempal said. He looked inside. 'We should have brought a torch.'

'It would have gone out in the wind,' Marna said. 'Or in the tunnel.'

'The passage isn't long,' Kris said. They were a distance from the Ness wall of at least five men lying on their backs. Marna didn't believe him.

Sempal covered his fingers with his sleeve to push aside the thorny branches. Kris and Marna helped him move the rocks across the entrance until he could squeeze in the gap. Kris anxiously kept watch behind them.

'You'll be fine,' he said once Sempal's behind disappeared, leaving Marna to find her way in. Afraid that she might get her head stuck, she decided it would be wiser to sit down and go in feet first, bumping her way along the low tunnel. The flagstone walls were damp and smelt of mouldy cheese. Droplets of cold water and what she presumed were creepy crawlies fell onto her head. There was no room to lift a hand to brush them away. She could hear scurrying between the stones and when her foot touched something soft, she hoped it was Sempal's sealskin cloak. She kicked it and heard her friend grumble.

Sempal edged his way one hand then one foot at a time. Marna dug her heels into the earth in front of her and pulled her body forwards, worrying what her mother would say about the mud gathering on the seat of her tunic. As Kris promised, the tunnel widened and Marna was able to swivel onto her knees. Dim beams of light shone in from the far end.

'I hope we don't scare Ralfe,' Sempal whispered, twisting his head to address Marna. His voice bounced across the walls, growing deeper and louder until it sounded like a family of man eating ogres. Marna didn't reply, fearful of a spider crawling into her open mouth. They crept on. Suddenly Sempal stopped and Marna banged her chin into his back.

'What now?' she asked.

'It's a dead end.'

'I can see light. There must be a way out and into the room. Didn't Kris tell you?'

'No. You were there too,' Sempal said, knowing Marna would accuse him of not listening.

'Let me through,' Marna said, squashing against the wall to get ahead of Sempal. He leaned towards the side and held in his stomach. The wet hairs of their seal skin cloaks clung together. For a moment it seemed they would be stuck together and trapped. Marna tugged at the material. Sempal's hand fell against her leg and she jerked it off. Their faces brushed against each other. She felt his hot breath and for an odd flash she imagined kissing him. He pulled back and she was able to wriggle past. Once she straightened up, she tapped the stone in front with her knuckles. Thork had shown her how to test walls for their strength, listening to the changes in sound.

'Here.' She pushed against the stone. Nothing happened. 'I'm sure it sounded hollow.' She tried to convince herself.

'It looks like the light is coming from above, not ahead,' Sempal said.

'How can that be?'

'We must have travelled further under the wall

than we thought. Give me a leg up and I'll investigate.'

Marna interlocked her fingers to cup her hands. In the dim light and cramped space, Sempal struggled to find the foothold she provided and kicked her in the stomach. He was about to repeat the action. She grabbed his ankle and positioned his foot in her palm. He sprung with his good leg and bent his head to avoid banging it as he reached for a ledge. Marna couldn't hold his weight and let go. He had managed to grip the edge of a flagstone and hung in mid-air, his fingers clinging to the roughened stone. Using the side of the wall, he scrambled his feet up, dislodging pebbles onto Marna. She watched as his back then his legs disappeared.

'Aren't you going to help me?' she called. An arm reached down. The light was brighter than it should be and it was shining directly on her. She could see the stubby fingers with dirt beneath the nails. Taking hold of the hand, she allowed Sempal to pull her out.

'I didn't know you were that strong…oh.'

The hand was not attached to Sempal. As her eyes adjusted to the light she spotted her friend sitting on the ground across from her, rubbing the back of his head. A priest she didn't recognise stood over him with a torch, dripping hot oil dangerously close to his ears. Looming in front of her, arms folded, was Hunkel.

Chapter 13

'What do you two fools think you are doing?' Hunkel demanded.

Marna planted her feet apart and folded her arms to match his. 'There is no rule against exploring the passageways in the Ness,' she answered, hoping her voice didn't betray the worms squiggling in her stomach.

'We'll see what Quint has to say about that,' Hunkel answered. He grabbed Marna's forearm above the elbow and turned to address his companion. 'You stay here and guard the prisoner.'

'What about him?' the man said, jerking a thumb at Sempal.

'He's not important. Throw him in with the other one.'

The man took hold of the front of Sempal's tunic with his spare hand and pulled him to his feet. Sempal struggled, but was unable to wrestle free. They were standing beside a door a few paces from where they exited the tunnel. Hunkel opened it to reveal a darkened room. The sound of heavy breathing reached them from the corner.

'You've got company,' the guard laughed, jostling Sempal inside. The door was pulled closed.

'Patro will hear about this,' Marna said.

Hunkel imitated Marna's voice then laughed. 'Patro is dead.' He started walking, dragging her beside him. It wasn't worth talking to him; the man was as brainless as he was brawny. He was taking her to Quint, which was what she wanted, although not in such compromising circumstances. Her tunic was damp and grimy from the passageway and her hair was a mess. Quint felt superior to 'girls' despite her being seventeen, a grown woman. It would be difficult to convince him to take what she said seriously.

Hunkel led her to the main hall. He lightened his grip on her arm as they entered. Quint was at the far end, in a room separated from the main chamber by deer skins bound together to make a curtain. Marna could smell the musky odour of the boar scent he applied to his body to make him appear stronger than the others. It may have worked for the boar, but it made Quint repugnant.

'Who is there?' Quint called. The curtain was drawn back. 'I said I didn't want to be disturbed.' He stared at Marna with one corner of his lips turned down.

'I caught your niece and her dumb friend

trying to reach the prisoner,' Hunkel reported.

'If you wanted to speak with him you could have asked me,' Quint said.

'It wasn't speaking they had in mind,' Hunkel said. 'I spotted one of the dyke workers creeping about when I finished my shift. I followed him and found the entrance to a passage leading below the wall towards the old house. I returned to warn Gilbin who was on guard.' He gave a snort. 'They didn't have the brains to come out in the prison.'

'I can explain.' Marna shook herself free of Hunkel.

'No doubt your story telling friend has invented a tale for you both,' Hunkel said.

Quint waved a hand at Hunkel. 'Leave us.'

Hunkel scowled, but he did as he was bidden. Quint approached Marna, closer than she would have liked. She took a step back and bumped her head against the bottom of a sheath of cereal grass tied with rope and hung from the rafters to dry. Not realising what it was, she let out a scream and jumped to the side, banging her ankle against a tree stump with a flattened top that held mace heads. One of the heads slid to the ground. She reached to pick it up. The stone was rough and the edge sharp.

The ceremonial mace heads were blunt and polished smooth. Quint gave an exasperated sigh and snatched it from her to replace it on the table. He cut his finger in the process and a drop of blood fell onto the felt floor covering.

Marna recognised the stump of wood. Patro was proud of it, and he enjoyed relating how he had tricked his hosts in Ireland into giving it to him. The solid oak was as wide as one of the flagstones on the floor. It was covered in a resin that had dried to protect the wood from damp. Its previous owner had polished the cut surface until it shone. Her mother would explode when she discovered Quint had moved it into his own space. The thought of her mother's temper encouraged her to speak up.

'The council have made a mistake. Ralfe is innocent,' she said. 'It was Phalt who killed the pirate on Hoy. He is the traitor, not Ralfe.'

'I see, and this Phalt somehow managed to throw a knife into Yarl's back all the way from Hoy.'

'It was a mace,' Marna corrected him.

'I don't believe a weapon was found, not according to Jolty.'

'I saw the body before he did,' Marna said.

'You seem to be good at finding bodies,' Quint sneered. 'However the weapon used is of no importance.'

Marna suspected that it was, but she didn't argue. 'Phalt couldn't have killed Yarl, I know…I mean…' She pictured Yarl's swollen body and her words deserted her.

'What do you mean? What do you know? Is there a traitor here at the Ness?' Quint asked.

'Do you believe there is?' Marna replied.

'No I don't and I will not have you spreading malicious lies. Ralfe is in league with the pirates. He as good as admitted it to the council when I questioned him. He was found guilty by the elders and he will be sacrificed at the next full moon. His throat will be slit and his blood will anoint the foundation of the remembrance stone to be raised for my illustrious brother.'

'Wait, your brother isn't dead,' Marna said.

Quint took a step back. The room was lit by numerous small torches, whale oil burning in coloured pottery bowls. In the flickering light his face looked pale. 'What are you saying? Who told you that?'

'A friend on Hoy. He has seen Patro. Your

233

brother is being held prisoner by the pirates.'

'There has been no demand for a ransom,' Quint said.

'You have to send fighters to rescue him,' Marna said. 'And Sylva too.'

'Who is this friend? Do I know him?'

'His father is a chief in Caithness.'

Quint's eyes sharpened. He stepped towards Marna. 'I need a name, girl.'

'I don't know his name,' she admitted. 'I call him Nuttal.'

'Nut all?' Quint mocked. 'Stupid girl, do you expect me to believe your fantasies? It is time you were married and concentrated on being a wife and in time a mother. I spoke about the matter with my brother before he left. He foolishly allowed you to make your own choices, to study with the priests even, but I shall not. My son Tura is without a wife. You shall marry him and by this time next year you will have his child.'

Marna gasped. She opened and closed her mouth twice before answering. 'You can't make me marry him.'

'The ceremony will take place in front of witnesses. I shall leave the rest to my son,' Quint

234

said. 'In the mean time, you will restrict your actions and conversations to domestic matters. I am told you are competent at making dyes. If you must mess around, mess around with those.' He flicked the back of his hand to dismiss her.

Marna was too shocked to move.

Marriage. To Tura. She hardly knew the man.

'Go,' Quint instructed. The word ended with a burp. Marna turned and marched out, swinging her arm towards the wood stump hoping to knock other objects off, but missed.

Tura. She repeated the name in her head. There was nothing she disliked about him, except his father. He was a year older than Thork and had his own friends and interests. He was studying soil and every time she saw him he was knee deep in a bog. Patro had invited him to dine with them once and they had talked about the outlines of ancient creatures being found imprinted on stones. Even her mother was yawning after the ale was finished, the fire was reduced to embers and there was no end in sight to the conversation.

Marna strode across the paving connecting the buildings, kicking the small stones in her path. As she walked past the cook house she spotted Tura

235

talking with a group of his friends. She wanted to avoid him, especially since her tunic was filthy from the mud in the tunnel, but the pebble she had booted across the paving landed against his foot. He looked up and their eyes caught. Ignoring him would make her look stupid.

'Hello,' she called as brightly as she could.

One of Tura's female friends scowled at her. Tura forced a smile.

'Hello, Marna,' he answered. She walked across to speak with him. He couldn't think of anything to say and neither could she. Her eyes were drawn to the mace he had stuck under his belt. He had advanced to being one of the senior priests and it wasn't unusual for them to carry ceremonial maces, but the stone head was rough and the handle was carved from hazel rather than the more usual willow. It was identical to the weapon Marna had seen dug into Yarl's shoulder blades. She felt sick. Putting a hand over her mouth, she hurried off, hearing the woman's sniggering behind her.

Maces.

Her brother was always going on about different maces, but Marna hadn't paid attention. The Ness was as lively as ants in a mound and she walked round examining every mace she saw, checking the smoothness of the heads and the make of the handle.

Willow, willow, birch, elm, willow.

With her eyes at belt level, she didn't see Jolty until he was beside her. 'You look intent on your task,' he said cheerfully. 'Can I can help you with it?'

'It's nothing,' Marna answered. She lowered her voice. 'Have you had success with what we spoke about?'

Jolty looked around then nodded. 'Ten men and three women are preparing to leave for Hoy. With aid from Orphir and folk from the settlement on Hoy we should have a force large enough to rout the pirates and rescue the prisoners.'

'Good,' Marna said. 'When will you be ready to go?' Jolty scratched his bald head. 'You should leave as soon as you can,' Marna advised. 'I have spoken with Quint. There will be no help from him.'

'You told him Patro was alive?' Jolty protested.

'He didn't believe me.'

'I shall have a word with him,' Jolty said.

'He doesn't want to believe it,' Marna said. 'Just as he won't believe Ralfe is innocent. I need to find out who killed Yarl or Ralfe will be sacrificed at the full moon.'

'What about Sempal? Will he be staying here or going to Hoy?

'Ah.' Marna remembered her friend's plight. 'There is a problem. Hunkel has taken him prisoner.'

'Why?'

'He thinks we were trying to rescue Ralfe.'

'Were you?' Jolty asked.

'Of course not.' Marna's blush belied her words. 'We wanted to talk to him. The guard wouldn't let us, so we found a secret way in, except the tunnel didn't go far enough.'

'Stop.' Jolty raised a hand. 'I don't want to hear any more. I shall order Sempal's release. The guards will listen to me.'

Jolty was as good as his word and Sempal was released that afternoon. Sempal had questioned Ralfe while they were locked up. Ralfe swore he was nowhere near the loch and Alekander could vouch for him.

'If Alekander would return to the Ness...'

238

Sempal began.

'He would be thrown in prison with Ralfe,' Marna finished. 'Jolty wants to know if you intend joining the fighters.'

'Of course, we need to discuss tactics.'

They found Jolty in his favourite haunt near the Stenness Stones. Sempal was full of ideas. 'We can march to Orphir in half a morning,' he calculated.

'We will need to take supplies. We won't have time to look for food when we get to Hoy and we will need spare axes and arrows,' Jolty argued.

'A couple of sleds should do the trip.'

'We promised the settlers supplies. We can't go empty-handed then ask the people to risk their lives.'

'They want dressed stones,' Sempal objected. 'We can't take those.'

'There are stones on Hoy that can be quarried. We can take the tools to do so and stones for sharpening them. Flyn, the stone mason's son has agreed to come with us and stay on Hoy to teach the folk there. We can take piglets, lambs and sacks of grain seeds. There will still be time to sow them for a harvest this autumn.'

'We *are* going to fight?' Sempal said.

'Yes, all I am suggesting is that we take the supplies by boat from here to Orphir.'

'Rowing would be faster and easier than walking,' Sempal admitted, unhappy that he hadn't thought of it.

'It is the only way we can take everything we need,' Jolty asserted. 'I shall ask Quint and the council for the use of boats.'

Marna wasn't able to listen in to the conversation between Quint and his father, but Jolty's expression was severe when he dined with them that evening. Lin, Henjar and Boda had been invited to dine with Norra, allowing them to talk freely of their plans.

'He has refused to aid us,' Jolty said. 'He told me I was an old fool, bent on following Patro to the grave.' He snorted. 'Fortunately he cannot prevent me taking the necessary supplies and tradesmen to Hoy. The council have allowed us the use of three of the oldest boats.'

'I'll check them over,' Sempal said.

'I can arrange the gathering of goods from the storehouses,' Jolty said. 'Marna, perhaps you can help me with that. You visited the settlement, you know what they need.'

After the afternoon of howling wind and hammering rain, the clouds had passed over the island to leave a clear sky. There was enough light after the meal for Sempal to walk to the bay to examine the sea-worthiness of the Ness boats.

He reported back early the following morning. Marna was helping her mother and Lin prepare healing potions for the voyage.

'There is a problem,' Sempal said.

'I know, I said we needed more oil,' Lin answered.

'I meant the boats. They all have tears to the skins or damage to the bindings and frames.'

'I thought the council had a boat builder to keep them in working order,' Marna said.

'They do, a man called Regha. Even he was surprised by the damage. He swore he checked the boats five days ago. '

'How many boats do you need?' Marna's mother asked. 'There are plenty of others you can borrow.'

'Quint won't allow that. Jolty asked him and he refused. He made excuses of needing them here.'

'You will have to repair the damaged ones,' Marna said. 'Regha and the other boat workers will help. It shouldn't take long.'

Sempal made a face. 'It will take at least two days.'

'To sew a rip?'

'That risks pulling the skins from the frame. We can't patch new skins over the old ones. We need to replace entire sections and waterproof them.'

'Any delay is a set-back,' Marna's mother fretted.

'Your friend Kris has built boats,' Marna said. 'He will know which skins can be repaired and which need to be replaced. He won't mind helping.'

'There is another problem,' Sempal answered. 'To stretch the new skins, we need the hot baths. Quint has refused us permission to use them.'

'I'm sure he has a good reason,' Lin said.

'He says they are needed to make ale for the feast to Patro,' Sempal replied.

Marna's mother snorted. 'Quint would prefer to have a feast than have his brother safely home.' She pounded the flower heads she was preparing, damaging the delicate seeds inside. The others

242

watched her, knowing it would be dangerous to interrupt. The pounding became less severe and she put the stone she was using aside. 'Marna, hand me ash from the fire.' Marna did as she was bidden. She was shocked when her mother used it to rub onto her face and hands, but she held her tongue. 'How do I look?' her mother asked.

'Awful,' she said, tentatively.

'Good. I shall go to Quint and insist that I am in need of a sauna. He cannot refuse the wife of the head priest.'

'How will that help?' Sempal whispered to Marna. Her mother heard.

'No-one is going to watch me having a sauna, are they?'

Sempal was slow to understand. Marna explained. 'We will be able to snag a hot bath for our personal use. You and Kris can use it to stretch the skins. The tubs are beside the loch. You will be able to keep the skins moist while you stretch them. I can help with the sewing, if you wish.'

'We'll manage,' Sempal said. Marna's face fell. 'We'll need a supply of needles. The tough skins break the tips. You could ask your friends in the workshop to make some.'

'I'll do that and then…'Marna smiled at her mother. 'I shall need a sauna too. I haven't had one for ages. I can't attend my step-father's feast without being cleansed.'

'I am not sharing a sauna with you,' her mother said playfully.

'Exactly. We will need two tubs.'

'I shall instruct Quint of our decision. Here.' Her mother handed Marna the broken flower heads. 'See if you can rescue these while I am gone.' She turned to Sempal. 'Why are you still standing there? Go and fetch the skins.'

'They will need to be prepared.'

'Nonsense – there are plenty of cleaned skins in the storehouse. I saw them yesterday afternoon. I took one to make Patro a new pair of leggings for his return. How many will you need?'

Marna's mother went to see Quint. She left him with a smirk on her face. He could not refuse her the use of the baths. She instructed two of the fire workers to follow her down to the loch to prepare the hot stones. Marna followed her.

'Quint will be surprised by the dirty water when we finish,' Marna said.

'You should see the water after Patro has a

sauna,' her mother answered. 'Full of dyes and sticky incense and whatever else he dresses his beard and skin with.'

'Yuck.' Marna wished she hadn't said anything.

Sempal, Regha, Kris and his friends got to work heating and stretching the skins to repair the boat. The damage was not as serious as Sempal had gauged, but it was tiring work. When they had punched holes and sewn the skins together with fresh sinews, they hammered them to the frames with wooden nails. They had to wait until they dried to waterproof them.

'If it is dry and warm tonight, we will be able to apply the fat tomorrow afternoon,' Sempal said to Marna and her mother. The women had strolled to the loch to watch the men work.

'Then they will be ready to leave?' Marna's mother asked.

'We will have to make trial trips to make sure the boats are sea worthy,' Kris said.

'How will long will that take? Perhaps you should leave the supplies for the settlement until later. You could march to Orphir with food and weapons for a few days fighting,' Marna's mother

245

said.

'If Jolty is going, it will take the best part of a day to get to Orphir,' Marna said. 'And he would need to rest before travelling on to Hoy.'

'Whereas it is a short journey by boat to Orphir,' Sempal concluded. 'We don't need to do all the tests. The trip is safe, if we keep to the coast. The folk in Orphir will have better boats we can use to cross to Hoy.'

Marna's mother was forced to agree. Sempal, Kris and their friends took turns to guard the boats as they dried. Marna was sent to collect dog roses and sweet smelling herbs, because her mother decided that she did indeed need a sauna. The boat repairers who were not guarding the boats were instructed to clean the water tank of the animal fat that had gathered from the skins.

The fire makers were called upon once more to tend the fires and rake out the hot stones when they were ready. Marna loved watching the heated rocks being guided down the chutes from the fire to the water trough. The fire makers warned her to keep her distance from the oven for fear of sparks, smoke and even exploding stones, but being close was part of the excitement. When they were hot enough, the stones came alive, letting out hisses and pops. Driving them down the chute was like herding animals and you had to be fast on your feet to avoid wayward rocks. She anticipated the splash when they hit the water and the squeaking sounds of the stones, like Boda when he was bathed in the loch.

She found a few dog roses in bloom and she scattered the petals over the steaming water before her mother entered the sauna. The soap of milkwort roots had been steeped in herbs and she handed a piece to her mother.

'Aren't you joining me?' her mother asked. Marna screwed up her nose. 'Then you can tell Sempal and his friends that they can use the water when I have finished.'

'I don't think the fire tenders will be happy to heat new stones for them,' Marna said.

'They will have to use cold water. It will get rid of the worst of the stink. I will not have Sempal in my house smelling like a cow's backside.'

Chapter 14

Marna remembered a rhyme her natural father had taught her when she was young to keep the rain away. She recited it several times that evening and the following morning, showing Boda how to clap his hands in time, which he thought was hilarious. It worked, because the weather held and the men were able to waterproof the boats with fat. Conscious of the warning from Marna's mother, Sempal did not take a hands-on role. He left Kris and Regha to complete the mucky task while he supervised the movement of supplies to the bay. It was late afternoon by the time the fat had set. The boats were loaded and the party was ready to depart. It was only one cycle of the moon until the solstice and the sun was still above the hills.

'Rowing will be hot work,' Sempal moaned.

'Delegate,' Marna answered. She looked towards the land. 'What is he doing here?'

Quint had come to see them off. He didn't venture down to the mooring, but stood with Tura a short distance from Marna. She could see from the way the younger man fingered the mace head in his belt that he would have liked to go with his grandfather. Whether it was to fight or to examine

248

the stones and soil on Hoy, she couldn't tell.

'Who can account for the foolishness of old men,' Quint said as Jolty boarded the last boat. He was speaking to Tura, but his voice was loud enough for everyone gathered to hear. Marna wanted to respond with a smart reply, but Jolty simply waved and smiled.

She watched the party row out with the tide, waiting until Quint and Tura left before making her own way to the Ness. Near the entrance she passed the foundations for the new standing stone to Patro. A stone had been chosen and cut from the cliff stacks near her village of Skara Brae. Two oxen and a group of strong men were pulling it towards the Ness. Ropes and pulleys were ready to hoist the sandstone into place. By her calculations it was three days until the full moon, but she wasn't skilled at counting. She should check with somebody and she thought of Tia Famel.

Tia Famel was a wise woman – even her mother said so. She had an upside down way of thinking compared to the other priests and her advice was often surprising. Patro put good store by it. She would know when the next full moon was due. She might even have a different view of Yarl's murder. She knew everything that happened within the walls of the Ness, hearing rumours and sniffing out anything of value.

Despite that, Marna was wary of approaching Tia Famel. The old priestess had been guiding her in her studies, but since Patro and her mother left to go on their travels, she had been neglecting them. Experimenting with seeds to produce new plants had seemed exciting when Patro suggested it, but the work was painstaking and the successes few. Compared to the pirate attacks, it seemed unimportant.

Tia Famel was alone in one of the smaller workshop areas, mixing green paste in a pot, which she heated using hot stones from the fire. She had her back turned as Marna entered. Although her ears were not as sharp as they once were, she could sense who was approaching.

'Ah Marna, good, you can help with the fire. I fear it will go out before I have finished.'

'What are you making?' Marna asked, lifting dried clots of earth from a stone box in the corner of the room to feed the flames. She sniffed the air. The green, mushy liquid smelt unfamiliar. It burned her nose and throat.

'Careful,' Tia Famel warned, a little too late. 'I am trying to find a green dye that will survive for more than a few days. Patro wants to send a gift of coloured pottery to his friends in Ireland.'

'You believe that Patro is alive?'

'I never thought he was dead.'

Patro had been absent from the Ness for several weeks. Marna was curious to know how the old woman could tell he wanted to send green pots to Ireland. Tia Famel answered before she could ask. 'He communicates with me,' she said, putting her pot aside and facing Marna. 'Tell me, what do you wish to talk with me about?'

Marna gave the fire a poke before sitting next to the priestess. She had intended telling Tia Famel selective pieces of information, but she found herself blurting out everything that had happened on Hoy. The words rattled out like a running deer and she overlooked details, which Tia Famel prodded her to return to. The order of events became muddled before she finished her account. Tia Famel took hold of her hand and examined her palms, as if she was reading the truth of Marna's words in the lines.

'I can tell that you believe Ralfe is innocent,'

Tia Famel said. She gave a hoarse laugh. 'That does not mean that he is.' She coughed over Marna's protests then continued speaking. 'You are allowing your feelings to get in the way of the truth. It is a grave fault you have.'

Marna freed her hand and stood up. 'I shouldn't have come,' she said.

Tia Famel returned to her pot, ignoring Marna. Marna didn't move. She watched the older woman stir the green dye. The colour deepened as it bubbled. She sat back down. 'I believe Nuttal's account of Phalt killing his friend Toomac. He had no reason to lie to me.'

'Yes, yes,' Tia Famel clicked her tongue against her few remaining teeth. 'There you go again "I believe". Stop believing what pleases you and start seeing what is in front of your nose.'

'How can I stop believing what I feel inside?'

'It's simple, once you learn how,' Tia Famel answered. She looked up. Her eyes had watered due to the smoke, but Marna saw a child like gleam in them. 'Take Patro – he believes he knows about the stars, but he is wise enough to realise that he could be mistaken. Or Quint, who believes his brother is dead, but makes plans for his possible return.' Her voice tailed off, as if she could see into the future and feared what she saw there.

'I understand, or at least I think I do.' Marna jerked aside as a spark jumped from a damp twig. 'But like you, I can sense things. There was truth in Nuttal's voice. I know it.'

The old woman nodded several times. 'You sense the death of the pirate on Hoy, and the murder of Yalt here at the Ness, are connected,' she clarified. 'That may be...' she nodded again, '...or it may not. You must weigh up both options.'

'I have.'

'Have you considered who among us had a motive for killing Yarl?'

'I know why Yarl was killed, if that is what you mean. He had information the killer didn't want made known to the council.'

'You must connect this motive to those who had the opportunity and means to kill Yarl. Motive, means and opportunity,' she repeated. 'Where they meet, you will find your culprit.'

Marna thought about this. 'Not everyone at the Ness knew Yarl had returned,' she said. 'His arrival brought a commotion and a crowd to watch, but he was dead before the news would have filtered far.

Few people would have had the opportunity to kill him.' She paused, waiting for Tia Famel's response.

The priestess urged her to continue. 'Names?' she asked. 'Who was at the gate when Yarl returned?'

'There were guards and a group of four or five priests. I can't remember who. Jolty was there and Quint came out later. They left and my brother Thork came looking for Jolty. He has a loud voice and doesn't keep secrets. He could have told his companions of Yarl's return. I know them, though, they are good folk.'

'And good folk don't kill?'

Marna thought of her mother's friend Wilmer, who confessed to killing four men. She brushed the memory aside. 'No,' she answered firmly.

'Was there anyone else at the gate that you might have missed?' Tia Famel said. 'Think hard and remember you were there yourself.'

'Am I a suspect?' Marna laughed. She closed her eyes, trying to picture the scene. 'Alekander and Ralfe were there, a little way off,' she remembered.

'They would have seen Yarl?' Tia Famel

asked.

'Yes,' Marna admitted. 'Yarl left to speak with Quint and the elders in private. He thought he could help in finding the pirate's hideout on Hoy. Ralfe and Alekander didn't follow him.'

'How long was this before you found Yarl's body?'

'I spoke with Alekander and Ralfe outside then returned to the Ness. Quint had called a meeting of the elders. I thought Yarl was with them.' Marna stopped to look up at Tia Famel. The old woman's eyes were as green as her dye. 'He couldn't have been, though.'

'What did you do once you were inside the Ness?' Tia Famel continued.

'I saw Thork and Sempal before they went to South Ronaldsay to fetch my mother. Then I took my dog Pip for a walk to the loch. That's when I spotted…it was horrible, puffed up like a bull frog. Luckily Jolty was nearby.'

'From what you say, I would suspect that Yarl was murdered on his way to find Quint.' Tia Famel rubbed the small hairs growing on her chin. 'Suspect, not deduce.'

'What is the puzzle?' Marna asked.

'If Yarl went into the Ness looking for Quint, as several witnesses claim, how did his body get in the loch? Somebody would have noticed if a dead body was carried there from the council chambers.' Marna pursed her lips, but didn't answer. Tia Famel continued with her ruminations. 'Yarl must have been waylaid and taken towards the loch, willingly or unwillingly, where he was murdered. There was no sign of a struggle and no-one reported seeing or hearing a scuffle.' She flicked her eyes at Marna.

'Someone reported seeing Ralfe at the loch,' Marna recalled what Jolty had told her.

'The Caithness lad, who gave evidence at the trial, yes,' Tia Famel agreed.

'What was he doing there?'

'Fishing.' Tia Famel turned back to her dye and added a sprinkling of ground charcoal. 'Yarl's killer must have been someone he knew.'

'Yarl was a senior priest,' Marna said. 'He knew most people here.'

'He was anxious to speak with Quint. Why delay the meeting?' Tia Famel asked.

'Someone he trusted told him Quint had gone there to reflect on the tragedy?' Marna ventured, wishing she could be specific.

'You said Jolty was nearby when you found the body.'

'Surely you don't suspect him. Why would he wish to harm Yarl?'

'It may be he blamed Yarl for not doing enough to help Patro. I agree that Jolty is not known to have a violent temperament, but in the heat of the moment, who can say?'

'I can. It wasn't Jolty. He was as shocked as I was at finding Yarl. Besides, he wouldn't have the strength to overpower a younger man like Yarl,' Marna was adamant.

'Perhaps Yarl was drugged first,' Tia Famel suggested.

'No-one knew Yarl was returning. The attack was carried out on the spur of the moment. The killer would not have had time to prepare a poison,' Marna argued.

'True, and being unprepared, he or she may have been careless. When you found the body, are you sure you found no clues with it?' Tia Famel asked.

'There was the mace,' Marna answered.

'No-one spoke of this at the trial.'

'I was the only person who saw it. I remember

it had a hazel wood handle. It fell in the water as Jolty dragged it out.'

'Did it?' Tia Famel smiled. 'I do not believe Jolty has the strength or stomach to launch a mace into someone's shoulders deep enough to kill them, but we cannot rule him out.' She added a pinch of charcoal to her mixture. 'What of your brother, Thork? He carries a mace and he was on Hoy. He could be in league with the pirates. He is a strong young man and could have brought Yarl down. Yarl trusted him and would listen if he said he had something to tell him in secret. Thork left the Ness shortly after.'

Marna felt her indignation rise. Out of respect for Tia Famel she struggled to hold it back. 'Thork left the Ness to fetch our mother and he returned afterwards. He is strong, but he is not a traitor or a coward. He wouldn't strike a man in the back.'

'I agree, that does not sound like your brother,' Tia Famel said. 'Perhaps it has to do with the news Yarl brought about Patro. With Patro gone, someone may have wished to take control of the Ness, other than Quint. They may have asked Yarl for his support and he may have refused.'

'But why kill him for that?'

'Yarl would have told Quint, who would not favour an opponent. In the heat of the moment anyone who isn't a friend could be considered an enemy.'

The reasoning was flimsy, but Tia Famel sounded convincing.

'Flemeer and Vill are keen to lead the council,' Marna said. 'Both would be capable, and also Kustan.'

'You don't include my name on that list.' Tia Famel said with the glint returning to her eyes.

'You didn't kill Yarl,' Marna answered. 'We should add Tura to the list. He is young to be an elected leader, but he has a mace similar to the one that I saw in Yarl's body. It is an unusual design.'

'He has been known to argue with his father,' Tia Famel moved a loose tooth with her tongue. 'If he still has the mace, it can't be the one you saw. Someone may be trying to implicate him.'

'I didn't think of that. What should I do?'

'You should ask him where or who he got his mace from. Apart from that, we need to watch and wait. You find out what you can about Tura. I shall keep watch on the council members, Flemeer, Kustan and Vill.'

Marna wasn't keen on getting close to Tura, even if it was to find out about Yarl's murder. She considered telling Tia Famel about Quint's proposal on his son's behalf, but the priestess had returned to her brewing. She had added too much charcoal and the mixture had turned black. Marna was dismissed and she felt miffed. She stood up and stretched her legs. 'You should add dock leaves,' she suggested. 'That works for me when I'm making dye.'

She headed to the door and heard Tia Famel mutter 'ruined' as she made her way out.

Chapter 15

Marna hurried along the corridor, impatient to speak with her mother, although she would have to guard what she told her. Her mother would have harsh words for Quint when she learned of his matchmaking and if she knew Tia Famel had accused Thork of wrong-doing she would never speak to the old priestess again. She was irked to find Lin and Henjar bustling around the house. It was impossible to catch her mother alone and the evening was spent with household tasks, amusing Boda and listening to gossip.

The following morning, she was woken by slobbers from Pip. Her mother must have left, or Pip would not have been allowed in the house. She couldn't hear snoring and assumed Lin and Henjar were awake. As there were no voices she knew she was alone. The room was smoky from the fire the previous evening. Lin had insisted on feeding it with too many dried clots. Marna rubbed her eyes, suspecting the others had gone out for fresh air. She took her time washing her face to cool her smarting eyes, combing tangles from her hair and straightening her clothes before making her way towards the loch. Pip skipped after her. Her mother would want to gather healing plants to refill her pots after providing for the Hoy expedition. Many of them grew in the marshy land near the lochs and she guessed she would find her mother there.

She had crossed the isthmus between the loch of Harray, that made its way inland, and the loch of Stenness that fingered its way to the sea, when she heard Henjar's voice. Henjar, Boda, Lin and her mother were sitting on stones near the water's edge. Marna waved and Pip lolloped over to give Boda a lick.

'Is this where you found the body of that priest?' Lin asked.

'Mum!' Henjar nudged her to keep quiet.

'No, it was further along towards the new stone circle,' Marna answered, sitting on a clear patch of ground beside them.

Lin pretended to shiver. When no-one responded she added, 'Of course, you are used to finding bodies in the loch, aren't you, Marna?'

'Come, it must be time for Boda's breakfast,' Marna's mother said.

'It's such a lovely morning, I'm sure we can stay longer,' Lin argued. None of the others stirred.

'I shall go and prepare porridge,' Marna's

mother stood up and rubbed down her tunic.

'I'll go back with you,' Marna said.

'You have just arrived,' Henjar objected.

'I need to talk to my mother,' Marna answered.' She stood up and called Pip. The dog couldn't decide whether to follow Marna or stay with Boda. Boda reached to stroke Pip's head and he settled beside the boy.

'I'll watch him,' Henjar said.

'Don't let him go in the water,' Marna warned. Henjar nodded and Marna and her mother made their way back to the Ness.

'Henjar is helpful and Boda is a joy, but I do wish Lin would go home,' Marna's mother said once they were out of hearing. 'She is driving me mad. She has her heart set on finding another husband among the priests, preferably a senior one.'

'Like Quint?' Marna laughed.

'It is no laughing matter.' Her mother said. She strode on then slowed as they neared the buildings. 'What did you want to speak with me about?'

'Quint,' Marna answered. 'He wants me to marry Tura.'

'Who told you that?'

'He did.'

'Tura?'

'No Quint.' Marna was exasperated at her mother's lack of outrage.

Her mother ran her tongue round her mouth. 'Tura is a good man,' she said. 'Patro thinks he will make head priest – in time.'

'Really?' Marna stopped walking.

''I had hopes for Thork...' her mother broke off. 'Of course, I'm not suggesting you marry Tura for that reason. He is in strong health, pleasant looking, smart...'

Marna didn't want to hear talk about marriage. It was pointless discussing serious matters when her mother was in a childish mood. 'We can talk later. I have to go,' she said. 'I've remembered that I told Maisel I would visit Barnhouse and collect a shawl to dye.'

'A summer wedding celebration would be lovely. You would be garnished with flowers, Thork could play his drum and Patro could give a blessing.'

Marna could see from the look on her mother's face that she would be planning a feast and discussing possible preparations with Lin and

Henjar all afternoon.

'I might stay the day in Barnhouse with Maisel,' she decided.

She left her mother and walked in the opposite direction, sneaking looks back until her mother was out of sight then stopped. Pip was jogging towards her. When he reached her she saw he had a daisy chain around his neck. She bent to remove it. He shook himself and the flowers fell away. Marna was left holding one, which she examined.

She hadn't thought of Tura as head priest material. If Patro had spoken to him about it, he may have seen Yarl as a rival. Quint was old, Tura could wait a few years to take over from his father, but Yarl had many active years ahead of him.

She plucked a petal from the flower.

That was stupid. Despite what Tia Famel said, there was nothing to prove that Yarl wanted to be leader.

She pulled off another petal then another.

Quint wasn't popular. If Yarl's knowledge of Hoy led to the defeat of the pirates, the other priests might elect him leader.

She finished destroying the plant. 'Patro isn't dead,' she reminded herself, speaking aloud.

Yarl didn't know that. Quint didn't know that at the time and Tura wouldn't have known, unless he was in league with the pirates.

She couldn't imagine Tura being a pirate. Nothing made sense. She threw down the flower stem and bent to pick one of the others that lay on the ground. When she stood up she saw one of Tura's female friends coming towards her. She was walking purposefully and when she reached Marna she gave her a shove in the chest with both hands. Marna stumbled, but kept her footing. Pip bared his teeth to snarl at the woman and she moved back.

'It's fine for some,' she accused, standing a safe distance from Pip.

Marna regained her composure. She was about to ask the woman what she meant, but she supposed Tura had told her of his father's plan.

'You've got it wrong, I don't want to marry Tura,' Marna said.

The woman folded her arms. 'Why not, isn't he good enough for you, Patro's-little-darling, the stuck-up High-Priestess-in-waiting?'

Marna was taken aback. She certainly wasn't Patro's favourite and hadn't dreamt anyone thought that about her. She wanted to answer the woman back, but she couldn't think of the girl's name. It might have been Braesha or Braeya. 'It's not about being good enough,' she said. 'He has already promised he will marry you.' She hoped that was true.

The woman glared at Marna, but her frown softened. 'Aye, he has. Who told you?'

'Nobody told me. I've seen you together. It is written on your faces.'

'His father will never agree to our union,' the woman admitted. 'My father is a potter and my mother a sewer of skins. I can dress birds and make goose pie, but I have no knowledge of stars and planets. I will not make a good wife to a senior priest.'

'I'm sure you will. Priests do have to eat, you know. My mother is always making fancy pastries for Patro. I could speak with Patro. He may be able to influence his brother.'

'Now you mock me,' Braesha or Braeya said then dropped her voice. 'Unless it is true and you *can* talk to the dead.'

'No, I meant...' Marna didn't feel like explaining to the woman. Luckily Braeya - Marna was sure now that was her name – didn't expect a reply. They heard voices approaching, one of which was Tura's, and the girl rushed off. Tura was with three other priests.

If he was Yarl's killer, he would have been hard pressed to find a time on his own, Marna thought. He was constantly followed by his friends.

She managed to dodge out of sight before Tura spotted her. Speaking with Braeya had roused her mind to an idea. She couldn't speak to the dead and ask them who had killed them, but in the past she had been able to find clues by examining dead bodies and returning to the scene of the crime. In Eynhallow she had risked her life in the burial cairn, trying to examine the bodies and she had found pipes belonging to the Irish woman, Erin, at the Loch of Stenness where Jona's body was discovered.

She wanted to examine Yarl's body and the weapon that had killed him, except the mace was at the bottom of the loch and she didn't know what the priests had done with Yarl's body. That was odd, as usually the whole community was involved when someone died, offering gifts or dressing the body with sweet-smelling oils. It hadn't been left to decompose at one of the sacred sites for the bones

268

to be interred in due course, and there had been no burial ceremony. She suspected something was being hidden and wondered why no-one else complained. She marched on, working out her next move.

'Unless Patro can be brought home before the full moon, Ralfe is as good as dead,' she said to Pip. He gave a yap as if he had understood. 'It isn't that easy,' Marna said. 'Jolty and Sempal will barely have left Orphir by now. Once they reach Hoy, they will have to walk across the island to meet up with Thork and Alekander. I can't see Jolty making the trek in less than half a day. Nuttal may not have been able to find Thork. Then they have to fight the pirates. If the pirates suspect a trap they will lie low rather than fight. There are more things that can delay them than you have paws or I have fingers and if everything does go as planned, they still have to get home. It is down to us, Pip, to find Yarl's killer. To do that we need to find a body.'

Pip cocked his ear and sprang over the heather to where a rotten, half-pecked carcase of a bird was lying. He picked it up and brought it to Marna. She crouched down on her knees and patted his head. 'A human body,' she said. 'We need to find a dead man.'

'What good is one of those?' a cheery voice said from behind her. She stood up and turned round. The young man coming towards her from the loch was swinging a rope with three fish attached. His face looked familiar. From his full head of hair and lack of a beard she knew he wasn't one of the priests, but his cloak was of good quality seal skin and was kept in place by a carved antler brooch that any of the elders from the Ness would covet.

'Who are you?' Marna said. Realising her tone was abrupt, she smiled and added. 'I haven't seen you around here before?'

'I've been fishing in your loch,' the man answered, avoiding Marna's question. He was beside her and she saw from his smooth skin, marked by the few scraggly hairs sprouting from his chin, that he was barely into manhood.

'Where are your parents?' she asked cheekily.

'At home,' the boy said. His voice showed no signs of taking offence.

'Where is that?' Marna asked.

'Over there.' The boy pointed south towards the glowering hills behind them.

'Hoy?' Marna said.

'Better than that - Caithness.'

'That's strange.'

'Why? What is wrong with Caithness?' The boy's eyes were bright. He was amused by her response.

'I met someone from Caithness not long ago,' she said.

'There are more of us than you think,' the boy teased.

'Actually, he looked like you. Do all boys in Caithness look the same?'

He frowned and Marna realised she had gone too far. 'Perhaps he was family?' she added.

'Was he here at the Ness?' the boy asked. Marna supposed he hadn't come alone and would have kinsmen with him.

'No, it was on Hoy,' she answered.

'Hoy? That's the island back there, with the hills?' the boy clarified. 'Maybe I should go there.'

'I wouldn't,' Marna said. The boy raised an eyebrow. 'Not at the moment. There's trouble,' she explained.

'Trouble is my name, or so I've been told.'

'That's what the folk in your village call you?'

Marna said.

'My parents call me...,' he hesitated, reluctant to tell Marna. '...Fergeas. My father is Kennet of Camster.'

This was the witness at the loch.

'You aren't what I expected,' Marna said.

'Oh?'

'Jolty spoke of you. I'm Marna.' Marna answered. 'Marna of Skara Brae. My father is Patro of the Ness.'

'You are not what I expected,' Fergeas answered. 'I have heard about you from Quint and others.'

They eyed one another, making serious faces, before they both burst out laughing

'Are you here to study or just fish?' Marna asked. 'I could show you around. I'm studying root plants, at least I should be...Pip, come here.' Pip had been hiding behind her legs, but while she was talking he had ventured out to investigate the young man. He balanced on his back legs and reached his front paws up onto the boy's thighs.

'That tickles,' Fergeas laughed.

Pip sniffed the air. His tail became rigid and he began barking.

'We've got dogs at home,' Fergeas said. 'He can smell them on my tunic.' He put a hand out to stroke Pip's head. Pip growled and twisted his head to snap at his fingers. Fergeas' smile faded. He reached for his stone knife.

'That's enough, Pip.' Marna grabbed him by the scruff and drew him away. 'I'm sorry, he doesn't like men.' She emphasised the word 'men' to flatter the boy.

'It's fine,' Fergeas said. He cut the tail off one of the fish and offered it to Pip, tossing it out of hand's reach. Marna let go of Pip and he snaffled the titbit.

'Like I said, we've got dogs at home.' Fergeas' grin returned.

'Where are you staying?' Marna was keen to make amends for Pip's bad behaviour. 'You could stay with my mother and me, but we have visitors from our old village.'

'It must be hard on your mother. I heard what happened when I arrived. I'm sorry.' He paused.

'She is strong,' Marna said, not wishing to confide the latest news about Patro to a stranger.

'I haven't come to study,' Fergeas said. 'My father Kennet sent me to discover what the priests

273

know about the pirates who are terrorising our coasts and what they intend doing about them. I have been here two weeks, but see no sign of retaliation.'

He clearly hadn't heard about Jolty and Sempal's plan. Marna was about to tell him, but hesitated. 'Two weeks is a long time. It is strange I haven't seen you or your kinsmen before.'

'It isn't that strange,' Fergeas explained. 'My father requested that my presence here be kept a secret. I'm travelling with one companion, who is staying in the village beside the old stone circle.'

'Barnhouse?'

'Is that what it is called? The folk there aren't as friendly as the Ness.'

'The elders take a bit of getting used to,' Marna agreed. 'Their settlement is older than the Ness or even my village of Skara Brae. That makes them feel better than the rest of us.'

'I can understand that. We have people at home who think the same,' Fergeas said.

Marna was keen to steer the conversation back to the pirates. 'You must have been here when Yarl was murdered?' she said, pretending not to know he was a witness. 'Do you think that had anything to do with the pirates?'

'No.' Fergeas brushed over her question.

'Then what?'

'I don't know, an internal power struggle, perhaps. The priests have their man. The business is over.'

'Not until he is sacrificed at the full moon,' Marna answered. 'Will you be staying for that?'

'I doubt it.' The boy made to move away, but Marna positioned herself in his way, expecting an explanation. 'I have a brother, Caordhu,' he said eventually. 'We are close in age and looks, but not in temperament. He argued with my father before storming out of our house. My father believes he has joined the pirates to spite him. I have been sent to find him and persuade him to return home - before he gets himself killed.'

'I see,' Marna said. 'Does he look like you?'

'You said all men from Caithness look the same to you,' Fergeas answered. 'Caordhu is taller than I am, but not as good looking.'

'Is he older or younger?'

'Caordhu is younger in age,' Fergeas licked his lips, warming to his description of his brother. 'If you saw him though, you would think he was at least two years older than me. At home he shaves his beard with a knife, but if he is with the pirates he may have let it grow.'

Marna tried to remember what Nuttal looked like. He didn't have much of a beard, from what she recalled.

'Do you think the man you met on Hoy could be my brother?' Fergeas asked. 'I have found out nothing here. My hopes rose when I heard that the messenger, Yarl, had returned with news of the pirates. I was told he was at the loch and I went in search of him. Before I could speak with him he had been drowned.'

'He didn't drown, he was murdered with a mace,' Marna said. There was no point pretending any longer. 'You were the person that spotted Ralfe at the loch,' she accused. 'You must have seen Yarl's body in the water.'

'Not then.' Fergeas took a step back as Pip sniffed round looking for another piece of fish. 'I didn't know Yarl was dead at the time. I only saw his body when it was brought up from the loch and laid out in the council chamber. Quint asked one of the priests who is knowledgeable in the ways of the body to examine it. He pointed out the froth at the nostrils and water in the throat and concluded that Yarl had drowned. There was no bruising to show he had tripped. The priest believed he had been held down in the water. I didn't see a mace or signs of a wound. There was a green staining on his tunic, but Quint put that down to the algae in the water.'

Thoughts were buzzing in Marna's head. She had seen a mace. It wasn't her imagination. Quint had told her it was a knife. He hadn't said anything about drowning. How could the elders find Ralfe guilty, if they weren't given the proper information? She grabbed Fergeas' sleeve. 'Do you know where the body is now?'

'You will have to ask Quint or Jolty. I believe the priests moved it to one of the outer workshops. They didn't want the rotten stench inside the walls of the Ness. It smelt sickening when I saw it. There were maggots coming out the nostrils.'

Marna screwed up her nose, pretending to be upset by his description. She was more bothered by the fact that Jolty hadn't told anyone about the mace. She recalled his tone when he told her he knew Ralfe was innocent, but could do nothing to help. There was something going on that she didn't

277

know about. Jolty wasn't here to answer her questions and she wondered if he had volunteered to go to Hoy to escape whatever hold Quint had over him. Fergeas shifted his arm and she realised she was still pulling it. She let go.

'I should be going,' Fergeas said, lifting up his string of fish. I promised these to Norra, but I can give you one if you want.' He untied one of the fish and handed it to Marna.

'You know Norra?' she asked.

'That's who I am staying with.'

'She didn't mention you to me.' Marna was put out. She considered Norra a good friend.

'My visit here is secret.'

'A secret everybody knows except me, it would appear. Now we've met, I'll see you around I expect.'

'I won't be staying much longer.' Fergeas said. 'I think I need to head to Hoy.' He waved as he walked off, giving Pip a wide berth.

Marna walked in the opposite direction, towards Barnhouse. She didn't hurry, taking a stroll round the old stone circle of Stenness first. She wanted time before meeting Maisel to think about what Fergeas had said, although she had the fish to think about. Fergeas had told her his travelling companion was staying at Barnhouse. She wasn't sure she believed that, but she could ask Maisel. Fergeas' answers to her questions sounded reasonable, yet at the same time they didn't. Nuttal hadn't mentioned a brother or a fall-out with his family.

It took twice round the stone circle for Marna to pinpoint what was niggling in her head. Fergeas had said he heard about Patro when he arrived, but if he had been at the Ness for two weeks, that was days before Yarl brought the news. Who had told him and how did they know?

Chapter 16

Although he could stalk deer or wild boar for hours when he was hunting, Thork was not patient by nature. Days of inactivity had driven him to collect more fresh water than they could store, gather piles of branches too wet to burn and climb to the top of the hill looking for an eagle egg. Nuttal was content to sit whittling arrows from hazel branches or sharpening and polishing stones. Despite a chesty cough, Patro couldn't have been happier trudging round the Dwarfie Stone with his arms spread to measure distances. At night, the heavens smiled on him with clear skies filled with glorious crimson and purple sunsets.

'Once you've seen one pattern in the sky, you've seen them all,' Thork grumbled on the morning of the third day since they had met Nuttal.

'You could go hunting,' Patro suggested, keen to get him from under his feet as he worked out the direction of the sun as it shone on the entrance to the cairn.

'We have more meat than we can eat for a week,' Thork answered. 'No matter how much time Marna wasted in Orphir with Caran or gossiping with mother at home, the men should be here by now. Maybe things are great at the Ness and nobody wants you rescued.'

Patro ignored his jibe. 'There may be sufficient meat for our needs,' he said, emphasising the "may", 'But do you think the fighters will wish to do battle on an empty stomach, or one filled with dry bannocks and burdock leaves?'

'Oh, I hadn't thought of that,' Thork admitted. 'How many men will come over?'

'None, according to you,' Patro said.

Nuttal was nearby, enjoying the morning sun and listening to the conversation. He couldn't help laughing. 'Why don't you see what game you can hit with your stones and spear?' he called to Thork. 'I fancy a hunk of roast boar tonight.'

Patro grunted at Nuttal's poor humour. Thork had bored them the past two nights with epic tales of how he could throw a stone ball an arm-span further than the strongest man in Orphir or of how he managed to hit a target with his spear despite having his eyes covered and with Caran distracting him with kisses.

'Even his abominable drumming practice is better than his story-telling,' Patro had complained to Nuttal.

'Wild boar it is,' Thork declared.

The other two watched him cover his face and arms with mud to conceal his presence in the peaty ground. Nuttal tossed him a spear and he tested the edge.

'You call this flint sharp? No wonder the men from Caithness have the worst reputation for hunting,' Thork denigrated. He spent time making serrations and sharpening the edge before starting out. 'I'll be back by supper time.'

Nuttal and Patro cheered him off. 'When do you calculate the fighters will arrive?' Nuttal asked once Thork had disappeared.

Patro looked to the sky. 'So far the weather has been good for travelling, but I feel a storm gathering.'

'How so?' Nuttal asked. 'There are few clouds.'

'There is excitement in the air. I can smell it. Any priest who has a nose could.'

Nuttal raised his eyebrows, but didn't disagree. 'I haven't had your training,' he answered.

'Marna has. We must assume that even she can appreciate the need for haste in this matter.' Patro twiddled with his fingers, pulling the joints into

282

place. 'If the fighters don't cross the Sound today or tomorrow morning, they may not be able to later.'

'They might wait until the sun sets and the sky darkens a shade,' Nuttal said, hoping to prove he knew something of tactics.

Patro nodded. 'My guess would be an early morning march. We should look out for them before noon tomorrow.'

'In which case, I should leave you after our hog supper tonight,' Nuttal said. 'Your fighters should be able to cross in secret at the southern end of the island, but a large group of strangers won't go un-noticed for long. To take the raiders by surprise, we must draw them here by late afternoon, if you are sure of your calculations and prediction of a storm.'

'I am sure of those,' Patro said haughtily, 'But no man can predict the unpredictable. There could be a delay at the Ness. The priests often take time to deliberate.'

Nuttal frowned. 'At home, when my father says fight, our people fight. They don't deliberate.'

'That sounds a perfect way of doing things,' Patro agreed. 'One which I wish I could adopt at the Ness.'

'If you kill a few objectors, the others will fall into line,' Nuttal explained.

'If I killed a few objectors, I would be the one falling,' Patro sighed, but his mood changed. 'When my brother Quint hears of the attack on my party he will be quick to rouse a fighting force.'

'He is a loyal brother?'

'No, he is a greedy one. He will want to retrieve the chalk, pitch stone and furs the pirates stole.'

'Should I leave tonight or not?' Nuttal wanted an answer. Patro looked to the top of the hill. He closed his eyes and muttered words to the gods.

'Yes,' he said. 'But try to delay your compatriots. A battle at dusk, amid thunder and lightning strikes, would suit our plan better than one in full light.'

'Thunder and lightning, is that what the gods have promised you?'

'Don't be cheeky, Fergeas son of Kennet, or I shall tell your father.' He gave Nuttal a light tap on his chest.

'I don't know if I can make promises,' Nuttal said. 'It will be hard enough convincing the raiders to trust me again.'

'I have been thinking on that. You will need a better lure to bring them here than an impoverished settler village. They have adequate supplies of stone from the loot they stole from me.'

'What do you suggest?'

'Tell them you have spotted me hiding out in the ruined huts across the burn. I heard them talking when I was held captive. The attack on my party was no coincidence. They knew where we would be and when. The pirate leader, Lional, was ordered to kill me and the goods they stole were their reward.'

'Why didn't he kill you?' Nuttal asked.

Patro did not appreciate the question, but he answered. 'Lional is greedy too. He hoped to bargain for more. He will not want my return to the Ness.' He bent to pick up an odd shaped stone and examined the lines.

'Did Lional say who he was working for?' Nuttal asked.

'I didn't hear,' Patro answered. 'I have an idea.' He threw the stone towards the entrance to the cairn. It hit the entrance stone and cracked.

'I'll do my best to bring the pirates here,

Lional with them,' Nuttal said.

'That will be good enough,' Patro answered. 'If we rid these waters of pirates, even for two or three years, the people in Orkney will have much to thank you for. I shall pay a visit to your father bearing worthy gifts.'

'There is only one gift my father wants,' Nuttal said. 'It may or may not be within your power to give.'

'What would that be?'

Nuttal had moved away when he finished speaking and pretended not to hear Patro's question. He returned to preparing his arrows and Patro didn't press him. Thork returned as the sun dipped behind the hills. He hadn't managed to bring down a boar, but had birds and smaller mammals strung together in a bundle which he carried over his shoulder.

'I don't think there are any boars on Hoy,' he said. 'Not this side of the island.'

'What is that?' Patro turned his nose up at a furry rodent the size of his thumb.

'It's a vole,' Thork answered. 'My mother adds them to our stew, without skinning or gutting them, to give it flavour.'

'Really?' Patro's face turned a slight greenish colour. He stared at the vole and the creature's glazed eyes glared back. 'I'll leave you to do the cooking tonight.'

Patro kept watch as the meal was being prepared and Nuttal readied himself to return to the pirates. The raiders had abandoned the cave their prisoners had escaped from, but Nuttal and Thork had made scouting trips and discovered another hideout in a cave a short way along the coast. Lional was with them.

'I've told Thork to keep back the best of the game for you to take as a gift,' Patro said. Nuttal nodded in approval at the larger birds and smiled to see the vole among the intended offerings.

'It would have been better if you could have taken them brooches or seal skins from this 'village' to prove it is worth attacking,' Thork said. 'All we have is Marna's useless whistle.'

'I can give them these arrows I have made,' Nuttal said.

'Giving weapons to our enemies doesn't sound like a good idea. Won't we need them?'

'Not these arrows. They have crooked shafts and the tips are designed to fall off before they reach a target.'

'You are definitely your father's son,' Patro approved. 'I am glad you are on our side.'

Thork narrowed his eyes. 'You are on our side?'

'Don't worry, you can trust me.' Nuttal looked at the moorland bird Thork had prepared for dinner. There were feathers poking from the half-cooked breast that Thork hadn't bothered removing. His stomach twisted and he left before the meal began.

Thork sat near Patro, keen to impress his step-father. He recounted how, on the hillside, he had been surprised by a stag in full antler. Patro was dubious as the rutting season when the males fought wasn't until September and the stags would not have grown their antlers back yet. He was more concerned to know how his wife had been when he left her. He was also keen to hear about Caran and their new child.

'The baby is noisy and never satisfied,' Thork complained.

'At least there is no doubt that you are the father,' Patro answered jovially then added, 'Not that anyone has thought otherwise. Does she have a name yet?'

'Caran is keen on combining our names. She likes Thora or Thoran.'

'Thoran is a nice name,' Patro agreed.

'Better than Cark,' Thork answered. 'That sounds like something to gather rain water in.'

Patro decided it was wiser to change the subject and turned his attention to the Dwarfie Stane. 'It would be good to get inside the cairn to study the carving on the stone. I imagine it will take a good five strong men to move the entrance stone, with ropes to pull it and seaweed to lubricate it.'

'I shouldn't think you would need more than three men,' Thork disagreed. 'Two to push and one to direct the movement.' He bit into a wing of the cooked bird. The outer skin was charred from being skewered and thrust into the flames, but the inner flesh was cold and raw. He noticed that Patro hadn't eaten any of his portion. 'Mum wraps the bird with herbs in some sort of leaf and bakes it in the embers,' he said, putting his wing down. 'I'll need to ask her how she does it.'

'Good idea,' Patro said. 'I think I shall retire for the night. Here, you can finish mine.'

When Patro woke the following morning, Thork was standing at the entrance to the cave looking towards the Dwarfie Stane. He rose and stood beside him.

'I've a mind to try and shift it,' Thork said.

'It is heavier than it looks,' Patro warned.

'I've spent the night working out how it can be done.' Thork walked towards the stone and Patro followed him. Thork gave the entrance stone a shove with his shoulder. There was no discernible movement. He tried again with his other shoulder. 'If Ralfe were here and maybe Alekander too, the stone would shift with no problem.'

'Would it?' Patro said. He wasn't thinking of the cairn. He was staring at the barren hillside around them. 'What do you see?' he asked Thork.

'Heather and hills. Rocks. There's an eagle on the summit and that looks like a doe behind the gorse bush. Why? Do you want me to get my bow?'

'No, I was thinking how exposed the land is. We should collect leafy branches, large enough to shield men against the hillside. The pirates will be expecting old men and women with bairns. Our aim is to surprise them with fighters. According to Fergeas there will be thirty of them – a large enough band to retaliate once they realise the ploy.

If our people are concealed by what could be construed as trees, we would have a better chance of victory.'

'That is ludicrous. No-one would believe...' Thork paused then snapped his fingers. 'Men hiding behind branches could pretend to be trees,' he repeated as if it was his plan.

'Brilliant,' Patro answered. 'Why don't you go and cut down branches?'

'Shouldn't we stay together?'

'I can see a copse of hazel trees from here,' Patro pointed a distance off down the valley.

Thork squinted against the rising sun. 'I don't think that's a copse. There wasn't one there yesterday when I was hunting.' He raised an arm to shield the light. 'It's moving.' He pulled out his axe and made to rush towards the copse. Patro managed to grab hold of the side of his belt and drag him back.

'One man against a forest?' he argued.

'This isn't fair. Hiding behind trees was my idea,' Thork huffed.

'They haven't spotted us yet.'

'What do you suggest? That we run or hide?' Thork said with disdain.

'I suggest we find those herbs and burdock leaves and reheat the left over bird for breakfast.' Patro let go of Thork and started walking towards the oncoming trees with his arms out in welcome.

Thork deliberated whether to stand and fight with his axe or rush to the cave for his bow. The branches fell to the ground and he recognised Jolty and Sempal at the head of a band of men and women from the Ness and Orphir. Patro embraced his father.

'We have come to rescue you,' Jolty said happily. 'It seems you have saved us the trouble.'

'I'm sorry you regarded it as trouble,' Patro answered. He cast an eye over the group. 'I had expected more. Is there a problem at the Ness?'

Sempal was about to answer, but Jolty spoke first. 'Nothing that Quint can't handle.'

'Patro is safe, but the pirates still need to be routed,' Thork said. 'Fergeas has gone to trick them into coming here, believing they can attack a poorly armed village.'

'Fergeas?' Jolty asked with surprise.

'The son of Kennet of Camster,' Patro said. 'You remember him. He gave us three white oxen, two carved horns and a pouch of flint the last time we visited.'

'I know who he is,' Jolty agreed, 'He has travelled fast to get here.'

'He has been on Hoy since the raid on the settlement,' Thork answered.

'Impossible,' Jolty began, but Patro interrupted.

'It's a long story. We can tell it over breakfast – if you have someone with you who can cook.' He eyed Thork, who glared back.

'We set off from Orphir at first light and have been marching since we landed. A break to eat would be welcome,' Jolty replied. 'We have brought supplies.'

'I'll let the others know,' Sempal said. 'We need to eat, but we also need to make ready for the pirates.'

'We have a plan to surprise them,' Thork said to Jolty.

'If this plan involves the man you call Fergeas luring the pirates here, they will not be surprised no matter what traps you set,' Jolty answered.

'What is your problem with Fergeas?' Patro asked.

'I have no problem with Fergeas, son of

293

Kennet,' Jolty said, 'Indeed, I find him an extremely amiable young man, but while we were preparing our boats to leave the Ness, Quint was showing him our pottery workshop.'

'I don't understand?' Patro said.

'He has been at the Ness for two weeks. He cannot have been here since the raid, unless he is in league with unnatural forces, which I do not believe. I don't know who your man is, but he is not Fergeas of Camster and I doubt he can be trusted.'

Chapter 17

'I knew it,' Thork slapped his thigh. 'Marna should never have trusted him.'

'Ah, this is the 'friend' that Marna spoke of. The one Ralfe accuses of murdering his fellow pirate, Toomac,' Jolty said.

Sempal came towards them. 'I heard Marna's name. What is the problem?' He had organised the men and women into small groups to set up camp. They had left the heavy supplies in Lyness with the boats, bringing only enough food and water for their immediate needs. He instructed some to unload sacks of bere, others to light campfires to cook the food. A few were ordered to keep guard while fresh water was collected from the stream. Satisfied with the arrangements, he had rejoined Jolty, Patro and Thork.

'You met the lad, Fergeas, didn't you?' Thork said.

'He didn't give us a name,' Sempal admitted. 'Marna called him Nuttal.'

'That was the name of our father's dog,' Thork said.

'He sounds like a rogue,' Jolty said.

'It was a good dog,' Thork answered.

Patro was silent, rubbing his chin. 'The boy looks like Kennet,' he said. 'He has the same gap between his teeth and crooked nose.'

'So does the lad at the Ness,' Jolty said.

'There is another boy, Caordhu, spoilt by his mother and allowed to run wild when I saw him as a youngster. I think we are being played a trick on,' Patro said. 'Who is the real Fergeas? Which lad should we trust?'

'How many pirates are there?' Jolty asked.

'Nuttal told us there were thirty, twenty men and ten fiendish women,' Sempal answered.

'He told me the same. I believe that to be a genuine number,' Patro said. 'Based on what I saw when I was held captive.'

'We have twenty five,' Jolty answered.

'Is Alekander here?' Sempal looked around.

'No,' Thork answered. 'After we rescued Sylva and Patro…' A snort from Patro reminded him who had done most of the rescuing. '…Alekander and Sylva went back to the settlement. It may be that he will bring men here to aid us.'

'May?' Sempal showed his disapproval. 'We are doing this for the settlers.'

296

'Our numbers should suffice.' Patro didn't sound convinced. 'I think we shall need a better plan though.'

Jolty moved a few steps past him and surveyed the scene. 'I remember hearing about the burial cairn. There are chambers inside.'

'Where did you hear that story? The entrance stone is sealed by a massive boulder, untouched since it was put in place generations ago. We haven't managed to get inside,' Patro said. 'It will take oxen and pulleys to shift the stone.'

'No, there is a technique for opening it,' Jolty said. 'It should require two men, three at the most.' Patro spotted Thork smirking and looked away.

'Thork, did you bring your drum with you?' Jolty asked.

'No. Marna wouldn't let me.'

'Then I would ask you to get to work making one.'

'I can't make a priest's drum in a few hours,' Thork protested. 'It takes weeks to mould the frame, cure the skins, soak them to stretch and fit over the wood and nail them in place. That is before I carve designs and colour them.'

'Nobody is asking for a precision instrument,'

Jolty said. 'I want something that makes a loud banging noise. Can't you fashion a block of tree trunk or arrange stones of different sizes to hit together?'

'You can't call those drums,' Thork moaned.

'No-one will take you to task over them,' Patro put in. 'Certainly not the gods.' He was beginning to gain an inkling of his father's battle plan. 'This might come in useful.' He reached to find the whistle he had stowed under his belt and raised it to his mouth.

'I can't hear anything,' Thork said.

'Not outside, but in there, with a slight modification...' He pointed at the Dwarfie Stane. 'You did say you and your brawny friends could move the entrance stone, with the right technique.'

'I see,' Thork nodded. 'You want us to play music INSIDE the cairn.'

'We can't all hide in there,' Sempal objected. 'Rushing out would scare the pirates, but we don't know when they are coming. If we wait inside from now until midday or later, we'll terrify ourselves. We'd trip over trying to get out and be unable to fight.'

'The way the weather is turning, you may be

298

glad to be sheltered,' Patro said.

'What if the pirates work out our plan and trap us inside? We could be buried alive,' Sempal said.

'I'm not afraid of a dark tomb,' Thork said.

'Nor am I,' Jolty said. 'But Sempal has a point. We can't all hide in the cairn.'

'We don't all need to,' Patro said. 'It will take no more than three or four musicians, playing at full strength, to produce a distorted echo. I am not familiar with this cairn, but I am aware of the cacophony which can be achieved in other tombs. There is a dolman in Kilkenny, with the entrance facing the summer solstice sun, where I was convinced that every spirit in Ireland was rising to greet the morning until I saw the solitary pipe player emerge. Again in Ireland, this time in Down…'

'Indeed,' Jolty cut short his son's reminiscences. 'We shall have to warn our fighters to protect their ears from the other-worldly groans.'

Thork cast another look at the tomb. 'Fergeas, or whoever he is, left last night to make contact with the pirates. We believe they are hiding along the coast. Whether he can be trusted or not, he will bring them here to fight us. We have to assume they could arrive at any time. They may feel attacking in the morning gives them time to win their spoils and be off home before the sun goes down. We'll need to start now, if you want the stone moved far enough to let folk to crawl in.'

'Well said, boy,' Patro praised Thork although his look reminded him that he had boasted the stone could be shifted easily. 'But first we shall eat.'

Breakfast was gulped down. Afterwards, the men and women were given jobs unfamiliar to the priests among them, who were used to studying or crafting. Patro had not been head of the Ness for several years for no reason. He proved to be a skilled organiser and encourager, as was his father. Timing was essential. Patro was aware that there was no point rushing to complete the preparations, making errors and leaving tired workers who would be caught napping when the enemy struck. He posted lookouts at either end of the valley, ready to give warning when the pirates were in sight.

If Fergeas was not who he claimed to be, he would lead the pirates along paths the Mainland folk were not aware of. Without having anyone familiar with Hoy to guide them, Patro warned the lookouts to watch for unusual behaviour among the birds.

'They are our allies,' he advised. 'They will gather to defend their nesting sites from intruders.'

This proved to be the case. A colony of terns gave the first indication of trespassers. The colony was small in number, but not in audacity. Their screeching could be heard across the hillside, waking the guards who had come off their shift and been allowed to rest.

'Time to hide,' Patro instructed Jolty, who was in charge of the musicians who would conceal themselves in the cairn.

With directions from Jolty, Thork and three helpers had moved the entrance stone a sufficient distance to allow a person to slip inside, but no further. It was decided not to replace it, as no-one was keen to be trapped without an escape route. Once the chosen men and women were inside, the others would build up a pile of smaller stones of the same hue to give the appearance of closure from a distance.

Thork had constructed a make-shift drum from the skull of a stag he found on the hillside. The hollow bones allowed the noise to echo.

'Who is going to play it?' Thork asked.

'You, naturally,' Jolty answered.

'I don't want to be stuck in a hole when everyone else is fighting,' Thork complained.

'The drumming is the major part of our plan,' Patro said. 'Not anyone can beat it to achieve the proper vibration inside the tomb. It needs a skilled musician.'

'Whereas anyone can fire an arrow at a fleeing foe,' Jolty added.

'I see.' Thork looked from Patro to Jolty. They both nodded solemnly. 'This has nothing to do with my mother, has it?'

'Think how proud she will be, if your drumming wins us the battle,' Patro answered quickly.

Thork accepted the argument and he was the first to enter the cairn. He was followed by a woman with a horn, a man with reed pipes and Sempal, who could make a noise like seals singing. They had volunteered, although Sempal had only done so to show he wasn't scared. He had memories of finding a murdered body inside Maeshowe at his brother-in-law's internment. If it hadn't been for Marna he would have shamed himself by fainting. Jolty was the last to squeeze in.

He had Marna's dog whistle and once inside had demonstrated to the others how to make a high pitched vibration. The noise jumped from wall to wall, getting louder then softer, sounding like a snoring giant.

Patro took charge of the fighters. He had them placed in a wide circle round the tomb, hidden among the hills and overgrowth with branches to camouflage them.

'Do not attack until I give the signal,' he reiterated until everyone repeated the order under their breaths whenever he approached. 'When they are close enough to be trapped, the pirates will be panicked by the 'spirits of the dead' inside the tomb. They will drop their weapons and flee. That is when we will be ready for them. None must escape.'

Nuttal was the first to come into view. He was treading lightly over the moorland, talking to another man. Behind them, the motley band of pirates made no attempt at camouflage. Their voices were loud, with their intentions to do battle resounding across the hillsides. The terns did not put them off. They waved their weapons at the birds flying overhead out of reach and diving to a hair's length of the men and women before rising again.

Patro watched until the entire group was in view – thirty one people, including Fergeas. They were outnumbered, but the pirates were unruly, expecting only to scare helpless villagers and easily re-capture the injured head priest. As if preparing for the battle, clouds appeared over the tops of the hills and the sky darkened. Patro had to concentrate to keep track of the enemy. It was easier to see movement than individual warriors.

Despite his warning, one of his men lost his nerve and released an arrow before Patro gave his signal, which was to have been the whooping sound of a curlew. The arrow fell short, but the pirates stopped to a man. Fortunately they were close enough to the Dwarfie Stane for Patro's plan to be put into action. The pirates had scooped mud to use on their faces as war paint, but they hadn't let it harden. Little of the mud stuck and the splashes that did gave them the look of wallowing pigs. Who could be afraid of those?

Patro gave his call, repeating it twice. He waited for Jolty's response. He knew his father was hard of hearing, but someone inside the cairn must have heard. They had to react before the pirates could regroup.

There was a flash of forked lightning, the tip prodding the top of the hill. At the same time a low groan, like the rumble of falling rocks, rose from the tomb. The pirates fell back. A few crumbled to their knees. Nuttal ignored the lightning and continued his conversation with the lead pirate. The crash of thunder silenced him.

'Look, the stone is moving,' one of the pirates shouted. 'It is alive.'

'The giant is waking,' a second man called.

The lead pirate raised his arm. 'Stones do not move unless they are pushed,' he declared. 'Prepare to attack.' The others fell into straggling rows with their weapons drawn. They stood motionless, waiting to follow Lional. Nuttal pointed to a spot up the hill, behind the Dwarfie Stane. 'There.' The clouds leeched together overhead, seething like a wronged fire master. The first rain was released in one magnificent spit of hail, obscuring the view.

The pirates raised their shields to protect their heads and faces from the pounding. The soft wood cracked as hail stones the size of beach pebbles bounced off them. Combined with the thunder and the moaning rising from the tomb, even Patro feared the gods were waking. The pirates screamed and their rows unravelled. They slipped on the newly wet ground as they scrambled to escape.

Lional and the braver pirates advanced towards the Stane, commanding the others to follow. Patro signalled his archers to move into a position to fire. They put aside their branches and crept forwards to get a good aim at the pirates. The hail had softened to rain, but the wind blew it in sheets towards them, giving strength to the backs of the advancing pirates. Patro had not taken the wind direction into consideration, a point he disclaimed when recounting the tale later. For the moment he cursed his miscalculation. The archers could not fire against the wind and he signalled for them to draw back and prepare for close combat with their maces.

Lional and half his band were upon them. Patro was at the head of his band of warriors. He could see the grimace of rage on Lional's face as he raised his axe to strike. Intent on organising his fighters, Patro had no weapon to hand apart from his make-shift staff. He raised it to protect his face.

As if this was a sign, a drum roll from inside

the cairn threatened to bring forth armies of un-dead. The screeching of the pipes echoing around the walls stopped the pirate leader. The hesitation was only for a heart beat, but it gave Patro time to seize the mace from his belt and thrust it into Lional's chest. He dropped his axe and staggered back, blood oozing from his wound. Two of the Ness men crowded upon him.

The fall of their leader served to halt the pirates. Those who were able retreated back.

'Don't let them get away,' Patro called hoarsely, his voice lost in the struggle.

Nuttal could not hear Patro, but he understood his need. He raised a cry to rally the pirates. 'Onward,' he called. The pirates floundered. 'Are you men or gutless worms?' Nuttal shouted.

The strongest pirates were willing to fight against dead spirits, but the wiser ones weren't. As Patro had hoped, fighting broke out among them. His own men had re-organised their battle lines and were advancing in numbers. The wind had blown its course and the archers took up new positions to fire upon the cowards fleeing. Separated from the main group, it was easy for the Ness bowmen to pick them off.

When the remaining pirates saw their comrades being slaughtered as they ran, they roared and flung their weapons with force. With the thunder growing nearer and the supernatural sounds rising to meet it, they weren't sure who they were fighting. The shattering sounds gave the impression of a monstrous force of the living and the dead. Patro passed word along the line of his fighters to make as much noise as their lungs allowed.

One of the stockier pirates had assumed leadership. He called for a final rush and ten men attempted to run up the hillside, hacking at anything that moved. Four of them fell headlong into the heather. Patro spotted Fergeas taking the opportunity to 'disappear' into a crag in the hillside. Once he was sure the boy was safe, he gave the order for fifteen of his fighters to rush at the pirates. The close fighting didn't take long. The pirates were drenched and exhausted. Seven of them, including the four fallen and the leader were killed.

The last of the pirate band were desperate. Patro counted eight of them scurrying towards the coast. His archers were unable to stop them, but luck was with them. The men from the settlement village at Rackwick, led by Alekander, were making their way towards the Dwarfie Stane. They had sheltered from the storm lower down the valley. As the rain lightened, the clouds moved on and the sky cleared, they ventured on and met the retreating pirates head on. The pirates had lost most of their weapons and were easily routed.

A cheer from the settlers told Patro that the fighting was over. He tried to raise a shout to tell his men to stop their advance, but his throat was dry. The woman beside him took up the call. A priest was sent to the opening of the cairn to tell Jolty and his musicians to stop their ungodly playing. The noise faded. Thork was the first to step out, followed by Sempal, who tripped in his haste. The piper and the horn player looked shaken. Their faces were pale and they wobbled until they adjusted to the outside world.

'I'm glad the entrance stone was left open,' Sempal said. 'I might have had a fit. There are dead bones in the chambers covered in cobwebs.'

'Better than live bones,' someone answered, but nobody laughed.

'That was weird,' Thork said in a high pitched squeak. 'My head is splitting. I feel like I've aged twenty years in less than an hour.'

'The blood has been rushing around my body. I feel like a man half my age,' Patro answered.

'There is something on your tunic, Thork,' Sempal said. It was caught in the fabric and he picked it out. It was a decomposing finger bone. 'Aargh. He dropped it and jumped away.

'What are you doing?' Patro snapped. 'Removing bones from a tomb is not only disrespectful, but dangerous.'

'I didn't put it there,' Thork objected.

Patro bent down to retrieve the bone. He wiped it on his tunic. 'I shall return it. Once everyone is out we shall have to re-seal the tomb with due dignity. Where is Jolty?'

Patro strode towards the stone. A foot appeared at the entrance and Jolty was helped out by the pipe player and the woman with the horn. He looked like a corpse himself, but hearing of the victory brought back his colour. Patro moved past him to enter the cairn.

Thork, Sempal and Jolty recovered their senses and stood on the open hillside waiting for Patro to emerge.

'It can't take that long to replace a finger,'

Sempal said.

'I'll give my drum a beat outside the entrance,' Thork said. 'That should hurry him out.'

He was advised by Jolty not to do so.

Patro appeared with a ruddy glow to his face. 'Amazing,' he muttered. 'Quite spectacular. I wish Katbar could see it.'

'Who is Katbar?' Thork whispered to Sempal.

'Your mother, I believe,' Sempal answered.

'Oh, of course!'

Some of the Ness fighters had received minor cuts. None were serious enough to threaten risk to life. The healing ointments Marna's mother had prepared were brought from the bags which had been stored in Nuttal's cave for safety. Jolty commandeered two of the priests who he knew were familiar with preparing dressings and they tended the wounded. The men from the settlement collected the axes, maces and stone knives from the dead pirates. Patro instructed that the bodies should be laid out properly on the hillside. He spoke words for their spirits to pass unhindered.

It was evening before the tasks were finished and the first of the crows and gulls were circling overhead.

'Pity there are no enemies alive to recount the battle with fear in their throats,' one of the younger men said.

'Killing a fleeing enemy is not easy,' Patro answered, 'If even one had escaped, mark my word, they would have raised a new band and returned to seek revenge.'

'Talking of the enemy, where is Nuttal?' Thork asked.

'I can't see his body among the dead,' Sempal said.

'Just as well,' Patro added, with a look to his father. 'Kennet would not be happy if we hacked down his eldest son.'

'Should we look for him?' Thork asked, his voice betraying his wish to return to the Mainland and his family rather than search the hills for a possible murderer.

'No,' Patro replied. Jolty looked at him askance. 'He knows where we are. He will find us when he wishes to. We will have supper and rest here tonight.'

'Our folk will investigate the pirates' caves along the coast for anything worth salvaging,' Alekander said. 'They will have left pots and

312

cooking ware as well as boats.'

'The boat with the chalk and pitch stone belongs to the Ness,' Patro said. Alekander and the settlers moved into a huddle. Alekander tapped his mace head against his palm several times. 'You are welcome to have it for your settlement, with our gratitude,' Patro added.

'We have brought over the supplies you were promised,' Jolty said. 'They are stored at Lyness, with Flyn, a stone mason who is willing to spend time here teaching you his craft.'

The settlers showed their approval with a cheer.

'How many boats are there at Moaness?' Patro asked.

'Three,' someone answered. 'They were hidden from the pirates.'

'Good. Tomorrow morning, Jolty, myself and those from the Ness that the boats can carry shall return via the bay of Ireland. It will be faster than trekking to Lyness, rowing to Orphir and hiking back from there.' Patro's tone showed that comfort rather than speed was his main consideration. 'The folk from Orphir should go home the way we came, with our grateful thanks, which will be manifest as

313

material rewards in due course.'

'I'll go with the Orphir folk, if that is fine with you,' Thork volunteered. 'I want to make sure Caran and the baby are well.'

'I shall leave you to arrange the various boat parties,' Patro said. 'Jolty, perhaps you can take over the cooking arrangements and Sempal, could you ensure everyone has somewhere to sleep tonight?'

'The ground is wet. We'll need to find shelter in caves.'

'There are odd huts and "things" across the way there,' Patro pointed obliquely. He was already making his way back towards the Dwarfie Stane.

The rain stayed off and the mainland folk were able to light fires to cook and dry their drenched clothing. Sempal was able to locate the run-down huts and with help they constructed make-shift roofs for the least damaged ones, using material from the other huts. Small caves were discovered in the hillside that could shield sleepers from the wind. Patro returned from studying the Stane and organised watches, although he didn't fear an attack.

The night passed peacefully. In the morning,

314

Jolty, Sempal and the party leaving from Moaness prepared to set out. Patro could not be found.

'I'm not looking for him in there,' Sempal pointed to the Dwarfie Stane.

'Hasn't it been re-sealed yet?' Jolty asked.

'There he is,' Thork pointed to two figures striding across the moorland towards them. One carried a wooden staff. Nuttal and Patro were deep in conversation and laughing as they approached the make-shift camp. Thork, Sempal and Jolty went to meet them.

'Where have you been?' Thork accused, poking Nuttal in the chest. 'I didn't see you do any fighting yesterday.'

'You didn't see anybody fighting from your position inside the Dwarfie Stane,' Patro reminded him

'You managed to get out of the hand-to-hand combat?' Nuttal returned the jibe. Thork fingered his knife and Nuttal backed off. 'I thought it safer to keep out of the way once the arrows started arching over.'

'Sensible,' Sempal agreed. 'Not everyone is as hot-headed as you are, Thork.'

Thork turned to Patro. 'Are you sure he is on

our side? Why didn't he come out and help us clean up the mess?'

'I am happy with what Fergeas has told me,' Patro said. 'He has agreed to return to the Ness with us, as my esteemed guest.'

'Esteemed?' Thork objected until Patro raised a hand, allowing no further argument.

'What about the boy at the Ness who also claims to be Fergeas of Camster?' Jolty asked.

'Fergeas and I have discussed that,' Patro answered, 'Which is why, for the moment, Fergeas will be disguised as one of us.'

'The others will know at once he is a fraud,' Jolty said.

'Will they? There are over forty priests working or studying at the Ness. Many others come and go. Fergeas will not be with us for long and will not bring attention upon himself unless he has to.'

'I'll look odd with my hair cut off,' Fergeas laughed. 'I suppose it will grow back.'

'If it gets a chance to,' Thork muttered, keeping hold of his knife.

Patro looked around the site. 'Have the settlers returned to Rackwick?' he asked.

316

'Some have stayed to march with us to Lyness to collect the supplies,' Jolty said.

'Good,' Patro answered. 'I need a couple of them to do me a favour and take a message to Caithness. We shall also have to re-seal the Dwarfie Stane before we leave. I have learned a great deal from it. It must now be returned to the way it was left by our ancestors.'

Patro, Jolty and Fergeas walked off. Thork hung back and took Sempal aside. 'I will be delayed in Orphir,' he whispered in what was marginally quieter than his usual voice, but could be heard for several paces. 'Keep an eye on Fergeas, or whoever he is, in particular when he is anywhere near my sister.'

Chapter 18

Marna couldn't visit Barnhouse without getting the feeling she was being spied upon. The village was the oldest in the area and somewhat run down. Only a few families lived there, but twenty eyes peered at her as she made for Maisel's house. She could sense them watching through the walls when the door was closed and ears listening through gaps in the walls. Maisel laughed when she told her this.

'You have a strange imagination, Marna. My folk are wary of strangers. There have been visitors from the Ness, who think our store house belongs to the priests and they can take what they want from it.'

'Talking of visitors, is there a man from Caithness staying here?'

'No,' Maisel shook her head. 'Does he know one of the families here?'

'His companion is staying at the Ness.'

'Then I can't see why he would stay here. There are empty houses, but the Ness is not short of room.'

Marna had given Maisel the fish Fergeas had gifted her, which she chopped into chunks and added to the pot of stew on the hearth. She ran the

318

wooden spoon round the inside rim of the pot several times.

'The visitor to the Ness is the son of a chief. I do not think his companion has such a lofty position. Quint may not have thought he was sophisticated enough for the Ness,' Marna said.

'Mmm,' Maisel thought for a moment. 'There was somebody in the old jeweller's house about the time of the new moon. There isn't a family there. It is used as a work place and storage house. I thought it was another traveller helping himself. He didn't stay for more than a day, not that I blame him. There is something cold about that house.'

'I shall have to investigate. Your husband won't mind me staying here for a few hours, will he?' Marna asked. Grif was a skilled mason, working soft and hard stone with his hands and turning slabs into tools or building stones, but he made little use of his tongue. Marna had heard him speak no more than three or four words in the years she had known him.

'Not at all,' Maisel answered. 'He is helping with the new standing stone at the Ness, but he should be back for lunch. He has work in the village this afternoon.'

'What about Pip? I meant to leave him at home, but he followed me here.'

'Grif likes dogs,' Maisel reassured her. 'I think he likes them better than people. He certainly likes them better than priests.'

Marna laughed. Grif returned home shortly after noon. The meal was prepared and he didn't speak while he ate, but slipped Pip a piece of gristle.

'The fish was from Marna,' Maisel said. 'She has come to collect my shawl to dye.'

'I could have taken it to the Ness,' her husband said, not looking up from his bowl.

'I wanted to catch up on the chat,' Marna said.

Maisel's husband made a noise through his teeth to suggest that women never had anything better to do than talk. He finished his food and left. Marna helped Maisel clear up the bowls then collected the shawl. She left to investigate Wilmer's empty house.

A shiver ran down her as she saw the empty stone cot where she had lain, drugged into sleep by Wilmer's 'poisoned' honey, while Jona was murdered. She felt the chill Maisel spoke of. There was no evidence of anyone having lived there. If the stranger had lit a fire, he had cleared the evidence.

She moved piles of pots from one side of the room to the other. The sacks of grain were too heavy to shift although she tried to shuffle them across the floor to look beneath them. A broken comb was sitting at the back of the dresser, gathering dust and cobwebs. Marna recognised it as one of Wilmer's designs. She picked it up and rubbed the whalebone on her tunic. It was a double-sided comb although half of the centre teeth were missing. When she held it on its side, it gave the comb the look of a yawning dog.

'Look Pip, it is going to bite you,' she said, wriggling the comb towards her dog. She had meant it as a game, but Pip took fright. He had been sniffing around the hearth, nose to the ground. When she spoke he spun round and gave a yelp, knocking against one of the grain sacks. It tumbled over and the precious meal fell onto the floor. Marna tried to scoop it up and replace it, but she managed to get pebbles and dog hairs into the sack as well. She put her fingers in to dig out one of the pebbles when her hand felt something hard. She dug round the grain to expose an axe head, crusted with a dark red stain.

The handle was missing, or else further down the sack. Marna didn't feel she could empty the grain out to find it, although if the axe had been used to attack someone and the stain was human blood, she didn't feel she wanted to eat any of the bread made from the grain. She put the axe head in the pouch she kept attached to her tunic belt.

'Good boy.' She patted Pip on his forehead. 'You have found a clue.'

She didn't know what it was a clue to, but it seemed significant. There was no point hanging around Barnhouse, she had work to do finding out what it meant. Her mother might be able to help. As she left Wilmer's house, she was aware of someone watching her from the door of the adjacent house. She smiled and waved and the door was closed.

It didn't take long to return to the Ness. Maisel wanted her shawl dyed a bright colour for the summer and she thought about which dyes to use. Bramble root would give a rich orange, or marigolds would make it sunny. She had decided on yarrow and bog myrtle roots to give a deeper yellow when she reached the door of her house. She heard a screech and as she entered she had to duck to avoid a felt cushion her mother had thrown. It flew over her head and out the door. It took a moment for Marna to spot Lin. Her mother's friend was crouched at the end of one of the beds, her curly hair visible round the side of the flagstone support. She was using it as a shield.

'How dare you!' her mother shouted. 'You jumped up little ...' Her mother spotted Marna and didn't utter the insult. She was holding a pot in her right hand, ready to toss the contents which smelt sour. She put it down and straightened her hair. 'Lin and I were having a chat.'

'I can see,' Marna said. 'Do you want me to come back later?'

'No, no.' Lin stood up and Marna noticed a scratch on her cheek that was dripping blood. 'I am leaving. Henjar and I need to go home.'

'Don't you want to wait on Sempal's return? Marna asked.

'No.' Lin crept testily past Marna's mother to the door and walked out.

'What was that about?' Marna asked.

'The woman had the nerve to ask for my bearskin. Do you know what she wanted it for?' Marna shook her head. 'To show off to Quint -

Quint of all men, I mean…' Her mother's temper was cooling and she realised how ridiculous the scene must have looked to Marna. 'I do hope you are right about Patro. What is taking Sempal and Jolty so long?'

'They have only been gone a day. They would have left Orphir early this morning,' Marna said. 'They probably haven't found Thork, or the pirates, yet.'

'I know, but I don't like the look of the sky. There will be a storm before nightfall.'

Marna sat on one of the cots. Pip had slipped into the room to join her. 'I met the lad from Caithness on my way to Barnhouse,' she said. 'Fergeas of Camster.'

'He is a weird boy. He isn't here to trade or study, yet he seems to be everywhere, asking questions,' Marna's mother said. 'I have asked Quint, but he tells me nothing.'

'Norra knows about him,' Marna said. 'He is staying with her.'

'Is he? To be honest, I haven't visited my friends since returning.'

'Well you should,' Marna said. 'They want to support you.'

'I don't feel up to that yet.'

'You could find out something important. Unless we discover who murdered Yarl, Ralfe will be sacrificed in two days time. Tia Famel told me.'

'If Tia Famel said it was so, who am I to disagree? What do you want me to do?' her mother answered.

Marna sighed. 'I don't know. I like this Fergeas lad, but I don't trust him. His being here, when this is going on, seems strange although his explanation makes sense. He seems friendly – I don't think he killed Yarl – but he lied about his companion and I found this at Barnhouse. It was hidden in a sack of grain in Wil... in one of the disused houses.'

Her mother raised a finger to stop her. 'I know what you need,' she said. 'My special ale of hawthorn, skullcap and nettle.'

'That sends me to sleep,' Marna complained.

'Which is what you need right now. Your mind is all over the place.'

'It isn't time for sleeping,' Marna objected.

'Take a rest and who knows – something may come to you while you sleep. Patro is a great believer in listening to dreams.'

'Usually only the good ones,' Marna argued. 'If I take a nap, will you find out what you can about this?' She produced the axe head. Her mother examined it.

'That looks like blood on the edge,' her mother said.

'I thought that too,' Marna said. 'Will you speak with Norra?'

'Yes, if I can find her.'

Marna helped her mother prepare the brew and added a drop of honey to the mix to sweeten the taste. She drank it while it was warm and settled down with Pip snuggled at her feet. Her eyelids were heavy and soon she was dreaming of dyes and plants. When she woke, Pip had gone.

'Is it evening or morning?' she asked her mother, stretching her arms in the air.

'It is still a beautiful afternoon,' her mother replied. 'You haven't been sleeping long, but I can see you look better already. I have been gathering duck eggs from the loch side.'

Marna could smell them cooking. She got up. 'You seem in a cheery mood.'

'I couldn't find Norra, but Tia Famel was at the loch. She read good fortune in my aura.'

'Did she give you any messages for me?' Marna asked.

'No, should she have?'

'She was keeping an eye on Flemeer, Kustan and Vill.'

Her mother laughed. 'You can't suspect these three of anything apart from big-headedness. Vill can't put a spoon in his mouth without three students copying him. Kustan needs someone to tell him how wise he is and Flemeer is worse. If he had killed Yarl he wouldn't be able to keep quiet about it. The whole of the Ness would be given a demonstration of how it was done.'

Marna laughed as her mother took on the roles of the three senior priests. 'Somebody killed Yarl, though,' she said seriously. 'Did you ask Tia Famel about the axe head?'

'She believes the blood is too old and ground in to have come from Yarl,' her mother answered.

'I knew that,' Marna said. 'Yarl was killed by a mace, not an axe.' She went to the dresser for her comb and pulled it through her hair.

'Tia Famel thinks the blood on the axe head is from an animal.'

'How does she know the difference?'

'I don't know. She is a wise woman.' The eggs her mother was cooking were ready. She had scrambled them with goats' milk and the mixture was bubbling in the pot. She spooned a ladleful into a bowl for Marna and stuck two bere bannocks on top to look like Pip's ears.

'I'm not a child any more,' Marna said lightly, taking the bowl and a wooden spoon.

Her mother sat next to her, blowing on her eggs to cool them. 'Yarl was a good man and a good friend to Patro,' she said. 'He did his best to save him when the pirates attacked. Patro will be upset and angered to hear of his death.'

'You mean he won't care who is blamed, as long as someone is,' Marna said.

'I said he would be upset, not vengeful. He is not hot-headed like you. What I was about to say before you broke in was that, to my thinking, Yarl was killed to stop him telling the senior council where the pirates could be trapped on Hoy. Who would want to prevent him from speaking?'

'Someone in league with the pirates,' Marna said.

'Exactly.'

'I knew that,' Marna dragged her voice.

328

'There were no reports of pirates before we left, or else Patro would not have set off. When did the raids begin?' her mother asked.

Marna thought about the question. 'It wasn't long after you left for Stonehenge -five or six days, no more.'

'Someone knew we would be away from the Ness for while,' her mother said.

'Everybody knew that.'

'No, only the senior council members,' her mother countered. 'And you and Thork. I told you to keep it secret.'

'I did,' Marna said. 'I imagine Thork did too.' She hesitated. 'Oh, I told Sempal, but he wouldn't tell anyone.'
Her mother sighed. 'He's a storyteller, Marna.'

'He makes these tales up. He doesn't give away proper secrets.'

'I can't see anyone on the council being part of a pirate crew,' her mother continued.

'People are greedy,' Marna said.

'There is plenty of feasting here. We have food enough for everyone. The Ness dogs are fat from the table scraps. If someone suddenly had extra skins or jewellery, it would be difficult for them to explain where they came from.'

'Unless they were in power,' Marna said, following her mother's argument. 'They could claim they were gifts from visitors. You agree with Tia Famel that someone who wants to take over the Ness is in league with the pirates. That is why Tia Famel was watching Flemeer, Kustan and Vill.'

'Who is the more obvious candidate?'

'Quint?' Marna said. She wasn't convinced 'He wouldn't have his brother killed. You are looking for an excuse to blame him because you don't like him.'

'I have heard him speaking with Patro. There is no brotherly love between them although Patro tries his best to be fair.'

'You are taking sides, mother.'

'I believe that Quint hoped we would encounter hostility down south and fail to return. When Patro sent a messenger ahead to tell him of our return, he made plans with unscrupulous people to attack us. They would have demanded goods in return, so Quint bribed them with stories of the gifts Patro would bring back. He would have told them about the settlement on Hoy which would be easy pickings for supplies and haematite.' She paused for a second. 'That may have been a reason for starting the settlements. He could have been planning this for months, waiting for an opportunity.'

'You can't prove it,' Marna said. 'Besides, there wasn't a messenger to say you were returning.'

'Patro sent Barnard ahead a week before we left Stonehenge.'

'He didn't arrive here,' Marna answered.

'What could have happened to him? We need to get that lad to tell us more, the one from Caithness.' Her mother eyed Marna in a way she knew. It meant the job was down to her.

Once her mother had a plan, or even the smidgen of an idea, she was keen to work on it straight away. Marna was scraping the remains from her bowl when her mother took it from her.

'Someone your age shouldn't be sleeping during the best part of the day,' she chided, handing Marna the new shawl she had brought from her travels. 'Here, use this pin.' Her mother offered her one of her ornate clasps.

'I'm going to question him, not to flirt with him,' Marna said.

'The two aren't separate,' her mother answered. 'You need some way of loosening his tongue. This works for me.' She gathered rose petals from a bowl and scattered them over Marna. Marna started brushing them off, but her mother stopped her. 'Men are sensitive to sweet smells. Once he has a nose-ful of my roses he will do anything to impress you. He will give you the information we need.'

'If he is able to,' Marna said.

'Show some enthusiasm. All you have to do is find out what knowledge he has gleaned from Quint.'

'He may not be here,' Marna said. 'He spoke of travelling to Hoy to search for his brother.'

Her mother returned the empty bowls to the dresser. 'Do you believe this brother is the lad on Hoy that you met?'

'Yes. The two look alike and come from the same area. Nuttal said he was sent by his father to find out about the pirates, which is exactly the same as Fergeas told me. Fergeas said his brother had been led astray. I believe he can be led back.'

'You can't trust him. He didn't even tell you his real name,' her mother said.

'You haven't met him,' Marna argued. 'I have.'

'Your instincts are often right,' her mother allowed. 'Speak to Fergeas, but don't do anything foolish or rash.'

Marna made her way to Norra's house. Fergeas wasn't there, but Norra guided her towards the loch. She spotted him with three of the younger priests, including Tura. Marna assumed they were fishing although she didn't see any nets or spears. They were too close to the bank and making too much noise to catch the larger trout.

'Hello,' she called.

Fergeas looked up first. He gave her an awkward smile as she approached. Tura moved to prevent her getting near the bank.

'What's up?' Marna tried to dodge past him. 'I need to speak with Fergeas.'

'Marna, there has been an accident...' He shielded her view. She pushed past, stopped by the rotten stink from the bank. She put a hand over her mouth. Lying on the bank, entangled with slime and watched over by Tura's friends, was the remains of a dead man.

Chapter 19

'Who is it?' Marna asked, holding back the egg which threatened to rise from her stomach. 'Do I know him?'

Tura stepped between her and the body. 'It has been in the water many days. It is not a pretty sight.'

The men had dragged the body out and laid it face up on the grassy bank. The build and clothing showed it to be a man, but the features weren't clear. Dank hair covered the skull, so it wasn't one of the Ness priests. The face looked as if it had been burnt. The skin was puckered and one eye was eaten away. It reminded Marna of Roben, the fire maker in Skara Brae who had lost an eye when a hot stone exploded in his face. She edged closer to examine the body. The two young priests took hold of her arms and lifted her away, with her feet walking in mid air.

'Jengon has gone to tell my father,' Tura said. 'He will know what to do. Here he comes now.'

The priests let go of Marna. She turned to see Quint striding towards them surrounded on three sides by his priests. His face was a fierce as a stag in rut and she could imagine antlers attached to his head, braced ready to lock with anyone who got in his way. While she was watching him she felt a hand on her forearm. It belonged to Fergeas. 'Come, we're not needed here,' he said.

'There is something bigger going on,' Marna began. Fergeas put a finger against his lips.

'Not here,' he said.

Marna tried one last time to get a closer look at the body, but Quint's priests had flocked round like starving crows. 'Fine.' She followed Fergeas away from the loch in the direction of the stone circle at Stenness.

Fergeas was the first to speak. They hadn't gone far, but were out of hearing distance from the priests. 'You told Tura you needed to talk to me. Have you news of Caordhu, my brother?'

Marna hesitated, pretending to find her footing among the stones and long grass. She wanted to know about the body, but she would have to answer his questions first. 'Yes,' she said, rejecting the offer of his hand to steady her. He waited for her to explain. Her mother's warning against being rash and foolish bounced in her head. She considered how much to tell him. 'He is on Hoy.'

'Do you know that for certain? Is he with the

pirates?'

Marna wasn't sure how much to tell him, but a cunning idea came to her. Patro didn't like her telling tales. Her mother would understand, though.

'I know he is on Hoy. I don't know if he is working with the pirates or against them. You will be able to ask Patro today or tomorrow. He is on his way back.' Fergeas either choked or gave a strangled gasp. 'I have heard from my friend Sempal,' she affirmed, hoping he didn't demand details of how Sempal had managed to send her a message from Hoy.

'Patro returning – that's impossible. He is dead.'

'He was struck and fell in the water, as Yarl reported, but he didn't drown in the sea. He made it to land and was captured by the pirates. Jolty and the folk who set out from here were able to overcome the pirates and rescue Patro.'

'Pah.' Fergeas blew air through his clenched teeth. 'The pirates are too strong for the pathetic band of stragglers Jolty managed to raise.'

'They journeyed to Orphir before crossing to Hoy,' Marna said. 'The men there are strong and the women don't shirk from fighting.'

Fergeas rubbed his chin. It was something he did when he was worried, Marna had noticed. 'I meant that the pirates are not like us. They are brutes. They would have killed anyone washed up on the shore.'

'Even a High Priest?'

'Especially a High Priest,' Fergeas answered. 'Your information is false, Marna. Your friend Sempal is trying to trick you, or he is dead and an enemy sent the message.'

'Why would they do that?'

'I don't know. I'm not one of the pirates.' His face had turned pale and the confidence in his voice had faded. 'I must be going. I...I...have to speak with Quint.'

'Wait - don't tell him what I said,' Marna pretended to plead. She reached for his hand, remembering what her mother had said about flirting. 'I don't want to raise his hopes up, if my news is wrong.'

'If Patro were to return, it would come as a shock to Quint,' Fergeas admitted.

'Oh?' Marna looked at him with wide eyes hoping he would tell her what information he had without the need for her to bombard him with questions. Fergeas made faces, lowering his eyebrows, puckering his lips and running his tongue round the inside of his mouth. Marna kept her gaze on him. He looked away and his shoulders slouched.

'It wasn't meant to be like this,' he said.

'Like what?' Marna said softly.

Fergeas didn't answer at once. He pulled himself up. 'My brother, Caordhu, has been foolish, but he is not a bad man. He is adventurous. Farming didn't appeal and he hated being told what to do by our father. He joined the pirates as a way of getting back at him. He was keen to show his strength and courage.'

'Murdering and pilfering from defenceless villages isn't bravery,' Marna said.

'People can get caught up in bad things when their blood is hot. They do things they shouldn't. I don't mean Caordhu is stupid, he isn't, but…'

'But what?' Marna asked.

'His head could be turned,' Fergeas answered. 'In Caithness our father is a chief, but we live simple lives. Not like here at the Ness. The influence of the priests goes beyond these islands. People travel from distances to come here. They trade, share knowledge, learn, but also wonder at the buildings, the colours, the organisation. Priests, like Patro, venture to foreign lands. They bring back ideas for tools, farming methods, musical instruments and the like, as well as an understanding of the stars, nature and the realms of the living and the dead. To someone like me, it has opened up new worlds I never dreamt existed.' The boy's eyes lit up as he spoke.

Marna brought him down to earth. 'What has this to do with your brother?' she asked.

'The senior priests have influence and power. Others would like this for themselves.'

'The pirates are rough brutes, as you said. They can't think they can take over the Ness,' Marna answered.

'They don't want to. Someone has made it worth their while to help them take control. That man in the water - Tura wasn't sure because of the state of the body - but he thought he was with Patro's expedition south.'

'He wasn't a priest. Who was he? What was he doing here?' Marna tossed the questions at Fergeas as if she were collecting shellfish in a pot.

'Tura mentioned a name, a man called

Barnard.'

'I know him,' Marna said. 'He works with the cattle, or he did. Patro takes an interest in farming and they often shared ideas on husbandry. He went on the expedition to learn about the lighter framed animals in the south. I don't remember seeing him with the others when they returned. Tura said he had been in the water for many days.'

'Tura suggested he might have been sent ahead by Patro to tell the Ness of his homecoming. Patro was arriving earlier than anticipated. It makes sense that he would send a messenger to let people know.'

Marna snapped her fingers. 'You are right. My mother told me earlier. I had forgotten.' They had been walking as they spoke and had arrived at the stone circle. Marna rested against the largest stone to think. 'Except Barnard told the wrong person and that was his downfall.'

'Yes. I'm guessing that person sent a message to the pirates telling them to look out for Patro's boats and attack them.'

'Someone already at the Ness?' Marna said, gripping his arm. Something was stirring at the back of her brain. 'How was Barnard killed?' she asked. 'Did he have an axe wound?'

'I don't know. The body was a mess, as you saw.' Fergeas pulled away. 'I have to go.'

If the axe she found in Barnhouse was the weapon that killed Barnard, it meant the murderer was Fergeas' companion from Caithness. 'Hold on a moment.' She rummaged in her pouch to find the bone pin Thork had removed from Toomac's body. 'Do you recognise this?'

Fergeas glanced at the pin. He shook his head.

'It has a carving on it.' Marna urged him to look closely. He took it from her and turned it over in his hand.

'The pattern is similar to those used in parts of Caithness,' Fergeas said. 'Where did you get it?' He closed his fist over the pin.

'I found it on Hoy,' Marna said.

Fergeas stared into her eyes. She could tell he knew she was hiding the truth from him. 'I need to prepare for my journey,' he said coldly. 'It was nice meeting you, but I doubt we'll see one another again.'

Marna moved to stand in his way. 'Tell me about Yarl's death,' she demanded.

Fergeas didn't answer.

'You told Quint you saw Ralfe at the loch side. What else did you see? Don't say "nothing" because I don't believe you.'

'Yarl had served his purpose. He told the council of Patro's death, which I imagine he believed. If he had been allowed to speak further he would have given the priests knowledge of the caves in Hoy where the pirates were hiding.'

'I had already worked that out. Tell me who killed him.' Marna insisted.

'When I heard that Yarl had returned, I was eager to speak with him. I was told he had headed out of the Ness with one of the senior priests, so… I followed.

'Who was he with?' Marna interrupted.

'I don't know.'

'But you saw them kill Yarl.'

'Let me finish. I saw two people walking towards the loch, but I only saw their backs. The second person was smaller than Yarl and was pointing towards where the swans gather. I kept a distance back. I don't know why, but I didn't want to be seen. It seems odd saying that now. I had nothing to hide, but I suspected something wasn't right.'

'What happened?' Marna hurried him.

'While I was taking care not to be seen, I didn't realise someone else was doing the same. You know the clump of gorse near the little bay. I was about to sneak behind it to listen to the conversation when a cloaked figure leapt out of it. They stuck something into Yarl's back.'

'A cloaked figure?'

'I didn't see a face.'

'Didn't you rush to overpower him or help Yarl?'

'The attacker was gone before I could react, but I hurried to Yarl's aid. The mace, or whatever it was, knocked Yarl into the loch. He was thrashing in the water when I reached the bank.'

'What of the priest who was with him?' Marna asked.

'He was trying to drag Yarl out. He called me to give a hand, as he wasn't strong enough. I waded into the water to help. The priest had panicked and did more to hinder the task, banging Yarl's head against a rock and trapping it under the water. When we got Yarl out, he was dead.'

'What are you saying?' Marna tried to imagine the scene. 'Why didn't you tell anyone this?' she

343

demanded. 'Why was Yarl's body returned to the loch?'

'The priest feared we would be accused of the murder. I am a stranger here and had followed Yarl in secret. Quint would have blamed me for the drowning.'

'But...but,' Marna felt indignant. 'How could he?'

'Quint is keen to blame the pirate attacks on anyone from Caithness.'

'He has to be stopped. People trust the priests,' Marna said. 'If folk know the head priest is spreading rumours, they will not be generous with their gifts or support. You should have spoken up at the council gathering, not blamed an innocent man.'

'I did see Ralfe near the loch. He could have been the cloaked figure.'

'Was he wearing a cloak when you saw him?'

'No, but he could have thrown it away.'

'We are wasting time. I have to tell my mother what you have told me. Who was the priest with Yarl? You have to say.'

'I promised I wouldn't.' Fergeas was adamant. 'Why should I trust you, anyway? You are Quint's

344

niece. There is nothing I can do here. I'm going to Hoy to find my brother.'

'What of the pirates?' Marna said.

'According to you, the fighting is over. If my brother has died with them, I need to find out for my father's sake.'

Marna watched him walk off, stumbling on the rocks. Afraid that he would look back and see her watching, she gazed over to the hills of Hoy. They were glowering under a thick cloud and she gritted her teeth as she thought of the task Sempal and Jolty had ahead of them.

The fighting may already be over, she told herself. Fergeas was no more than a speck in the distance and she began her own way back to the Ness, thinking over what he had said.

Could she believe him?

He was frightened of Quint, yet he had seemed more concerned by Patro's return, which was odd since her mother had said Patro was a friend of his father's. Her mind returned to Barnard.

Barnard must have returned as she and Thork left for Hoy. Fergeas and his companion had arrived roughly at the same time, perhaps a little before. It was possible his companion was Toomac, who killed Barnard then returned to the pirates to warn them of Patro's return. If so, who was he working for and did Fergeas realise his friend was a traitor?

Chapter 20

By the time Marna reached the wall of the Ness she had smoothed out faults in her thinking and was convinced Toomac had killed Barnard. It made sense. Why else would Phalt have killed him? Toomac could not be recognised back at the Ness. Marna was certain she was on the right track, but she was missing the vital link that would save Ralfe. It was at her fingertips, if she could reach far enough. She wished Sempal was with her to say something unrelated that would jolt her mind in the direction she needed to go.

The clouds had been spreading across the sky and first rain fell as she reached the gates of the Ness.

'Best get indoors,' the guard warned her. 'It looks like a storm is coming over from the south.'

That would stop Fergeas from leaving the Ness.

The thought pleased her, but there was little she could do apart from wait on her friends' return. She should get to work on Maisel's shawl. She was low on most of her yellow dyes as she hadn't had time to pick marigolds. The priests coloured their bodies in reds and yellow ochre for ceremonies, except Patro who insisted on having a blue dye specially made up from rare plants. Ochre was fine for use on skin and stone walls, but it wasn't suitable for a woollen shawl. She thought of Tia Famel and the green paste she had been working on.

Hadn't she mixed in a yellow dye to lighten the colour and bring out the spring hues?

She decided to ask her advice, but Tia Famel was not in the small workshop. Instead, one of the potters was pounding a lump of clay.

'She will be at the meeting of senior priests,' the man told Marna. 'I have been shooed from the potter's hut because it is too close to the meeting hall for Quint's liking. He is afraid they will be overheard. It is useless working here. The dust from Tia Famel's powders will ruin the clay before it is fired.'

Marna knew she would have to wait. It was a shame Henjar and Boda had gone home. Her mother was waiting to hear her news when she returned to the house.

'What kept you? Did you speak with the lad from Caithness?'

'Tura and his friends found another body,' she

348

reported.

'I heard that,' her mother answered.

Marna's face fell. 'How?'

'Jengon has as loud a voice as Thork. I was passing Quint's rooms when he brought the news.'

Marna didn't ask her mother what she was doing there. She suspected Quint would have wished to keep the find secret.

'They say it is Barnard, Patro's messenger,' her mother continued.

'That is the name I heard too,' Marna admitted.

'From Fergeas?'

'I saw the body,' Marna said. 'It had been in the water long enough for the fish to get fat on it. The face was melting, but it had Barnard's dark hair.'

'You didn't find Fergeas then?'

'Yes, I mean no. I did find him. He was with Tura when they dragged the body from the reeds.'

'Was he? Where is he now?' her mother asked.

'Gone.'

'Gone where?'

Marna shrugged and turned to poke the fire. She had been excited to tell her mother the news,

349

but she already knew as much as Marna did. Her questions were probing and Marna didn't want to answer. Her mother got the message and began busying herself separating dried leaves she could grind to make healing potions. Marna offered to help and they spent the evening mixing powders without mention of the murder, each waiting on the other to ask the first question.

They were preparing breakfast the next morning when there was a rattle at the door. It was open, to allow for the smoke from the fire, and the overpowering stench of the garlic her mother liked, to escape. A trainee priest was standing in the doorway, getting his breath back.

'What is it?' Marna's mother asked brusquely.

'There are boats… in the bay… approaching the landing… at Wraith.' The boy stuttered his message out.

'Pirates? Have you told Quint?' she demanded.

The boy had doubled over, sucking in air. He looked up and nodded. When he was able he added, 'They are not pirates. The lookout recognised Jolty…and Patro.'

'Patro.' Marna's mother stumbled back and covered her mouth.

'Go, go tell the others.' Marna edged the boy away and closed the door. She moved to steady her mother.

'I need to be ready for him. I must look awful. I smell of garlic and my hair is a mess.' Her mother was flustered. 'Quick, go to Tia Famel and get me eye powder and nail colouring while I wash. I should have asked the boy how close the boats were. They couldn't have been far out, if the watchman recognised individuals.'

'What about breakfast?' Marna said.

'It will keep. Mushrooms, we need mushrooms. Patro loves mushrooms.'

Marna left her mother blabbing to herself as she went in search of Tia Famel. The old priestess had a habit of lying in bed late. Luckily she was awake and in her room although none too happy to be disturbed.

'What are you doing here?' she asked crossly.

'I'm sorry, I know it is early, but have you heard the great news? Patro is home. His boats are in the bay. I need make-up for my mother.'

'Do you now?'

Marna was bewildered. Tia Famel was usually keen to offer the women the face preparations she made, with advice on how to apply them. She glanced round the room and her eyes fixed on a pot of green powder. 'Is that ground malachite?' she asked. 'I heard a pot of stones had been brought from Burray.'

'No!' Tia Famel snatched the pot and shoved it at the back of her dresser.

'We can give you a pot full of clay beads in exchange,' Marna offered. 'They have been pierced, ready for sewing and...' She couldn't finish the sentence as her eyes were fixed on the pot of green powder. All she could see were the green marks on Yarl's throat. She sensed Tia Famel could read her thoughts.

'Beads, pah.' The priestess moved to close the door. She stood between it and Marna, barring her exit. 'You and your mother think you run this place. You get whatever you ask for. You can think again when Quint takes over.'

'What do you mean?' Marna asked. 'Patro is home. He will be at the Ness before the sun is much older.'

'Will he?'

Marna wished Tia Famel would stop being cryptic. 'The lookouts have spotted him,' she repeated.

'Patro may have survived the pirate attack by an act of wonder. He won't be helped by the gods again. A skilled bowman is lying in wait ready to shoot him when he steps off the boat.' She laughed. 'The deed may have been done.'

'But...? Quick, the guards must be warned. They could stop this bowman.' Tia Famel didn't move. 'I don't understand. Patro is your friend.'

'While he was here I followed him. When I believed he would never return, I gave my allegiance to his brother. It is too late to change things. Quint will be high priest and I will be there by his side.'

'Why is it too late?' Marna didn't like the way Tia Famel was herding her towards the corner. 'What do you know? Who told you about this bowman?'

'The lad himself.'

'The lad, you mean Fergeas?'

'Don't sound surprised. He is better with a bow than with a mace.'

'A mace?' Marna felt stupid, repeating everything Tia Famel said, but her brain was burning her head open. 'You mean he killed Yarl?

Impossible, he saw the cloaked figure.'

'He lied to you. There was no cloaked attacker. Fergeas threw the mace although Jolty managed to convince the council that his wound came from a knife. That way the settler could be implicated. Why muddy the water with a mace, or bloody it in this case?'

'This doesn't make any sense. Fergeas had no reason to kill Yarl and Jolty had no reason to cover up what happened.'

'Fathers do have favourite sons.' Tia Famel laughed, but stopped suddenly. 'I am not saying that Jolty had anything to do with the pirate attack on Patro, mind. Quint thought that up himself. When Jolty spotted the mace, he suspected the Caithness lad was involved and he didn't wish to implicate a son of Kennet of Camster.'

'Quint is behind this?' Marna was astonished.

'You underestimate your uncle's lust for power. Quint has a hold on everyone here. The lad had joined the pirates. Lional sent him and his companion to the Ness for instructions. His companion disposed of Barnard. It was time for the lad to prove himself, but he didn't have the heart for it. His throw was weak. There was no need for

354

Jolty to lie. Yarl died by drowning. I saw to it myself.'

'The green fingernails in Yarl's flesh. You were the priest who lured Yarl to the loch. Fergeas said it was a man.'

'He lied about that too.'

'Fergeas won't kill Patro,' Marna said. 'As you said, he isn't a murderer.'

Tia Famel made a sound something between a snort and a titter. 'He is in too deep to allow Patro to live. If the lad does not do what Quint says, Quint will reveal that he is a pirate spy. In addition, Quint has the boy's mace. Jolty took it from the body.'

'Fergeas is being blackmailed.'

'I thought you would have worked it out earlier.'

'I don't have time for your madness. Let me out.' Marna tried to side step Tia Famel. The old woman was more agile than she appeared, blocking Marna's way. 'Quint won't get away with killing Patro – not here, so near to the Ness,' she argued.

'Nobody, apart from you, me and the bowman know Quint is involved. The assassin will come to a sticky end, I fear. He will be caught and killed by one of Quint's men while making his getaway.'

'Are you going to kill me too?' Marna challenged.

'You could have an accident. That pot could fall and knock you into the fire or you could be given a slow poison and die in your cot in three days time, however I think it is unnecessary. I know you, Marna. You are no fan of your step-father. He makes you feel small, like a silly child.'

Marna clenched her fist. 'I hate him,' she said.

'That is because you are a woman with brains. You will have Tura as a husband, jewellery, make-up and a position of respect. Don't worry about your mother. She will be given cattle, pottery and grain to take back to Skara Brae.'

Marna's head was beginning to cool. She was listening to Tia Famel. 'What of Thork?' she said. 'He has ambitions to be a senior priest.'

'Now you are making sense,' Tia Famel smiled her toothless grin. 'I can't make promises for Quint, but I have influence.'

Marna strode towards the door, not quite trusting Tia Famel. The old woman moved aside and Marna banged into the wood. Tia Famel opened the door as Marna rubbed her forehead.

'We understand one another,' Tia Famel said.

'Indeed. Now, I wish to see my proud step-father being brought low.'

Chapter 21

Outside, Marna rushed towards the gates, pushing people out the way. A welcoming party was being organised and Marna spotted Quint inspecting his priests and giving instructions. He didn't look like a man who was about to have his brother murdered. When he looked up, their eyes met and he gave a slight nod.

She didn't speak, but marched out of the gate and ran towards the bay. Her chest tightened and she reduced her speed to a jog. The bay seemed further away than usual, even taking the shortcut across the rough meadow.

By the time she arrived the prow of the first boat was visible as the rowers steered it round the headland and into the bay. Patro was on board. He was at the bow directing the oarsmen. When the boat was in shallow water he stood up. The boat rocked. Marna waved her arms. Patro waved back. The boat rocked more.

She switched her gaze from the water towards the bank and further beyond, trying to identify a spot where Fergeas could be hiding.

Think like a hunter.

The best position was behind the gorse bush,

on the opposite side from where Marna stood. That would conceal an enemy, while allowing them a clear view of the target. She would need wings like a sea eagle to reach it before Patro was in range of an arrow fired from the spot. A hooded figure stepped out, armed with a bow, the arrow cocked ready to fire. No-one on the shore or in the boats spotted him.

Marna lunged towards the water in a vain attempt to shield Patro. 'No...oo...oo,' she yelled as she stumbled on the thick cow parsley bordering the rocky shore, lurched a few paces as she tried to right herself then crashed towards the ground. She flung her arms in front of her to cushion her face as she landed, but someone jumped from the boat and she tumbled onto a warm chest. 'You have to stop him,' she gasped.

'Who?' the voice asked.

'He's going to kill Patro.'

'Who is going to kill me?'

Marna regained her balance and her senses. She got to her feet and stepped back. She recognised Patro's voice, but the person beside her bore little resemblance to the man who had left the Ness several weeks before. His torn tunic hung from his bony frame and although he had attempted to tame his beard and tie it with a leather thong, the colouring had faded and it engulfed the lower part of his face. Blonde hair sprouted from the top of his usually shaved head.

Nuttal had stepped from the boat and was standing next to Patro. She hoped he was the person she had fallen against rather than her step father.

There was no doubting that Nuttal was Fergeas' brother. She could see the likeness around the eyes and in the crooked nose. Several more priests were wading ashore, dragging the boat to the bank. The scene was a joyful one of reunions and showing off battle scars. There was no sign of a killer. Marna felt silly.

'He was there, hiding,' she said, pointing towards the gorse bush. She turned back to Nuttal. 'It was Fergeas, your brother.'

Patro took a step towards the bush, before Nuttal put a hand out to stop him. 'I'll go,' he said. Patro stood aside to let him pass.

Patro glanced towards the Ness then turned to speak with Marna. 'Where is your mother? Thork told me she had returned safely. Is she well?'

'She is getting her make-up on,' Marna

answered. Her eyes were on Nuttal as he vanished behind the bushes. 'Where are Thork and Sempal?'

'Thork returned to Orphir to be with Caran and their child. Simple should be…'

'It's Sempal,' Marna corrected.

'He was in the second boat,' Patro answered. 'It wasn't far behind. There it is.'

The second boat approached the shore. Sempal and another man jumped out to pull it onto the pebbled beach. Jolty rose stiffly and was helped by a younger priest.

The sounding of horns could be heard and the official welcoming party from the Ness was seen approaching. The senior priests had painted their faces and woven strings of beads into their beards. Quint had taken the time to put on his best deer skin cloak, clipped with an antler horn brooch. He was leading the way carrying the High Priest's staff. He stopped suddenly when he spotted Patro.

Patro stepped forward to embrace Quint. Quint's face twitched and his muscles tightened. 'I see you have brought my staff, cleaned and restored,' Patro said. 'And thankfully there are no drums, although they did save my life on Hoy.' He reached out to receive the staff. Quint looked to the

361

delegation of senior priests. They were staring at Patro and realising he had no support, Quint handed the staff over.

'I am delighted you are well and back with us.' Quint forced the words through his teeth.

Patro kept his voice low, but reading his lips Marna was sure he muttered 'No thanks to you. We need to talk.' He raised his voice and spoke clearly to address the gathering. 'Thank you for this wonderful welcome home. We have fought the pirates and were victorious. They will not be harassing us again – not while I am here.'

Everyone gave a cheer. The younger men wanted to raise Patro on their shoulders. He managed to avoid their tribute and they lifted Jolty instead. Others in the group arranged themselves into an escort. Patro and the returning fighters were surrounded by well-wishers.

Marna found herself on the outskirts of the group. She couldn't get Patro's attention, but she managed to tug on Sempal's tunic and drag him back. 'What about Nuttal?' she asked.

'What about him?' Sempal asked.

'Did he help you fight the pirates?'

'That is a matter of opinion. Patro thinks he

did, Thork isn't convinced.'

'What about you?'

'I'm inclined to go with Patro, but we will find out soon enough. Where did he go? He was in the boat with Patro.'

'He went to find Fergeas,' Marna said. There were people close and she didn't want to say more.

'He ran after himself? He told us he was Fergeas, the son of Kennet of Camster.'

'Fergeas is his brother's name. He is called Caordhu.'

'You've got it mixed up. It's the opposite way round,' Sempal said. He seemed pleased to know something that Marna didn't.

'You have been fooled,' Marna countered.

'Don't look cross,' Sempal said. 'Aren't you happy that we have returned unscathed?'

'Of course, but...'

'Patro knows how to sort out which Caithness lad is which.'

'He would,' Marna huffed. 'There are things Patro doesn't know. Like who was behind the murders of Yarl and Barnard.'

'Barnard?'

'Patro sent him ahead as a messenger, to tell

Quint he was on his way home. Nobody saw him. His body was found in the loch a day ago. He had been dead for days. Toomac killed him then was sent to Hoy to warn the pirates.'

'He couldn't have killed Yarl, though,' Sempal said.

'I can't speak here,' Marna said. 'I need to talk with Patro before Quint twists the truth, but I don't know how.'

The parade had started its procession back to the Ness. Marna couldn't see either Patro or Quint among the crowd. Jolty had been set down and two of the lay workers were carrying him between them at the back of the march.

'We need your mother,' Sempal said. 'Can you run ahead and fetch her?'

'When I get my breath back,' Marna said. 'Luckily the parade isn't making much speed.' She bent to rub a stitch in her side. When she looked up she spotted the two lads she knew as Fergeas and Nuttal approaching. Nuttal was holding onto Fergeas' shoulder, pressing him forwards. The lighter boy tried to shake free. His head twisted behind him ready to flee if his brother loosened his grip.

'Fergeas!' Marna called towards them.

Her voice was loud. The tail-enders of the parade heard. They stopped and alerted the others. The parade came to a halt. A space cleared around Patro and Quint. Quint was the first to react.

'Guards, take these men captive,' he ordered.

'What for?' Patro objected.

'Those lads are part of the pirate set-up,' Quint declared. 'I was taken in by the younger one at first, but have been keeping a watch on him since Yarl's death. They are the ones responsible for the attack on your party, one here and one on Hoy, sending secret messages to one another.'

The priests in the welcoming committee were unarmed, but those returning from Hoy had axes and maces. They stepped into line, ready to defend their leaders.

'Take them alive or dead,' Quint ordered.

'Not so fast.' Patro raised his staff as well as his voice. 'These lads are the sons of a good friend of ours, Kennet of Camster. I will not have anyone harm them.' There was muttering at Kennet's name, with most of the priests recognising it. 'There has been, I believe, confusion over which brother is Fergeas and which Caordhu.'

'I am Fergeas,' the boy from the Ness spoke up.

'I have evidence to show he is in league with the pirates. No doubt they are in it together.'

'The matter will be resolved shortly,' Patro said. 'I have invited Kennet to the Ness.'

Marna glanced at the boys. The one she knew as Nuttal was smiling, but the other boy was scowling.'

'Both lads will be made welcome with us until their father arrives,' Patro continued. 'Neither will be permitted to leave until he does.'

The priests seemed content with Patro's judgement and returned their weapons to their belts. The two young men joined the group. Quint was chewing his lip, considering his move.

'The boy there,' he pointed. 'I have proof that his companion was responsible for the death of Barnard.'

'Barnard is dead?' Patro was shocked.

'You didn't know?' Quint said.

'How would I?'

'His body was found in the loch yesterday, but he had been dead many moons. The man, Ralfe, who murdered Yarl, has confessed to being in

366

league with the pirates. He has given us the names of his fellow conspirators,' Quint admitted. 'Fergeas and Caordhu were among the names.'

'He's lying,' Marna whispered to Sempal.

'And still blaming Ralfe for Yarl's death,' Sempal answered. 'You had better fetch your mother now, before Patro agrees with the council's decision to have Ralfe killed.'

Marna didn't wait to hear the rest of the accusations. With everyone huddled close to get a look at the two boys, she was able to make her way round the back of the gathering without being obstructed. She hurried along the shore of the loch towards the Ness. Her mother was coming out of the settlement as she neared the gate. She had pulled her hair into a bun and was adjusting a scarf over her head to keep it in place.

'What has taken you so long?' her mother demanded. 'Did you get my eye powder?'

Marna grabbed her mother's arm. 'You will have to do without. We have to hurry.'

'Where? Why? What is wrong?'

'I can't talk and run,' Marna said.

'I can't run at all with my hair like this. Stand still and explain what is wrong.'

367

Marna faced her mother. 'You were right. Quint is involved with the pirates and responsible for the murders. Tia Famel told me. She is in league with him. She drowned Yarl after the man Quint sent to do the deed failed. Quint sent Fergeas to shoot an arrow at Patro when his boat landed, but he didn't.'

'Slow down. Why would Tia Famel tell you this?'

'She tried to bribe me into keeping quiet. I had to pretend to go along with her to escape. Quint is trying to squirm out of taking the blame. I need to tell Patro what I know, but he is surrounded by the council of elders.'

'I see,' her mother said. 'It would have been easier to entice Patro away from the council if you had brought me the make-up.'

'Didn't you hear me? Tia Famel is evil. She is part of the plan to kill Patro.'

Her mother bent to pick a handful of marsh marigolds and fixed them to her cloak.

'Can't you walk while you do that?' Marna urged.

'And look a mess for Patro?'

'You didn't worry about your appearance with

my father,' Marna accused.

'Of course I did, you were too young to notice.'

Her mother finished adjusting her bouquet and began walking, picking up speed as they neared the bay. Marna struggled to keep up. They met the parade of priests as they rounded the side of the loch. Patro had worked his way to the front of the march and was the first to spot Marna and her mother. He hurried ahead to embrace his wife then put an arm round her shoulder to walk together.

Quint was unwilling to grant them space alone. He moved to walk behind Patro's shoulder. The cramp was out of Jolty's legs and he had dispensed with his helpers to walk beside Quint and join in the conversation. Marna was bundled out of the way by two of Quint's aides. She kept as close as possible, but couldn't hear what they were saying. Jolty's hand movements showed he was not happy. Quint glowered with a look that could freeze the lochs. His eyes, when she saw them fall on her mother, sparkled with hatred.

Marna couldn't keep up and slipped to the back of the march. She couldn't see Fergeas or Caordhu, but Sempal was hobbling towards the tail end. She fell in line with him.

'What have I missed?'' she whispered.

'Fergeas and his brother have gone ahead to the Ness with two of the priests. I don't know what they told Patro, but he gave instructions to prevent Tia Famel from leaving.'

'I didn't see anyone passing. I met my mother at the gate and we came straight here.'

'Patro advised them to take the long way, behind the stone circle towards Barnhouse then hugging the edge of Harray loch until they reached the new circle. They will back track from there and enter the Ness through the north gate.'

'Why is there a need for such secrecy?'

Sempal stuck out his bottom lip. 'You know what Patro is like. He makes a drama out of washing his hands.'

'This isn't a game,' Marna chided.

'No, but it will make an excellent tale to relate to travellers.'

The parade had reached the spot where the foundations had been dug for the Standing Stone to be erected in Patro's honour. The flagstone had arrived and had been cut into shape. It was lying on wooden boards with the ropes in position, ready to be hoisted into place. Patro stopped. He turned to Quint.

'What is this?' he asked.

'It was to be a guard stone erected as a memorial to you, brother,' Quint said. 'You will see it marks the way to Maeshowe. Now that you have returned to guide us, there is no need for a mere stone.'

Patro pulled on his beard, the way he did when he was thinking. He clicked a loose tooth with his tongue. 'The stone is here. It has been cut and prepared well. I like the hue,' he said. 'It would be an insult to the men and women who helped dig the foundations and bring it this far, if we didn't complete the work. There is no need to wait until I am dead. I am not considering dying for some time yet.' He squeezed his wife's hand and his voice sounded like he was jesting. His followers laughed, but Marna saw the dark look Patro gave his brother.

He took a pace to the right and held out an arm with his hand raised. Clenching his fist, he propped his thumb sideways and raised his index finger at a ninety degree angle to it. He closed his right eye then opened it and closed his left. 'I believe your calculations are slightly out. They can be adjusted

371

before the stone is raised.'

Quint gave an exaggerated sigh and rolled his eyes. Marna's mother tugged on Patro's sleeve. He turned to address the gathering behind him.

'I am honoured that you thought of me in this way.' He waved. Quint reluctantly raised a cheer and the others joined in with gusto.

The march continued until they reached the Ness. Inside, Patro invited the senior priests present to follow him to their gathering chamber while the others returned to their business. Messengers were sent to fetch those who hadn't joined the welcoming party. Marna wanted to wait to see if Tia Famel turned up, but Sempal pulled her away.

'Your mother will be at the meeting. You can trust her to speak her mind.'

'She doesn't know everything. I didn't have time to tell her.'

'The elders aren't stupid,' Sempal said. 'Neither is Patro. Your mother will report everything afterwards and no doubt you'll get your say. Being at sea has made me thirsty. I need a drink. We can go to Kris's house and I'll tell you about our adventures on Hoy.'

'I want the truth, not one of your fantastic

tales.'

'What really happened is more amazing than anything I could invent,' Sempal answered.

Kris and Tama were at home and eager to hear of the battle on Hoy. Marna listened to Sempal's tale of bravery and cunning in outsmarting the pirates, knowing she would hear the story several times, with an added embellishment at each telling. Part of her brain was imagining what Quint was telling Patro. She interrupted Sempal when she heard him mention Fergeas' name.

'Which Fergeas are you talking about?' she asked.

'I knew you hadn't been listening,' Sempal complained.

'I was. It's confusing, though.'

'Nuttal is the real Fergeas,' Sempal explained. 'He joined the pirates to find his brother Caordhu.'

'The lad at the Ness said he was Fergeas, sent to find his brother Caordhu,' Marna countered. 'Tia Famel could have been lying when she accused him of being in league with Quint.'

'What is this about Tia Famel?' Tama asked.

'Nothing,' Marna answered. 'Continue your story, Sempal.'

Kris had to return to work and Sempal cut the story short to finish his account.

'Rather you than me, inside the tomb, I mean,' Kris said. 'I would much have preferred to do the fighting.'

'And I am glad you stayed at home,' Tama said. 'No good comes of disturbing the dead.'

Marna could tell Tama had been disturbed by Sempal's story. 'We should be going,' she said.

'Come back here tonight,' Tama urged. Marna was about to object, but Tama stopped her. 'Your mother and step-father will want time alone.'

'You're right. I hadn't thought of that. I need to speak to my mother and find where Pip has got to. I'll be back before supper. I'll bring dried beef and honey cakes.'

'Sounds good.' Sempal licked his lips.

Sempal and Marna made their way to the Ness. Marna was keen to continue her argument about which brother was which. 'I will give you two flints if Nuttal is Fergeas,' she said.

'Fergeas is supposed to be the honest son. The boy *you* claim is Fergeas was hiding in a gorse bush, waiting for us to land,' Sempal said. 'I saw him as I landed.'

'He didn't fire at Patro,' Marna argued.

'It isn't normal to hide in gorse bushes,' Sempal said. 'He didn't shoot his arrow because his brother was standing beside Patro. He was afraid he would hit him.'

'They are on opposite sides.'

'They are brothers,' Sempal said. 'Brothers stick up for each other.'

'And sisters don't?' Marna huffed then said, 'Their father Kennet will be here tomorrow. He will tell us which brother is which and who he sent to look for the other.'

Sempal scratched his head. 'I think I know what you mean by that.'

Chapter 22

Kennet arrived at noon the following day, with a party of ten armed men. Look-outs had been placed to watch the bay although with the shouts and splashing, their approach across the Flow was heard before they were spotted. Marna had stayed overnight with Kris and Tama. In the morning Kris returned to his work on the dyke. Sempal was cutting drift wood and Marna was helping Tama hang game when they sensed the excitement and went to greet the visitors.

Fergeas had described his father as a chief, but it was difficult to tell which of the men he was. They all wore felt tunics and skins, all had thick beards and long hair and all carried stone axes and maces with hazel handles. She tried to recognise the man most like Fergeas and Caordhu. Three of them bore a resemblance and she guessed they were related.

'Will there be trouble at the gate?' Sempal asked Marna. 'Strangers are not permitted to take weapons inside the Ness.'

'I wouldn't want to argue with them,' Marna replied. 'I suppose they aren't strangers if Patro knows them. Good, there's my mother.' Marna pointed at the entrance.

Sempal laughed. 'Everything will be fine.'

Patro appeared behind Marna's mother to personally welcome the Wick folk to the Ness. Her mother was wearing her new bearskin. She had patterns painted on her cheeks and green powder round her eyes. Patro had on his best tunic and bone jewellery studded with polished amber. His beard was trimmed and dyed a greyish blue, although he hadn't shaved his head. Despite his recent trauma he stood erect. Marna had to admit they were an impressive couple. Patro embraced one of the men, whom Marna assumed was Kennet. He was smaller than the others and Marna thought puny in comparison. The party laid aside their axes and maces at the gate although they were permitted to take in their knives.

'Come on.' Marna nudged Sempal before hurrying to the entrance. Sempal followed at a distance. She waited for him at the gate.

'You won't get to be part of their meeting,' he said, when he caught up

'Why not? I'm one of the main witnesses.'

'Witness to what?' Sempal said.

'Everything.'

Marna didn't find it easy to get into the discussion chamber. She didn't know the priest on guard and he hadn't been instructed to let her in. It was impossible to slip past. Fortunately Jolty hobbled along late and she persuaded him to let her enter.

'I'll be as quiet as a hunting hawk,' she promised.

'That I doubt,' Jolty replied. 'Please do not make accusations in front of Kennet that you can't prove.'

Patro spotted them as they entered the hall and waved them over. 'You know my father, but you won't have met my daughter Marna,' he introduced her to Kennet. Marna wasn't sure how she was meant to greet the chief. Kennet flung his arms around her shoulders in a hug. She stood motionless until he released her.

A feast had been prepared and the Caithness men made short work of the meats, fish, bread and pastries set before them. Kennet sat between Patro and Marna's mother, switching his attention between them as he made jokes. Thork had returned from Orphir and was seated on her mother's opposite side. Marna took a place beside him. She could see her mother and could tell she wasn't amused when the fat spurting from Kennet's open mouth missed her bearskin by the width of a finger. Patro tried to turn the conversation towards the elaborate burial cairn at Camster, asking questions about the interior and the alignment of the walls. Kennet was more interested in talking about an upcoming competition to throw stone balls across a field.

'My son Thork is a champion ball thrower,' her mother said, taking Thork's arm.

'I didn't know you had a son, Patro,' Kennet gave Patro a friendly punch.

'A step son,' Patro answered.

'You will have to come over and pit your strength and skill against our champion,' one of Kennet's companions said to Thork.

'Is he here?' Thork asked.

'It is Kennet's son, Fergeas.'

Marna could see Tura among the younger men, but Kennet's two sons were not in the room. Neither was Quint nor Tia Famel. She was surprised to see Ralfe gorging himself on pig ribs in the corner. Kennet was eager to raise a toast to the heroes who had vanquished the pirates. It wasn't a

379

custom that the folk at the Ness were used to and it took a moment for them to fill their beakers. Extra ale had to be sent for, which didn't please Marna's mother. She feared her guests would think she was unprepared or had been stingy.

The fighters were congratulated and beakers refilled. Kennet praised the quality of the ale as he drained his pot for the fifth time. Patro decided it was time to call for Fergeas and Caordhu before a sixth toast could be proposed. The two young men entered the room together. They had washed and were wearing smart skin tunics and wool cloaks.

Kennet rose and lurched forward to greet his sons. He handed his beaker to one of his men, and put a hand on Nuttal's shoulder.

'This is my youngest lad, Caordhu,' Kennet said.

Patro had already been told this by Kennet and did not look surprised. Marna smiled, thinking of her bet with Sempal.

'And this,' Kennet paused to put a hand on the other lad's shoulder, 'is his cousin Greegar, my brother's boy. I adopted him four years ago when his parents died.'

'So who is Fergeas and where is he?' Marna

asked. She hadn't meant to speak aloud.

Kennet laughed. 'Fergeas, my eldest boy, is at home minding his mother and the cattle.'

'I didn't like lying to you,' Caordhu spoke to Patro. 'I knew Greegar had been spreading tales about me and I didn't think you would trust me if I said I was Caordhu. The rest is true. I was sent to find Greegar, who I regard as a brother.'

'Aye, that he was,' Kennet agreed. He moved his hand from Greegar's shoulder to pull the boy's ear. Greegar gave a yelp. 'What have you to say for yourself lad?'

'I didn't do anything,' Greegar grumbled.

'You ran off when you were needed on the farm. You got up to who-knows-what. Mischief, most like. You pretended to be your sensible cousin and Caordhu put his own life in danger searching for you...'

Kennet gave the boy's ear a tug with every accusation. He would have gone on until the ear came away, but Patro stopped him. 'I'm sure once Greegar is safely home in Camster with both ears intact, he will be able to listen to your words of advice. I am afraid my own brother Quint was guilty of encouraging him in his deeds.'

Kennet grunted, but let go of his son's ear. 'Where is Quint?' he asked.

'My brother is on his way to Ireland with Tia Famel and others. He had been waiting for my return to depart and didn't wish to delay his mission any longer. The signs suggest the weather should be fair for the crossing. His expedition will travel from the north to the south of the island, sharing knowledge and learning about Irish cultures. It will keep them from the Ness for several years. They may not return.'

Patro was addressing Kennet, but he raised his voice to make sure everyone in the room heard. Marna hoped that Hunkel was one of the 'others'. Patro called it a 'mission', but it was banishment.

Patro took Kennet's beaker and signalled for it to be filled before handing it back to his friend. 'I shall raise a toast to Caordhu. Without him we would have been unable to free our waters from the terror of the pirate attacks.'

Marna drank her toast to Nuttal with the others. She wasn't used to drinking so much ale at one time. Her vision was blurring and she felt light-headed as well as a little nauseous. It was going to be a long evening of drinking. Since the official business was over, she was thinking of a way to retire without being noticed when she heard her name. Her hearing was muffled, but she wouldn't mistake that. Nuttal was speaking. He was raising a toast to her, telling Kennet, Patro, her mother and the rest of the gathering that she had saved his life on Hoy. Without her aid, his wounds would have become septic and he wouldn't have survived in the wild. Her face burnt as everyone stared at her.

'Aye,' Ralfe called from the corner, 'And a toast to Thork, who prevented me from killing him before she had time to treat him.'

The room was silent. Marna thought she heard Patro groan, but her head was fuzzy.

'More ale,' her mother called and there was a cheer. Marna managed to squeeze out of the room as another hunk of roasted beef was brought in. She ripped a piece off with her knife to give to Pip.

Marna collapsed on her cot and was asleep before she could go over everything that had happened. Patro and her mother did not return to the house that night. They were not at home when she woke. She couldn't think about preparing breakfast, but her stomach rumbled. She decided to visit Norra. Norra made wonderful cheese and she always had plenty in her house. Marna took a handful of her mother's bere bannocks to go with it.

'I hope you don't mind me joining you. I couldn't face cooking after last night.'

Norra laughed. 'I haven't drunk as much for years, if ever. Patro had his best ale served. The brewers boil the ale and gather the vapours. When they cool, the ale is stronger. It is worth savouring, but not in such quantities.'

'Kennet appreciated it,' Marna agreed.

'Just as well,' Norra said. 'Kennet can be hot-tempered. It took all of Patro's diplomatic skill to keep him placated over the business with Quint and Tia Famel.' She handed Marna a beaker. 'It is water,' she said. 'I will miss the lad, Greegar, although I had my suspicions about him. His companion, Toomac, called him Gee, which he said was a nickname, short for Gus. I offered to make room for both of them, but Quint did not want Toomac seen at the Ness. He sent him to stay at Barnhouse. Shame, he seemed like a nice man.'

Norra's tone implied that she blamed the poor influence of Barnhouse on what happened.

'He murdered Barnard then returned to the pirates with instructions for them to kill Patro,'

384

Marna said. 'Caordhu recognised him when he returned to Hoy. He wanted to keep a close watch on him. From what I remember from yesterday's conversation, Caordhu didn't take an active part in the raid on the settlement. He kept hidden until he saw Toomac fall then injured himself in order to stay with him. I had suspected he was feigning the injury to his shoulder as it had healed without treatment. The wound on his leg was nasty. It must have taken courage to inflict it.'

'Rather him than me,' Norra agreed.

Kennet and his party planned to leave the Ness shortly after noon. Kennet had business at home and was in no mood to linger. Patro supplied them with groove ware pottery, whale bones and oil to make their trip worthwhile. Three sleds transported the gifts to the boats and one of the Ness boats with its rowers was needed to take everything to Caithness. Kennet promised to send across his builder and designers to explain the intricacies of the Camster tomb to Patro.

Marna hoped to talk to Nuttal, or Caordhu as he was, before they left. She went in search of him after leaving Norra. The guests had been sleeping in the buildings at the north end of the Ness. The men had risen early and were busy loading the sleds and preparing to leave. Caordhu and Greegar weren't among them. Marna was directed to one workshop then another, but failed to find him. She ventured outside to look for Sempal and found him with Jolty.

'We were talking about the Dwarfie Stane,' Sempal explained.

'I heard you fainted when you were inside,' Marna said.

'Did Thork tell you that?'

'Maybe. Have either of you seen Nut... Caordhu?' she asked.

'Why?' Sempal asked.

'I wanted to say goodbye.'

'Camster isn't far away,' Sempal said with an air of mischief. 'You could visit him.'

'I think I should leave you two to your ...' Jolty circled his right hand, unable to find a word that wasn't "argument". He gave an awkward smile and walked off.

'Are you going to tell me where Nuttal is or not?' Marna demanded.

'He was with Patro, admiring his horse,' Sempal answered.

'It's a pony,' Marna said as she started to walk away.

'That was before breakfast.'

Marna turned back. 'You don't want me to see him, do you? You're not jealous, are you?'

'Jealous of a good-looking, intelligent man who has caught your eye? Never.'

Marna smiled as she left Sempal. She continued her search for Nuttal but was unable to find him. She returned to her house and at noon went with her mother and Patro to see the Caithness party off. Caordhu and Greegar were with Kennet. She waved at them. Caordhu smiled and waved back. Greegar pretended not to notice her. Patro and her mother went over to give their goodbyes and Sempal appeared at Marna's side.

'I wouldn't like to be in his boots when he gets home,' he said, nodding towards Greegar. 'The word is that Toomac did what Greegar told him to, not Quint.'

'It doesn't matter. Quint has gone, the pirates are defeated, Ralfe is safe, the settlement on Hoy has been promised support and Patro and my mother intend staying home for a while,' Marna said.

'Speaking of returning home, it is time I went back to Skara Brae,' Sempal said.

Marna pouted, but she knew he had work to do there. He was one of the village elders, responsible for making sure the older boys did their share of the work. The days were longer as they neared the solstice. It was time to take advantage of the light to tend the crops for a rich harvest in autumn and to make repairs before the winter storms.

'There is no rush to go today,' she said. 'It is a gorgeous afternoon. Once Kennet has left we could take a picnic to the loch. You could fish and I could...'

'Eat the picnic?' Sempal said.

'I was going to say, I could gather plants and exercise Pip.'

'Someone will have to guard the food or I know what hungry hound will snaffle the best bits.'

'If we're agreed, I'll go and fetch ale and bannocks,' Marna said. She gave Sempal a peck on the cheek.

'I'll find Pip and I'll ask Tama if she has any cheese or cold beef to spare,' Sempal said.

The Caithness boats slid out of the bay. Marna returned to the Ness and was packing nuts and bere bannocks in her basket when she heard her mother's voice outside the house. She popped a skin of ale into the basket before opening the door. Patro had his hand round her mother's waist and they were both laughing. They tried to stop when they saw Marna. Patro furrowed his eyebrows and pursed his lips and her mother burst into a fit of giggles.

'What do you find so funny?' Marna asked.

Her mother couldn't answer for sniggering. She pointed at Marna's basket of food. Patro leant over and took a handful of nuts and her mother put her head against his arm to hold back her amusement.

'You have been drinking,' Marna said.

'We had to see Kennet and his party off,' Patro said.

'And give a toast for a calm sea,' her mother added.

'And a fair wind, and a safe landing and welcome home...' Patro said.

'I like that custom,' her mother hiccupped as she spoke and laughed again.

Marna was not impressed. 'You go away for ages and all sorts of horrible things happen and when you get back all you can do is laugh.'

Her mother stared at her wide-eyed then bent forwards to kiss Marna on the forehead.

'What has got into you?' Marna demanded.

'Nothing. Can't I give my only daughter a kiss?' Marna made a face. 'It's good to be home, with my family,' her mother said seriously.

Marna continued to look cross.

'Talking of family,' Patro said, 'I heard you were interested in marrying my nephew Tura. Quint has been banished from the Ness – rather, he has been sent to Ireland with my blessing – but that wouldn't prevent a union between you and Tura.'

Marna felt her blood rise. She was about to make her opinion known when she saw Patro wink at her mother, who burst into more laughter.

'You think that is funny too?' Marna said. 'Tura is promised to Braeya.'

'It's Braesha,' Patro corrected.

'Why don't you go and find Sempal?' her mother suggested. She took hold of Marna's free hand and edged her out the door as she and Patro entered. Patro had a hand on the door, ready to shut it after her. Her mother offered her a shawl.

'Take your time,' Patro suggested. The door

was closed before she could answer.

Sempal and Pip were making their way to the house when Marna met them. 'Parents, who would have them?' Marna complained.

'You can stop worrying about them now.' Sempal took the basket to carry.

Once they were far enough from the Ness, Marna stopped to breathe in the air, free from dust, smoke and the odours of cooked meat. The wind blew from the west, taking the earthy aroma of the midden towards the stone ring at Brodgar. They decided to head towards the loch of Harray.

Sempal put his free hand to his ear. 'Can you hear that?' he asked.

'Hear what?' Marna said. She could make out the lowing of the cattle and someone nearby was hammering stone with a rhythmic thud.

'It sounds like pipes.'

'Don't be silly,' Marna said. 'You must have been in that tomb too long. It has damaged your ears. Who would play pipes here? The faerie folk?'

'I'm being serious.'

Marna listened. After a moment she heard a melody drift through the air, rising above the whistling of the breeze. It sounded familiar.

391

'Look,' Sempal pointed.

The sun was in Marna's face, casting a glaze over the path from the loch. She shielded her eyes. A figure was walking towards them. The music got louder as the figure approached. Marna couldn't make out the face, but Pip gave a yelp and hung back behind Marna. The music stopped.

'Hello, Sempal my darling,' a woman's voice said.

Marna froze. 'Erin, what are *you* doing here?'

Other books in the Marna Mystery Series:

Maeshowe Murders

Evil in Eynhallow

Printed in Great Britain
by Amazon